I0763427

Tangled Web Of True Love Tales

Tangled Web Of True Love Tales

A Tantalizing Tale
by Micole Williams

Tangled Web of True Tales
by Micole Williams

Second edition and E-book edition published 2014
Third edition and E-book edition published 2019
Third edition Editor Geri Felder
Third edition Front Cover Illustrator Alisha Brumfield 2018
Third edition Front and Back Book Jacket Designer Micole Williams 2019

ISBN-13: 978-1-7333023-0-2 Softcover
ISBN-13: 978-1-7333023-1-9 Hardcover

www.micolewilliams.com

to all those who have rooted for love

to win

Seven "Her" Stories

Black Widow - Nadia's herstory
Pushing Buttons
Bite Me
In My Head
Pure Illusion
Venom
Black Christmas
Rubik's Cube
One Love
SINtinel

PhDepressed - Dr. Lynne's herstory
Recapture
Silly me, tricks are for kids

Forces of Nature – The story of the elements that be
Journey
Faithful fate
Colossians 3:23-24

Illusions of the Pure – The story Autumn and JT
A Dime a Dozen
Exposure
A.D.D and Pedigree
What's wrong with a laughing smile?
Options (open)

Sometimes I feel Like A Fatherless Child – Autumn and Hendrix's Story
Song in my head
Summertime
The good, bad and the ugly
When I think of homecoming
Birds of Paradise

These are the Tales of Seven Deadly Women and the men they love…to hate.

The saga begins…
the drama continues…

tangled web

Stuck in a sticky situation
Turned out to be a brilliant work of complication
Just a love triangle spun out of control
And the mystery has yet to unfold

Trapped in circles of confusion
Confused on what's real or illusion
Intertwined in a perplexed state of mind
your way out, is getting hard to find

But game was pretty tight
Not tight enough to win the fight
Of the battle that constantly plagues your mind
Strings unattached have now multiplied

Now it's deeper than deep, steeper than steep
The web of lies and deceit, greed and defeat
Have got ya caught up in heat, so much heat,
Look who's laughing now

So what you gonna do, what you gonna do
When the joke is really on you
Love is not a game; love is not a game
But you insist to play

So what you gonna do, what you gonna do
When the joke is really on you
The love you once knew, was so true
But now a tangled web is what you are crawling through

SEASON'S CHANGE

Autumn's Herstory

**"For everything there is a season,
and a time for every matter under heaven…"
(Ecclesiastes 3:1-2)**

Epiphany

Seems like people don't even hear me until I write.
Seems like I don't even hear myself until I do.
I know you are probably wondering "what am I talking about?"
That is something I am used to.
Years ago, no one really knew me.
I didn't really know myself.
Life has a funny way of flashing before your eyes when you are met with the thought of death.
If I had opened my eyes sooner,
I would have seen what life was really about.
I would have seen I have so much more to live for...
so much to live without.

It's a long story.
I'll give you the short version…

The Hurricane was coming. IKE was its name; it sounded vicious for obvious reasons, though premature.

Memories of past hurricane seasons flooded the thoughts of twenty-four year old optimist, Autumn White. She looked around the bedroom that was bursting at the seams with memorabilia of three important periods in her life: her childhood, college life and her current post grad days. She had consciously saved a little bit of everything from these three eras, as if she were storing jewels in the treasure chest that sat at the foot of her unmade bed.

The ever-evolving hopeless romantic found it hard to let go. She had a love affair with the past and fell in love frequently.

It was 2008 and the shaky month of September, Autumn's birthday month. Storms surrounded her birthday too often.

Things have got to change, she thought, with eyes fixed on the overstuffed box. Too many hurricanes had passed and she still wasn't where she dreamed she would be by now. She was still unapologetically living under her mom's uninspiring roof, still aimlessly searching for a full-time job that suited her artistic spirit and still deliberately trying to get over *him.*

Autumn knew she had some bad habits she needed to break in order for her life to transform her world; living vicariously through others was one of them. She knew the stories of others, but she needed to be a subscriber to her own. Known to pace her life to fit the rate of others' opinions, she was now ready to live by her own rules and set her own tempo.

Somehow, she did a good job of ignoring her mother's opinions. Precilla, a sharp and savvy inner city high school assistant principal, was far from amused by the fact that her daughter was juggling three entry level part-time jobs. Precilla, who had grown less stringent over the years, was still a force in Autumn's life. She had unpleasant memories of the expenses she'd shelled out for her daughter's college days at Prairie View A&M University, known casually as PV.

In February of her senior year at Chamberlain High, a spirited multi-cultural school in the suburbs, Autumn tagged along with a close friend to the PV campus for Panther Land Day. Not expecting anything special, Autumn came back with the realization that this school was the school for her!

Precilla cringed every time she thought about how her *usually fickle* daughter surely made up her mind to turn down two full academic scholarships to apply at the last minute to a school she knew nothing about. "*The campus called out to me,*" Autumn expressed whole-heartedly. Still to this day, Precilla's close-to-empty pockets wished the unknown voice had kept its mouth shut. Precilla hated to admit that she didn't understand her one and only offspring. Autumn was a bright girl with a gentle and kind spirit, who lived in two worlds and seemed stuck between a rock and a hard place.

Throughout grade school, Autumn's introverted spirit made it difficult for her to find her place. She had grown up in a black neighborhood and after elementary school, she attended more of a predominantly white school. One thing she found to be true at both, her mature body spoke for her. Developing earlier got her either teased by whites or the wrong kind of attention from blacks. For this reason, Autumn kept her body covered up in baggy clothes.

While the popular kids stayed after school participating in extracurricular activities, she went home, hit the books, watched reruns and drowned herself in music: all types of music and especially country, because of the stories.

She was looking for a change.

Autumn enrolled in PV with an undeclared major and for much of her time there, that was her status. She tried to make sense of herself. Her mind was clouded but her heart was clear. In order to attempt to make sense of her restlessness, she wrote. Writing was healing. Outside of that, she wanted to lend a helping hand. She felt peace volunteering her time at homeless shelters, retirement homes, and libraries. Helping was healing.

Declaring Social Work as a major seemed like a solution.

As she stood in the doorway of her own bedroom, Autumn could hear her eighty-something year-old grandmother's signature high-pitch laughter. Since Autumn was a sophomore in high school, her grandmother, Mama B, had suffered from Alzheimer's.

"Bright Eyes," said the seemingly fragile, yet spirited silver-haired lady sitting in a dim corner of the room, busily knitting a new piece.

Autumn was born in 1983 during Hurricane Alicia. Let Mama B, a natural story-teller, tell it and you would feel like you were there. You would witness the bullets of sweat on the newborn's face while Mama B and Precilla tried to maintain their cool during the nightmarish events.

Bright Eyes is what Mama B called her Autumn the moment she saw her. The two were kindred spirits. In the darkness, Mama B could see the newborn's inquisitive eyes following the flame that pacified her. Her big hazels rested on the flickering candle that sat in the far corner of the room.

Twenty-four years later, the three women sat inside Precilla's one story house, somewhat numb to worldly news, awaiting the newest tempest. The house happened to be surrounded by tall weeping willow trees. Autumn, not one to worry, actually found herself agonizing over the contents of the treasure chest. By the looks of things, she might not ever finish that project that was very dear to her heart, something that she had started long ago. If the hurricane was going to be as life-threatening as the meteorologists projected, she might not ever finish her project. There was too much to do in so little time, and the outcome did matter - *to her*. She *had* to finish!

Shamefully, she stared at the trunk filled with notebooks - her life lied in that box.

Back in 2005, during Hurricane Rita, Precilla's two younger sisters came to the Whites' residence with their children because the storm was not supposed to hit her area too hard. Precilla's sisters' husbands worked for the police department and both were on duty. Precilla's ex-husband, Autumn's father, was deceased, although he was dead to Autumn before he died, considering he didn't exist in her life.

During Rita, Autumn had remained at Prairie View, working as a community assistant for one of the apartment complexes on campus, helping residents who couldn't evacuate. It was her junior year - a turning point in many ways - the year she stopped writing. As a result, her life seemed to spin out of control.

As she stood, she ran both hands through her puffy hair. The rubber band that rested on her right arm soon wrapped around her chunky tresses to make a ponytail.

Autumn had a weakness. She was a hopeless romantic.

During the night of Hurricane Rita, JT Hudson, a fellow Community Assistant at one of the college housings on the campus was on duty too. According to Autumn, he somehow ended up taking shelter in her apartment. Letting him in had been her biggest mistake.

"Autumn, your phone is doing something," Precilla called out to her daughter after she noticed Autumn's cell beeping in the family room.

Hearing her mother, Autumn snapped out of her trance. Turning away from her memories, she began to walk out of her cluttered room and into the more orderly area of the house. Her spirits picked up a bit, hoping it was a call or text from someone she wanted to hear from, even though deep down, she seriously doubted it.

Holding her phone, she frowned at the text, knowing she needed to give up on the idea that *he* was going to call her again. It was over, or at least in his mind, and her wishful thinking was making her depressed. *She needed to let go.*

After seeing that the text was from her Aunt Deon, Autumn considered not opening the full message, predicting it was something work-related. This was going to be her last year working for her aunt.

It was Friday, and IKE had shut down the city. Her aunt's lavish salon, where Autumn worked as an assistant, was closed. The New Era bookstore, where Autumn worked the morning shift, was closed. Sampson's Department Store, where Autumn worked in the juniors and jewelry department was closed, too, but would probably open the minute the storm passed. Autumn needed to find a full-time job, but so far, Houston had nothing really to offer her and her dream.

Now, she read the text message: *I made it. Keep me informed. – Deon.* Autumn rolled her hazel eyes. Aunt Deon had escaped to New York to *avoid* the storm, while others endured it. Everyone was a bit nervous about what awaited them and were bunkering down, hoping for the best. Things felt different from the last hurricane. They had been lucky with Rita, but would IKE be as dismissing? IKE was coming at a different angle and they just happened to be in its path.

Autumn deleted the message and returned to the home screen of her phone.

Suddenly two text messages came through. Autumn couldn't help but laugh at how her close friends, identical twins, Kennedy James and Kyla James-Withers had texted her at the *same* exact time. They had a habit of doing that. She responded to the oldest twin, Kennedy, who was a TV producer working in a small town that she hated. Autumn let her know that she was okay. Kyla, who was a preacher's wife, lived in a nice house in Sienna Plantation, a community down the street from Autumn. Kyla had evacuated and was worried about Autumn. Autumn reassured her that she was okay. The twins were the big sisters Autumn never had. Autumn thought it was really a shame that the James' sisters hadn't been on speaking terms since Kyla's wedding in 2005. *We will get into this later...*

When she glanced at the clock, her heart raced. *Time was ticking past.* Autumn shook her head. She couldn't continue to let life pass her by. In two weeks, she would be twenty-five and didn't know where she was headed. She knew where she wanted to go – The Big Apple, where she would be closer to the job she dreamed about. This would be where she would fit in, because her attitude and her hair certainly didn't conform to the stringent standards of corporate America, the average 9 to 5 or better yet, Houston's humidity.

What she wanted to truly do, what her heart sincerely desired was a far-fetched reverie imprinted on those once-blank sheets of paper in the trunk. Last time she mentioned it, she was told she would have to *get the hell out of Houston* in order to really go for it. *Whatever* she needed to do, *wherever* she needed to go, as soon as the storm was over, she was setting her sights on it because more than anything, *life was short* and she wanted to experience the trueness of her love.

Under the Weather

Ignoring her mother's call, Autumn returned to her bedroom. Somewhat of a klutz, she found some way to stumble over her own feet. As she reached the center of her dumping ground, she opened the antique-carved chest and some tablets that kept it from being closed fell in her lap. The dust tickled her nose, but she didn't sneeze.

On impulse, she started pulling out the heavy contents, carefully holding pieces of her life in her hands. She sat each notebook down, one by one, and was soon surrounded by tablets of her penmanship; the sight of them brought back nostalgic moments.

As she sat, she held her hands close to her lips and her eyes panned the floor – taking in the optimistic childhood diary entries, naïve college poems, and post-grad journals of theories.

She knew she was torturing herself but she had to face it finally. *Where to start* is the question. Before Autumn could think, her hand was reaching for a tan leather journal – one that started her PV journey. As she flipped through the delicate crème-colored pages, she held her breath. It wasn't long before she was lost in her words that she had thought described love - a bitter-sweet experience. As she read her thoughts, she wondered *who this little girl was.* At times, she felt guilty for invading who she once was. Other times she felt guilty for letting that little girl down. She had known where she was going, but hadn't followed through. She had let *him* get in the way.

***

"Your room holding you hostage?" Precilla asked, standing in the doorway, intrigued by what had made her daughter go deaf for the past ten minutes.

Autumn looked up to see her mother looking at her quizzically. Autumn couldn't help but smile just imagining how she must look, sitting there, on the floor.

Her foot was waking up as she headed out of her room and into the family area. She knew she would have to return to reading excerpts from her college chronicles; the compulsion was too strong. For now, they would wait.

The television showed the updates of the storm. Mama B's eyes stayed focused on the strings of yarn that she manipulated with her needle. Autumn and Precilla watched the screen.

Autumn assessed the gray, violent water. Galveston looked more like the ocean than land.

"Look at that!" Precilla said, moving closer to the television. Autumn looked once more before going over to sit at the computer which sat in the library in the front of the house. She tried to sign in to her MSN account, but the signal was getting weaker as she clicked in her inbox. There were lines of junk mail and e-mails from a few friends and many co-workers urging her and others to stay safe. Autumn appreciated the need for concern and said a silent prayer for all.

Before she closed out of her account, something caught her attention on the home page. She blinked. It was an advertisement for a reality TV show that read, *looking for a new approach to television.* Being a reality show fan, she clicked on the text, but the signal was getting weaker and rain was getting heavier by the second. The webpage finally stabilized, allowing her to quickly skim the guidelines. It sounded like an interesting opportunity for someone. *"Do you have a concept for a new show?"* She knew that, now more than ever, reality shows were good for people who needed a way out of small towns or cities that *did* sleep. As she *tried* to click on the conditions and rules, her computer screen went completely white. The last thing she read was, *"What's your story?"*

Autumn sighed. Just a blank page sat before her. *Come on! Please,* she begged, closing her eyes and shaking her head. *Of course,* she thought. *Another tease.* Autumn didn't know if she had much of a story to tell, but she did want to know more about the competition.

Suddenly, the screen started to refresh. When Autumn opened her eyes to shut down the computer, she could see faint letters on the flickering screen. She scrolled the text and quickly read, *"Do you have a unique story? A different approach to television? A lesson learned?"* Autumn abruptly sat up to read as much as she could. So many fragments of ideas shot through her head as she continued to read.

Suddenly, the screen went white once more. Autumn clicked the mouse and hit the keys prompting the page to return. Ideas continued to spill out of her brain. She needed more details. But the screen remained blank.

***

Less than thirty minutes later, the wind picked up tremendously. The unwanted visitor was on its way, and when he arrived, he surely did make himself known. Like the door knock of doom, the sound of the increasing rain thumped the roof and hit the sides of the house, challenging anyone to go outside and meet it.

In the main room, the three women sat in their designated areas in the center of the house.

Once a whisper in the night, the howling sounds that surrounded them were now loud and impossible to tune out. There were noises that would have haunted Halloween. The cries grew sharper by the minute. Wishing she was hearing sound effects from a movie, Autumn listened as the winds whisked by like full-speed roller coasters, taking rubbish, dirt and sand along for the ride. Flying debris crashed against the fences around the house. The women couldn't help but jump after each thump. The lights began playing a far-from-amusing game of *now you see me, now you don't.*

Autumn's adrenaline was high. She had to see. She cautiously walked to the window at the front of the house, eager for a glimpse of what the storm looked like. She was amazed at how the defiant plants and trees held on for dear life as their contorting branches whipped the air. She had never seen anything like it. The window panes rattled as they bumped together.

Returning to the living room, Autumn glanced at her parents, *her mom and grandmother*, while the lightning struck.

A loud, bass-filled clap of thunder boomed, followed by an eerie silver streak of lightning that illuminated the three wide-eyed faces in the room. Autumn closed her eyes, and when she opened them, the family room went completely dark.

"Oh my," her grandmother said.

The women laughed, to ease the intensely sinister moment. Both Precilla and Autumn knew they were in for a long, shadowy night and that sleep was not coming for anyone. It was hard enough keeping up with Mama B on a regular day. For Precilla, during Hurricane Rita, keeping the stubborn yet sweet lady occupied was always a challenge. Ironically, tonight she just sat quietly with her knit work on her lap.

The lights returned.

There was a sigh of relief.

They held their breath as another *louder* clap of thunder shook the core of the house and the three ladies within it. There was another strike of light that entered the room, blinding them for a moment. As more flashes of light entered the room, it felt like the end of a live concert, each strike competing with the last, while highlighting the expressions on their faces.

"Time to make that unwanted transition to substitutes," Autumn said as she grabbed the flashlights in the center of the room. They turned on battery-operated fans and radios to keep cool and listen to the news.

After a treacherous clap of thunder, the room went dark...completely. The electricity said good-bye, and then there was a crackling noise outside. Autumn and Precilla both had the flashlights on...Then there was a new loud noise outside in the front, crackling and then crashing. Autumn used the flashlight to guide her and her mom to the front window. They peered out the open blinds but could not see anything. Autumn put the flashlight up to the glass, but was only met with a glare. She quickly stepped away, but stopped dead in her tracks when something else crashed in the front of the house.

"Mama, please stay here," Precilla pleaded to the woman who looked around at them from the other room. Precilla held the flashlight and this time, they were able to peer out. Autumn's eyes bucked as an eerie, yet exhilarating feeling took over her body. She quickly stepped away from the blinds.

"Maybe if we look out the front door," Autumn suggested.

Her mom was a skeptic, but knew, if she didn't look, Autumn would, so they would do it together.

"The wind is high, so we both need to hold on to the door so it won't swing and puncture the wall with the knob," her mother said. Autumn took a deep breath, getting ready.

When the women unlocked the door, they slowly and cautiously opened it but a heavy, prickly tip...the top of the tree that had once stood tall and proudly in the middle of the yard, now lay on top of them; and parts of it sat in their shaking hands.

"Oh my Gosh!!!"

They had to maneuver around it to let it fall to the ground. The wind blew so strongly that the door swung open, knocking a hole in the wall.

"Shit!" Precilla yelled.

Autumn hadn't heard that word come out of her mouth in years. She pulled the door handle out of the wall. Pieces of the sheetrock fell to the tiled entryway. Autumn gasped.

Mama B was rushing toward them.

"Everything okay?" she asked, trying to bend down and help the two.

"No! Yes, Mama! Don't worry yourself with this. Please go sit back down. We don't want you to get…"

Debris leaves, and dust suddenly whipped the ladies in the face as it flew into the house.

"Close the door, fast!" Precilla yelled.

Easier said than done. The heavy tree tip was in the way. Kind of hard to pick up a thirty year-old tree by its top, Precilla thought.

Since the door wouldn't latch they had to prop stuff against the door.

Another loud clap of thunder shook the house, leaving it rattling as the sound echoed. A bright streak of lightning showcased the frightening sight of the street.

"Lord Jesus, help us!"

Many trees were on top of people's houses.

The women pushed the tree, but it wouldn't budge. Tired of watching them play around, Mama B knelt down. The two ladies watched in confusion, *then in shock,* as Mama B got to work before they could protest. The silver-haired lady cleared the doorway and shut it behind her before walking back to her seat.

***

IKE was ruining the neighborhood, but it did allow for some to sleep in the wee hours of the night and early morning. As soon as the winds died down and the lightning and thunder calmed, Autumn returned to her notebooks to escape the present nightmare. She had something she needed to finish.

Before she knew it, she had read her freshman year journal, the one that she was the most reluctant to face. She read between the lines of the busy life that jumped off the page.

Undergrad freshman year was the memorable time that led to the beginning of her life. Bright days quickly turned gray. People she had loved made her hate her dreams, paralyzing the spirit that seemed to be present now. Autumn blinked. JT was the guy she spent countless pages writing and wondering about. The one she loved at first sight. Autumn swallowed hard.

Going back down memory lane had her stumbling over past loves and heartbreaks. Though emotional, it was also a therapeutic experience now that she was out of the situation.

Autumn clearly remembered the day when she first laid eyes on JT. Everything stopped. That was the *beginning.*

Then it was *homecoming…*

Then it was the *photo shoot…*

Then it was the *dates…*

Then it was their *night…*

Then it was… *nothing.*

JT, he was my mirage, she thought resentfully. Thank God Hendrix was there. If Hendrix St. John had not been there, who knows where she would be? Hendrix had been a good friend whom she loved dearly. They spoke the same language. As much as she thought JT meant to her, she realized the absence of Hendrix was what killed her slowly. Their friendship wasn't much of anything now, because of her and JT's ambiguous relationship.

She didn't blame Hendrix, but she did miss him. The music he made. The way he played. He was a musical genius and she loved how in tune they were with each other. Hendrix was a sensitive soul and her flighty attitude did nothing for his need for security. She learned the hard way, that she *couldn't have her cake and eat it, too.* She knew she had messed up stuff with him and anybody in their right mind wouldn't forgive her. She hated that she didn't realize it until it was too late. *Don't know what you got till it's gone.* Autumn was sure Hendrix was gone.

She hadn't talked to Hendrix since the last Hurricane in 2005, though she did receive birthday texts from him every year.

***

The candle flickered as she poured her heart into that pen and pad. She just wrote. She didn't think, she just felt. With no rules, she forged ahead on instinct. Most importantly, she felt her own sense of self returning, so she settled on the idea that she would complete the project she had always dreamed of. Forget the rules. Forget the critics. Forget the judges. She would create what she wanted to see.

The storm's urgency pushed the procrastinator to finish a project that she'd been fearful of producing. *Her story.* For once in her life, she had the focus needed in order to commit to the idea.

Soon the room seemed a little brighter. Autumn wasn't sure if it was actual sunshine or a mirage. She humbly soaked in its intense luster.

Bright Eyes

The next morning the lights were still out, which meant the electricity as a whole was gone. Autumn needed the internet! As Precilla and Autumn took Mama B back to the personal care home so she could take her meds, driving out of the neighborhood seeing the damage was heart wrenching.

After they returned, Autumn walked around the house anxiously. Determining who had power was pretty difficult with no way of communicating. She tried to call some of her friends, but her cell phone wasn't dialing out.

Some hours later, the two ladies were surprised to hear a knock on the door.

They both looked at each other.

"Who is it?" Precilla asked nicely as they walked to the door.

They could hear the voice of a man, somewhat muffled.

Autumn shot up and stood up straighter. She knew that voice. The sound of it made her heart beat faster.

She moved swiftly to the door to meet the person on the other side.

Precilla stood midway through opening, and fell back once Autumn brushed her aside.

There stood Hendrix St. John amongst all the fallen fragments. Autumn saw that many things had changed.

"Hello, Mrs. White," said the guy who stood six feet tall.

"Hello, Hendrix. Long time no see," Precilla said pushing her daughter out of the way to give him a big hug. "How are you?"

"I am doing well. And how about yourself?" he asked sincerely.

"Nothing's better than surviving a storm," she added.

"Ain't that the truth," Autumn and Hendrix said at the same time.

Precilla was happy to see the one she always envisioned as her son-in-law; Autumn was eager to have a moment alone with him.

"Well, it was good seeing you!" she quickly said.

Autumn smiled at her mom and then stepped down, shutting the door behind her.

There was an awkward moment that followed her mother's departure as the two schoolmates stood, facing one another.

Hendrix had a new look. He had let the puffy fro go. She had never seen him as the bald type, but he wore the shaved head rather well. It gave him a new edge. His formerly, clean-shaven, pretty-boy face was now framed with a dark and full goatee that gave him an air of mystery. He had packed on some muscle and he filled out the gray knit shirt rather nicely.

Autumn, on the other hand, probably looked a mess. She hadn't bothered to fix her hair because she couldn't really see in the house, let alone plug up a flat iron. So she just let her long, wavy mane stay free and wild.

Hendrix swallowed. He didn't know what to do. He wanted to hug her, but he had only come to see if she was okay.

"I have been worried sick about you!" the words left his lips before he could stop them.

He cautiously kept his distance. Autumn was aware of this, not wanting to overstep any boundaries.

"I'm okay! Are you?" she asked with a smile.

He nodded.

Suddenly the mood changed. They both knew why.

"Yeah, things weren't that bad, I was actually on my way out," Autumn said, feeling awkward.

"Out?" Hendrix said, with his same overly protective tone.

"Yeah," Autumn reassured.

Hendrix's eyebrow rose.

"It ain't much out there," he said.

Autumn laughed.

"Oh I know. I had to…take care of something. I need the internet."

He assumed she was referring to FEMA stuff, but knew Autumn better than that. It was probably something lighter.

Hendrix, as always, tried to help in whatever way he could. His mind searched all possible connections.

"I think I know where you can get on the net," Hendrix said. "I can take you if you'd like."

Moments later, Autumn informed her mother that she and Hendrix were going for a little ride. Hendrix opened the door to his champagne colored Tahoe.

"Thank you," she said graciously as she hopped into the passenger's seat. As Hendrix walked over to the driver's seat, Autumn tried unsuccessfully to smooth down her puffy hair. She hoped Hendrix wouldn't be embarrassed to be seen in public with her, wherever they were going.

Suddenly the sounds of the radio put them in a lighter mood. All it took was music to clear the air for the two old souls.

Smiles spread across their faces when one song in particular came to them through the air waves. It was an oldie, but goodie. The distinctive strings of *Love Ballad* by LTD held a special place in both of their hearts. For a Homecoming concert, Jeffrey Osborne was one of the artists who came to the PV campus.

The two best friends did their best Osborne impression.

"Uh um... hey a yeah..."

They rocked from side to side.

"I...have never been so much...in love...beforeeeeee..." They laughed between crooning.

"What a difference a true love made in my life...So nice...So right...Loving you...gave me something new, that I never felt, never dreamed of. Something's changed, no it's not the feeling I had before. Oh it's much, much more." They belted out notes that existed and some that didn't quite make the cut in the comfort of the SUV.

Soon the song was over and the absence of the familiar sound made reality hit hard. They used to have silly singing sessions in Hendrix's homemade music studio right outside of PV's campus. Autumn wished things were the same. She sat in many of his recording sessions, impressed with him and yearned for that opportunity again.

They began to focus on the sights around them even though they turned their stomach. As she rode with him, just being around him made her realize how much he added to her security. She had missed him dearly. At that moment, she so badly wanted to share this with him and fill him in. She wanted to spill the beans about the writing competition. She wanted to catch up. She wanted to do a lot. But all she could do was sit still.

This was the first time she could say she was *secretive* with him, but knew it was best for now because things *were* different.

Hendrix was quiet as he drove, deep in thought, keeping his eyes on the road. He was aware that she was occupied with something else, as always. He had grown accustomed to never really having her full attention and felt he would never really fit into her world.

Though Hendrix looked ahead, Autumn could see the grave expression on his face.

She could only imagine what was going on in his mind. The new Hendrix made her nervous.

After a forty-minute drive, Hendrix pulled up to the near-empty parking lot. This was one of the *Bushwik Services* offices. Autumn was curious to know how Hendrix found himself in such a place. She still was trying to figure out what he did, exactly. She didn't want to be rude and ask as he used his keys to open the front door.

"This is one of the locations I come to," Hendrix said. "My main office is in the inner city. I'm sure we have…" Hendrix unlocked the door and flipped on the nearest switch. "…power."

As the lights came on Hendrix said "Looks like you are in luck."

Autumn felt a huge sigh of relief. She would have hated to waste Hendrix's time, driving out to the outskirts of where she lived, for nothing.

As they walked to the back of the small, bland building, Autumn saw that this was maybe a data entry place.

In one of the offices in the back, there were several computers. It took Hendrix some time to re-plug the one that sat beside a laser printer.

"You want something to drink? Some of the bottled waters may be cool enough."

"Oh no, I'm fine," Autumn said, trying to stay focused on what to say and what not to say once she was online.

Soon Hendrix left her to type.

After a couple of word searches, Autumn rediscovered the screen that had her taking chances; she began to print the facts.

When Hendrix returned, she minimized the screen and stood protectively over the printer. She smiled graciously and kept her eyes on the documents. Hendrix weaved in and out the room, patiently waiting for her to let him know when she was done.

As each sheet shot out, she couldn't see the fine print from a far, but she could see the startling details in bold. The deadline! She had to get a move on. She needed to get it postmarked *today*.

Once everything was printed and read thoroughly, Autumn expressed the urgency to return to her neck of the woods. Hendrix looked empathetic, but once again heartbroken as it was time to disconnect.

Hendrix was determined to get her back home, safely. Autumn couldn't help but wonder if she even had a chance. The storm played a huge part in how she would get her story to the judges and she doubted the post office was open. She tried to push doubt out her mind and stayed positive.

"Did you get everything you needed?" Hendrix asked, looking over at Autumn as she read the rules of the competition. She was trying to map out a plan of action, not an easy task for the free-spirit, especially considering how her options were very limited.

"Yes, I…did," she stopped to look at someone she appreciated. "Thank you so much," she said.

It seemed like in a matter of seconds, he was pulling up in front of her driveway.

"The ride is always faster on the way back," Autumn laughed.

***

For Hendrix, it was hard to say bye to Autumn's mother. They both gave each other a heartfelt hug.

Precilla waved and shut the door, leaving the two outside on the front porch.

Hendrix kept it brief so he could let her be.

Autumn thought the least she could do was let him determine the flow.

"Hendrix, thanks for everything," she said.

"Oh it's nothing," he said.

"Not to me." Autumn hoped he understood her appreciation and words.

Hendrix smiled, but did not look at her.

"I won't hold you," he replied.

The words cut Autumn deeply.

After a moment of standing in awkward silence, he turned and walked away.

She reluctantly shut the door. It was time to get this show on the road, Autumn thought.

Her mother was curious. "What are you working on?"

"Oh, it's nothing." Autumn kept it to herself.

***

As she reached over to get the package with the Los Angeles address written neatly in the center sitting securely beside her, she stopped before placing it in the slit of the blue mailbox. For some reason she couldn't let go. She had to think. She closed her eyes for a moment, not sure what she was feeling, but the honking of horns behind her made her resist the emotion and soon her fingers released the package. *Whatever will be, will be,* she thought. The battle was half won in her mind.

As she drove her hybrid off the lot, she smiled a smile that was new to her. She felt lighter. The burden of her dream had been lifted. Now if only the burden of the other dream would do the same.

Pieces of a dream

As soon as she got back to the house that still lacked electricity, she took a cold shower, tried to settle down for the evening and then called Hendrix. He was the last person she had expected to see that day. As happy as she was to see him and be around him, she was proud of herself for not getting too attached. She was proud that she kept her secret. She didn't want to tell it out of season and that meant not mentioning it, period. The idea of him made her feel warm all over, then hot from pure shame. The phone just rang. Soon instead of Hendrix, she got his voicemail. Disappointed, she ended the call, but figured it was late and she wanted to put an end to the long day. Maybe she would get the sleep she had lost the night before.

Autumn placed her cell beside her bed on the nightstand. Without thinking she reached for her charger then remembered there was no power.

What a day, she thought as she kneeled beside her bed and began to pray.

Ten minutes later, Autumn was in her bed. She was out as soon as her head hit the pillow. Half way asleep, she heard her phone rattling against the top of her night stand.

Autumn, quite groggy, reached over to see who was calling. "Hello."

After the storm

The very next day…

"The water is contaminated," said the lady behind the counter of the burger joint. The only place that was open had dirty water. *Not a good sign*, Autumn thought. Hendrix and Autumn had decided to meet up, to talk.

"What do you have that is not...You know what? Never mind, don't even answer that," Autumn thought as she figured she was doing herself a favor.

They both scratched the food idea and settled on conversation. Hendrix drove to the nearest outside mall. They walked and found a seat together, away from the clusters of shops and restaurants.

Things seemed so different, for both of them. Outside of birthday texts, they had been out of touch with each other since 2005.

"I know we weren't able to really talk yesterday, so fill me in. What you been up to?" Hendrix asked as if it was at the top of his list.

Autumn hesitated before truthfully answering. She thought about the treasure chest of her writing and her recent project.

"Just trying to sort things through in order to let some stuff go. What about you?"

Hendrix paused, knowing she probably couldn't handle the truth. Trying to let her go was impossible for him. There wasn't a day that went by that he did not think about her. He tried not to, but failed miserably.

As he sat across from her, he missed her uncontrollably. She seemed alert and focused. Most importantly, she seemed happy. That was the wish he had the day he laid eyes on her. In his eyes, her beauty still overpowered her complex blues, but he wanted her to sing happier tunes. He tried his hardest to take away the sadness, knowing that he couldn't do it alone. He tried to be there for her when JT broke her heart. He tried to pick up the pieces, but she insisted that they stay there, as she recapped the moments of their end over and over again, like a broken record. But looks like that sadness was gone. He wondered who the new man in her life was. He was not the best at wishing. *Wishing was her forte.* Looking back now, he wished that he had rephrased it: not only make her happy, but happy with him. Finally he returned to the conversation that was on the table. "Working mostly. Got a new job. Miss the creative side," he said.

"You still do your music, right?" Autumn asked, concerned. In her eyes, he was a true artist.

"I try to make time for it. Lack of inspiration though. Not like while in college." Hendrix knew his real muse was Autumn: her fickle ways and unchanging beauty created pieces that he was proud of. Hendrix looked at her, wanting to know who was in her life.

Autumn looked at him shamefully. There was a look in his eyes that made her heart cry with guilt.

"I hope you can forgive me. That night. I was at a weird place. I didn't know where we stood," she slipped.

Hendrix was quiet.

"We don't have to talk about that," Hendrix said sitting up straighter and avoiding eye contact. He preferred that they didn't go there.

"I know, but I feel awful about what…happened. I was a fool."

"You weren't the only one." Hendrix tried to smile. "I knew you didn't see me the way you saw him, but I hoped that, maybe, maybe one day you would. I guess it was…wishful thinking."

"Hendrix, please know that I didn't see JT the way he was. The saddest part is that I didn't see you the way you were. I was blind, but now I do see." Autumn wanted him to understand her heart. "I just hope that one day, you can forgive me."

"I did the moment I knew," Hendrix swallowed hard remembering the moment that he knew that she had stepped outside their relationship.

Autumn blinked and thought back to the day they went their separate ways after her mistake. Any other man would be furious, not forgiving. This was news to her.

"I just let you go because I wanted you to be happy. As much as I cared for you, as much as I was hurt, as much as I wanted to be with you, there was one thing I learned the hard way - you can't make someone love you. I tried to make you love me. It didn't work. That is the only reason I let it go."

She never understood how Hendrix could be so mature, how he could see through the emotion and still move forward in the fog. She couldn't relate. It intimidated her from the start that he was not like all the other guys, who played games. He was honest. He was patient with her impatience. He showcased kindness by listening to her repeatedly vent. She was used to other types of guys. She entertained other types of guys. But with Hendrix, she felt she had wasted his time. He deserved better.

"I hate that you think I didn't love you," Autumn said. "You were the one I loved, once I learned. I am such a late bloomer in love. As much as I wanted it, I didn't realize - it wasn't defined correctly for me. It took me some time to see that what I felt with JT was not love at all. It was something shallow. At the end of the day, it was something I hated most - an unanswered question. *Was it there or wasn't it* kept me playing his guessing game. I couldn't figure out why someone would lie about how he felt for me. How someone would play with my heart for the fun of it. I couldn't fathom it."

Hendrix could.

She continued. But this was something new to his ears.

"Soon, I realized, I wanted answers from him, not a future. I was just so hurt and so confused. I tried to make sense of it, but I didn't and couldn't understand. But you know, now that I have settled on the fact that I don't need to know, some answers aren't worth having."

Hendrix looked at her, wondering if his heart could believe her - wondering if his heart could take any more of her. His heart said yes, but his mind said, *Leave while you can. Don't start this again.*

"It really kills me that for a moment you didn't know how much you meant to me. But I guess it would make sense because until I met you, I didn't know what love was," she said.

Hendrix felt so much in that moment. He couldn't deny that her eyes were focused on him, looking deeply into his soul. In seconds, her words were like bandages to his heart. He always wondered how she felt about him or if she felt anything at all. There were times when she was not emotionally available to him, even when they dated for a second, he wondered if she had feelings for him. He understood that now he had closure. The closure he properly needed to move on.

To have your cake and eat it too

Four days after the hurricane, many of Autumn's family who circled around her, had taken a break from storm clean up to celebrate her 25th birthday. Earlier that day, Mama B, who was still at her personal care home, had called to sing happy birthday and it warmed her heart. Autumn had gotten many birthday texts, but one she valued the most was not sent. Hendrix was already on her mind and not getting the usual text made the day more bitter than sweet. She really hoped that she could find her way back to his life.

Autumn, hypnotized by the flame that sat on her cake, watched it glow.

Her mind drifted back to a time where she heard him loud and clearly, without even knowing it.

> *Autumn was done with her last final for her freshman fall semester when she walked out of the classroom in Hobart Taylor, a building on the Prairie View campus. She headed off for a long walk back to the University College dorms across campus. She knew that even though it was the end of her first semester, she still was undecided on what to declare as her major since there were so many dishes exciting her taste buds. She knew that this was something that was not yet there. She couldn't rush, she thought as she prepared to head out the back entrance. Throwing her scarf around her neck, she heard a familiar sound - the sweet melody of the piano seeped through the closed door and filled the empty hall. She had been hearing it all semester long, every time she passed this room. She wondered if it was the same person each time pouring their heart out on the piano keys. Whoever it was, was skilled, dedicated, but most importantly, passionate. She understood the passion they had for their craft. Her curiosity had been killing her since the first time she passed the closed door. On the other side was where she wanted to be. Autumn figured, today was the day she was going to be. This*

could be the last day she would pass that room at that exact time and hear the sound. She just wanted to at least see who was supplying the music.

Autumn stood there, directly in front of the door.

Some students passed, looking at her like she was on something. Autumn knew she was. Music was one of her addictions. It made her understand things that were unclear in silence. If it were the same person, boy did they have more than her ear. Blame it on the set up. Autumn's family had somewhat of a musical and artistic background - her grandfather especially. Mama B had stories for days about their good old days yet she always advised against falling for a musician. Autumn played the piano for a short time. Mama B was frustrated with her granddaughter's fickle spirit and that she didn't keep up with it. Sometimes Autumn wished she had stuck in there, considering how much she adored the instrument and its versatility.

To quench her thirst, she slowly put her hand on the door, not even thinking about what she would say once she opened it. The knob turned, and Autumn began to push, but the door made a loud bumping noise, as it remained shut.

The sound of an intended intruder made the music stop.

Autumn, quickly coming to her senses, felt a sudden rush of guilt for childish, inconsiderate actions. What if she broke the connection for the pianist? Forgetting her own curiosity, she settled for the thought that maybe the person behind the door could regain their focus and forget she had even come by. She quickly walked ahead and turned the corner.

Marching Storm band member, double music/ computer engineer major, Hendrix St. John, from St. Lourdes, Louisiana slowly walked to the door, perplexed. He didn't know if he heard someone or not. It could have been one of his crab brothers. As he looked out, only to see a clear hallway, he shrugged his shoulders and turned back. Must have been imagining things, he thought as he sat back down and began to play Donny Hathaway's, "Song for You."

As her family continued to wait for the birthday girl to snap out of her trance, Autumn continued to let the flame dance before her eyes.

"Today please, we would like to have cake, on your actual birthday," Deon, who was back from New York, said. Autumn finally closed her eyes and made a wish she prayed would come true. *Hopefully, he would play a song for her again.*

Autumn laughed.

Then she blew.

Later that evening, Kennedy texted Autumn again, asking how her day went. Kennedy, *Miss Current Events,* was planning on attending Homecoming in a couple of weeks and was already prompting Autumn to attend with her.

Autumn laughed at the thought of the event that brought the two ladies together.

"Homecoming is the last thing on my mind considering the last homecoming I actually enjoyed was the first one that I attended," Autumn smiled.

Autumn knew this would not be the end of Kennedy asking, but this would be the first time she actually stuck to her gut. She'd have to decline the invitation.

How can you move forward if you are always going backward?

Just mentioning Homecoming had Autumn slipping back down Memory Lane, a place she was tired of traveling. With the help of friends, it seemed to be a frequent destination.

Beating to your Own Drum

Homecoming 2003

The drums of the percussion line tugged at Autumn's heart. The infectious rhythm penetrated her inviting soul. It was Autumn's first Homecoming and she was taking in all the illustrative sights and distinctive sounds! As her and her building mates sat in the iron stands at the game, Autumn sat on the edge of the bleachers tapping her gold, strappy, flat sandals.

She wanted to get a good look at everything and she did. The Royal Court was about to be presented. She watched Mr. and Miss PV wave to the crowd as they strolled down the green lawn. Autumn's building mates tried to appear composed as the wiggled with excitement while the Greeks paraded around, sprinkling the crowd with bright, bold and pastel colors.

The crowd of old and new spectators came showcasing their styles and pride. The fashion show still didn't top the long-awaited halftime show! Some people had come just for that purpose. Specifically, Autumn had come for the music.

Since Autumn had moved into the fairly strict freshman dorms, formerly co-ed, she had quickly learned more history of the school just by walking around with an open ear. It seemed like everyone there was a teacher of some sort, wanting to share their knowledge. Adjusting to her new life rather well, she had made an effort to talk to Mama B everyday. Even though her grandmother may not know what Autumn was talking about, or better yet who Autumn was, or who she-herself actually was, it always made Autumn feel better.

Although she was enjoying the PV scene, her grades were superb, as always.

Appreciating the atmosphere and what PV had to offer, Autumn had never felt so at-home, seeing so many beautiful black people, embracing each other. For the first time in her young life, she didn't feel out of place.

Beside her, sat her roommate. Tara Pelkin was from Dallas. They had been getting along really well for the most part, that is, when Tara was around. Autumn practically had the room to herself, considering Tara's routine visits to the upperclass housing at night. She returned when Autumn was in her morning class.

As the band played Earth, Wind and Fire's, "Boogie Wonderland" the freshmen girls danced in their seats as they eyed the cute boys they would later talk about once they got back to the dorms. Autumn blushed. She had never seen so many endearing boys in one place! The band followed up with an MJ classic, PYT.

"I want to love you, pretty young thang," the girls sang and giggled.

The guys there were cute, but Autumn suddenly remembered the one that she had filled her mind with all summer. She really regretted not being able to see him that last day of her summer vacation. That meant she most likely would never see him again.

She snapped out of it and returned to what was before her, literally.

When the game was over, the seven freshmen flocked off the field and headed to Alumni Hall.

Autumn and her remaining friends went on. Before they could make it past the gates, she saw a familiar face. The almost five-foot petite yet, athletically-built Kennedy James with a tiny hand and firm grip reached out and grabbed Autumn's shoulder while holding the mic in the other.

"You are the perfect person to ask," she stated. "Come on over here!"

Autumn stood a little confused as Kennedy pulled her over to a guy whose face was covered by a camera he looked into.

"This is your first year here, right?" Kennedy said peering through her glasses.

"Yes," Autumn said nodding at the young woman who stood in a short-sleeved fitted black blazer, snug jeans and appealing red pumps.

"Did you enjoy your first Homecoming game?" she asked with her thick, brown eyebrows arched over her black-rimmed glasses.

Autumn replied with a yes...

"Okay, well I am just going to ask you a couple of questions on camera!"

Autumn agreed. She didn't feel like she had a choice though. She took a deep breath, wondering how it would turn out. She wasn't the best at expressing herself verbally, but she was going to give it her best shot.

Kennedy straightened her clothes and her blazer and waited for the red light and the camera guy to point. Autumn turned to face the camera.

"Hi, I'm Kennedy James and I am here…"

For Autumn, Kennedy's voice started to fade as Autumn couldn't believe her eyes. She tried to swallow, but she lost her breath as she took in the face of the camera guy who had peeped from behind the equipment. As she stood with a microphone shoved at her face, the guy of her dreams stood! The guy she had seen all summer long was standing there! Autumn wanted to jump out of her skin! Her heartbeat raced as he stood looking at her with the camera in his hand, focused on her. Autumn blinked and turned away trying to get her thoughts together. She knew there were bullets of sweat beading down her face. She could not meet his glance. She tried to catch her breath and unintelligible sounds that came out of her mouth, as the camera continued to roll. She realized what a fool she probably looked like standing there. He looked at her probably wondering who this sweaty, messy girl was. She felt awkward with his eyes on her. Then to make matters worse, Autumn realized Kennedy still stood there looking at her, having seen everything. Then to have it on tape! Autumn knew she looked like a complete idiot! - a hot and sweaty idiot.

"I'm sorry, what was the question?" Autumn asked.

That was only the beginning of a complicated love triangle, Autumn thought.

Family Matters?

The sweet aroma of watermelon-scented shampoo and the scent of burning chocolate overwhelmed Autumn, but the sound of women chatting over blow dryers rang too familiar as she reluctantly entered Deon's salon. It was a Tuesday, Autumn's day off. She didn't know how to describe the feeling that came over her when she stepped into the salon, each and every time. It was a beautiful place, full of beautiful people, who aspired to look more beautiful than when they came in. Autumn looked forward to her lunch breaks out on the courtyard patio and never spent time in the break room like the other girlie-girl women.

Autumn looked at her watch. It was 1:29. As she smiled and waved to her co-workers, the stylists greeted her in unison.

As she walked past the glass waterfall fountain that read "Deon's Hair Divas Salon," which stood behind the empty receptionist desk, she tried to accept that Hendrix didn't send her a birthday text this year. In gold flip flops, Autumn's flat-feet slapped the perfectly-waxed mahogany wood floors that she had polished the day before. She was wearing a brown and yellow retro printed frock with matching yellow tights. Once past the never-ending wall splattered with press pictures of Deon's face in countless magazines and periodicals, Autumn reached Deon's private studio where she worked the magic that the whole town ranted and raved about. *This was the V.I.P section.* Not everyone got their hair done by Deon.

Deon, Autumn's dad's half sister, kept Autumn busy. For Autumn, besides being Deon's niece, she also happened to be the salon's business assistant/ receptionist/ shampoo girl/ guinea pig. Today she served as the guinea pig. Every time Deon was hiring, Autumn was the hair model for the rather extravagant salon. Deon said Autumn's hair could take it, but Autumn was never too sure if that was a good thing or not.

One week had passed since the Hurricane night and Deon had opened up her salon doors. Pretty much all of Houston was a dead zone. All the school districts were closed for a week. All the stores were pretty much shuttered. People were sitting in dark homes, waiting for life to return to normal, and some managed to start the process of picking up the many pieces.

The salon owner, who happened to be a couple of months shy of her 30th birthday and a person Autumn didn't want to work under when the new year rolled in, was waiting in her studio. Autumn pushed herself to get to work on time. Life was livable when you stayed off Deon's hit list, or better yet, *shit* list. The list was longer than ever since she wasn't taking turning thirty too well.

Deon was a local celebrity with a pinch of national attention. Her magical touch had earned her a pretty high profile. Far from modest, Deon did everything in a big way! Autumn figured it was probably to match her fluffy ego. She did work hair miracles for many, including Autumn's own unruly strands. But every day in the shop, Autumn was reminded of how this was just a job, and an uninspiring one she had had since her freshman year in college. She needed a change.

As Autumn reached the studio door, she came face-to-face with the hair vixen herself. Autumn could see the top of Deon's long inky hair as she read her watch. Deon looked up slowly. Through her signature thick bangs, she focused her smoky gray eyes on her honey-hued-haired niece who stood in the doorway with a silly smile that got on Deon's nerves.

"Hey," Deon said slowly in her deep, scratchy voice.

"Hello," Autumn responded knowing she was in one of her moods.

"You can have a seat…for now. She isn't here," Deon managed.

Autumn hoped the women would hurry. She pulled out the latest romance novel she was reading and picked up where she left off.

Moments later, Autumn watched Deon hug her clipboard to her cleavage, as her eyes targeted ahead. She swished her hips as she strutted out her studio, past Autumn and out to the main salon.

This bitch better not be late, Deon thought with a thin-lipped smirk as she reached the front. *Favors.*

"I guess 'Miss Tardy' isn't excited about the idea of working here," she announced to the salon. "That's what she's telling me."

Celestina, a Latina stylist, tried not to laugh. She was tired of paying her boss attention.

They all knew Deon was big on first impressions. In the main studio, the aftermath of the storm was more than conversation. The devastation had altered just about everyone's lives in some way. The living conditions for the majority of Houstonians were in shambles, but the women did what they did best, talked it out.

"My family and I have a beach house. We went to board up our Galveston home - the irony of it all. After the storm, there was no house at all. The stakes still stood in the ground, but the house had collapsed and floated into the sea," said a woman who had been going to the salon since 2006.

Deon took a final glance at her watch before heading back to her station where Autumn was sitting in the styling chair in front of the mirror, too comfortably for Deon's taste. Autumn was still reading when suddenly Deon's cell phone rang.

"Deon," the owner answered, without too much personality.

Autumn watched a couple of emotions run across her aunt's face. She wasn't sure how to read them, but she tried her best. Deon mostly listened with her eyes in a far away place although she occasionally responded with a murmur.

Autumn watched Deon as if she were watching one of her beloved soaps. Autumn could tell the news seemed to be overwhelming. She braced herself as she tried to patiently wait for the phone call to end so she could try to put her own imaginative mind at ease.

Still with her ear to the phone, Deon nodded her head as she frowned.

"Well, all I can say is…congratulations, girl!" Deon then forced a smile although her face looked like she was holding back tears.

"Good for you!" Deon said again. "I can't believe it!"

There was some listening on Deon's part that followed.

"Of course. I will," said the owner.

Autumn sat and watched her aunt end the call. Deon walked out of the room without any words or emotion. She headed to the nearest bathroom.

***

"Another one," Deon murmured as she headed to the bathroom to pull herself together. She needed a cigarette, bad. This would be her fifth time walking down the aisle as a friend of the bride and she wasn't really up for the stroll.

If one more of these heifas gets married before me…she shook her head.

***

Once Deon emerged from the ladies room, where she tried to powder her flushed face, she said nothing about the phone call so Autumn didn't feel comfortable asking about it. Her aunt was not the conversational type, that was for sure. Deon headed back to the front. Shocked that the girl she was willing to interview never showed up, she then headed back to her workstation in a huff.

"Right now I need to get my things together so I can head on out." Deon started to put down her clipboard and began rummaging around her workstation. Autumn probably knew where more things were than she did because she was always barking at her to fetch them.

"My 1:30 interviewee is late," Deon paused. "We can walk out together. Just give me a second. I need to do some things," she concluded.

The Devil Made Me Do it

A couple of blocks down from the salon, like a Black exploitation action star, twenty-nine year old Nadia Masters managed to look both ways before crossing the busy streets. She dashed across the lanes, feeling defeated as her boots pounded the pavement. She really pushed all caution aside and followed through on her mission despite the risk. She had to get away! She just hoped the cars would let her cross in one piece.

She couldn't believe what she saw! Nadia was frantic. Hurrying along, not even noticing the shocked faces of the people she ran past, she ran for her life.

Moving back to Houston had her feeling like she was walking through one of those carnival crazy houses. One of the carnival games embedded in her head had become synonymous with her life. Far from amused, she played real-life, non-stop "Whack a Mole." No matter how fast or hard she hit the little animals into the ground they kept popping up, one after another. They might disappear, but one-by-one, they popped back out when and where she least expected. One-by-one, the little creatures reappeared. One-by-one, they laughed at her useless efforts to pound something into the ground.

It was 1:35 in the afternoon and Deon and Autumn were heading out the front door of the salon, leaving the other stylists with their customers.

***

Deon stood outside frowning. "Oh hell naw, let me get my shades." As she turned, Autumn stood at the door and gazed outside into the busy street. Her eyes settled upon a tall, cocoa-brown skinned figure running along the crowded sidewalk adjacent to her. Her chocolate long, elegant, hair flowed in the wind. The fairly slender lady kept a steady pace, making her way towards the block the salon was on. She held on tightly to her purse as she bravely ignored the traffic signs.

Autumn gulped as she saw cars begin to take off as the woman ran like she had stolen something. She felt like she was watching a commercial. Maybe one for hair or make-up, Autumn thought. Autumn could picture the ad: *You too, can be in a rush, dodging cars, buses and bikes, and still look fabulous after a long day's run with danger! Get "whatever product" and you will stop traffic!*

"Autumn!" Deon's voice from inside the salon snapped Autumn back to reality and out of her make-believe advertisement campaign.

She tried to ignore the call that permanently strained her itchy eardrums, but she knew not to when she heard it again in a different tone. Finally, she turned to look back into the salon, quickly searching for her boss.

"Yes ma'am!" she yelled back, hoping that that was enough, but she knew Deon too well.

"Come here!" the scratchy, bass-filled voice yelled back.

"Okay," Autumn managed, while quickly turning back to the street to find only the running woman had somehow made her way across the busy street, injury free. Nadia was now running past the side of the salon, soon out of Autumn's sight.

"How did she...," Autumn frowned still wondering how the lady had gotten across the street. She had a wild imagination, blame it on the *Muppet Babies.*

***

Nadia pushed to the final corner of the street. As she made a quick right, in a matter of seconds, she saw what made her want to brace herself, but it was too late. She felt an extreme force push into her stomach sending her flying backwards. Nadia fell to the ground and close to the edge of the street. A car turning the corner honked, more for being annoyed than as a warning for the woman to get out of the street.

While angry cars swerved around her, holding her bag over her stomach, she rolled onto her back and closed her eyes, trying to breathe and regain her breath. Nadia ignored the pain in order to quickly position herself on the sidewalk and out of the street. She didn't even see the short, stocky woman who had knocked the wind out of her. "Oh, my gosh, ma'am I am so sorry, please let me help you," said Sheila in a high-pitched, thick, southern drawl.

Twenty-nine year old, Sheila Roberts wobbled over to Nadia.

On impact, moments earlier, Sheila's shoe had flown and landed in the busy street. It fell between the two outer right lanes. She peered at the tall woman she had crashed into when she made a quick left at the corner. Sheila covered her mouth with total shock when Nadia did not respond to her offer of help. She hadn't meant to do anything wrong; she had just been trying to get where she needed to go, an interview of a lifetime.

Nadia was regaining some of the air she had lost, but her entire body ached. Sheila reached out once again to Nadia, who slowly but surely managed to sit up. Eyes that had been squeezed shut, finally opened. She saw where it all happened. Before she could stand, the woman's eyes widened and her lips formed a perfect circle. Sheila swallowed. "Elaine?!"

Nadia's senses were jolted by Sheila's assured voice, but Nadia remained composed. She frowned as she looked at the woman who looked at her as if she were face-to-face with a ghost. Nadia shook her head, concerned. "No," Nadia whispered lowly, but loud enough for Sheila to hear.

Embarrassed, and with her eyes still fixed on Nadia's, Sheila tried to make sense of what was going on. "No? Oh, my gosh. I am such an idiot," she smiled. "You must think I am some mad woman. First, I slam into you, knock you down and then think you are someone else. My apologies. You look like someone I used to know."

Nadia was not really hearing anything but her mind telling her to get up and go! She quickly looked behind her.

"Let me help you up," Sheila's tender voice insisted.

Nadia quickly stood up without her assistance.

"Are you all right?" Sheila asked, not convinced.

Nadia was quiet as she nodded and brushed off her clothes - fitted jeans and a black shirt.

Sheila did not take her eyes off Nadia who had hair all in her face.

"I feel awful for being so careless! I am always telling my kids, don't run, you may hurt someone and look at me. This has been a crazy day!" Sheila had a lot riding on the job interview at the salon around the corner and she was already late.

Nadia smiled as she made sure she had all her belongings. Suddenly something incongruent grabbed her attention - Sheila's feet.

Sheila had forgotten about the shoes she had bought on sale the other day. One remained upright in the street. She looked both ways but before she could move, a car turned the corner and in just a matter of seconds, the pump became one with the cement.

"Oh no!" Sheila squealed, remembering how she had bought the last pair at Showstoppin' Shoes, a small store in Sharpstown Mall, before it went out of business!

As she turned back to the sidewalk, she stood alone. The stranger she had collided with was nowhere in sight.

***

Around the corner, Autumn stood still, shocked by how fast the woman had traveled in order to cross the street. *Faster than a speeding bullet, faster than a ray of light,* Autumn thought, smiling at the nonsense of her thoughts. She giggled to herself and shook her head in disbelief. *That's crazy.*

Suddenly, approaching from the corner, Autumn saw a tired looking woman with trendy hair limping forward with an apologetic smile on her face. Autumn hoped, for the woman's sake, that she was not the "Miss Tardy" Deon had referred to earlier. She didn't want to witness that collision.

Deon's voice trailed behind Autumn as she walked toward the front of her salon.

"Never mind. I found them. Thanks for nothing, niece," Deon called out as she approached Autumn, who was standing at the door. Deon looked puzzled when she saw the exhausted woman standing before her, wearing only one shoe. The girl certainly didn't look like one of the celeb-starlets she had styled while in L.A and here in Houston when she opened her business. This woman was fair, mediocre, and missing a very important accessory. The shoe she did have on was not a status item - looked like a firesale knock-off to Deon, who frowned at the girl's poor taste. Worst of all, she was late. Deon couldn't get over that.

"Mrs. DeVaulle, I apologize for being…" Sheila struggled with the word *Autumn* knew all too well. "Late," Sheila finally pushed out frantically trying to meet Deon's squinted eyes that were hidden behind thick blunt bangs.

Sheila had had a hell of a morning, that was for sure. She had prepared for weeks for the interview only to have her youngest out of three children come down with some bug she was still trying to treat. Sheila was rarely late and usually five minutes early. If only her common law hubby had done what she had asked him to do, and come home in time to help her with their son. But he had something else to do and Sheila had to ask her neighbors to watch her child until she could get back. Her baby had been on her mind since the moment she left the house.

"I am so sorry," Sheila explained. Autumn could hear the pain behind her words.

"I agree," Deon said pushing back her long hair, but not revealing her light eyes.

Sheila could see her whole dream becoming a nightmare. She knew this did not look good, but she really had been prepared.

"Ma'am, I can explain the situation."

"A situation that I don't want to hear," Deon said, closing her eyes as she eased on her shades.

Sheila swallowed hard as she watched Deon pull out a carton of Marlboro cigarettes.

"Honey, you're alive. The only excuse I would have accepted was if you were dead, or something of that nature," she said in her pitchy voice that had become harsher over time.

Desperately, Sheila continued to stand wanting to explain, but Deon pulled out a lighter.

Deon held her index finger over her lip. "You have said enough," she snapped as she lit her cigarette and then stuffed the box back into her purse. She took one last glance at the girl's ridiculous shoe.

Autumn looked at her watch. It was 1:39.

"Is there any way I could explain? I mean I really want to be able to at least…"

Autumn knew the answer to that one.

"I don't think you understand," Deon laughed loudly. "I didn't build this salon on excuses." Deon continued. "Maybe the *rinky-dink* shops you've worked in, maybe they take bull shit, but I don't and will never start accepting that. If anyone even thinks they have a chance to work at this establishment, they can't afford to be - you."

Autumn exhaled, and was embarrassed.

Sheila held her tongue. She felt weak. Standing on one heel was not helping.

"I'm always on top," Deon snapped.

Sheila frowned at the woman who now stared at her directly through her dark shades.

"Out of respect for Romeo, I gave you an interview. But baby girl, I advise you to get on top of your game." Deon put the cigarette in her mouth and started to walk off waiting on Autumn to follow.

Getting more used to purging, Autumn had found the most opportune time to let go. This was Autumn's last day working under her Aunt.

STRETCH MARKS

Sheila's Herstory

What year does a woman begin to have…secrets?
Secrets she can't even share with the closest of kin
Secrets she can't even pass to the ears of friends

The moment her life becomes her own
because shame is too much to share

It is the curse that is passed so effortlessly
Yet it leaves the longest imprint
It holds you at night the tightest; you wake up smothered in its scent

I remember seeing the look
The same look I have now, on my mother's face
A moment impossible to erase
Even if I tried

The far away look, a silent cry out for *why*
Why me, did this happen to?
She sits and rocks, the rhythm of despair
The unanswered questions, she listens to, lies hidden in her consciousness
The defeat of not being able to reach clarity
The suspense kills and as she exists, she slowly dies a silent, yet assuming death

I watched the burden she carried quite gracefully and
began to wonder too, what could have kept her so,
what secrets could she possibly hold?

I knew that with that grip, that tight lip, I wasn't getting the answer

When you allow a man

into your life
One that does not deserve an invite
When you deep down know, yet you still let go
that is the secret you can't tell. That is the secret.
The living hell.

Roots

The "talk" seemed to happen earlier and earlier for twenty-nine year old mother of three, Sheila Roberts. Sheila, former EMT, current beauty school student was a country girl who could whip up a good southern meal in a matter of seconds. She was also the type that avoided confrontation at all cost.

This conversation could not be ignored. Shaunie Davis was Sheila's middle child, and only nine years old, but already experiencing mature situations early in the middle of her school semester. It was October. These situations made her mother quite nervous, even more nervous to share with Shaunie's daddy, underdog underground gangsta rap typhoon, Dro Dean.

Dro sure didn't need another reason to flip out. Walking on eggshells was the story of Sheila's life, but her feet had grown plump and swollen from cosmetology school and lately, the former professional dancer's footwork was far from fancy.

As far as Sheila and Shaunie's "woman to little woman" talk, Sheila remembered how she had skipped the talk with her fourteen year old daughter, Portia Smith. She lived to regret that everyday. All Sheila could do was brace herself for when she would have to bring it to the two year old son, Tony Dean, but her baby boy had some ways to go.

But Shaunie was only nine, and taking after her mom, had the body of a seventeen year old woman. However, athletic Portia, a replica of her former NBA basketball playing dad who was not in her life physically, but was monetarily present, was tall and lanky.

This was the last conversation Shaunie wanted to have and she was almost as nervous as her mother.

Sheila knew there was not a "birds and the bees" blueprint because she would have owned a copy and relied on it to feed her words she could recite line by line. Being a good mother was a challenge. She hoped to break the vicious cycle with her kids, which had continued in her family for generations. She had her kids at the same age that her mother did. Fifteen years old. Her mother's mother had done the same.

But Sheila knew there were grand differences between herself and her own mother, Lisa Roberts, whom she hadn't seen in years.

Sheila turned all her attention to the beautiful girl who sat before her, wearing the latest hairstyle, which Sheila jazzed up daily. Shaunie was a popular girl with a lot of friends and she naturally rolled with the "in crowd." She was proud that the hormonal boys called her "the finest one" in the group, but it made her wonder if they saw her intelligence.

Sheila was determined to make her daughter see that she had to be the brightest in the group as well. Shaunie naturally brought home A's, but her focus had started to drift and Sheila knew that as her mother, she needed to make sure it reverted back to academics. Her children's future was her focus and they meant the world to her.

"Shaunie, pleasing men can get you in a lot of trouble. Sweetie, it is the type of trouble that your heart or mind can't handle if you are not mature enough."

Sheila felt sick to her stomach as she thought about the call from Shaunie's teacher earlier this week.

"Mrs. Roberts? Your daughter Shaunie was caught in the boy's bathroom..." Sheila had cried like a baby when she heard the rest.

"I taught her better than that..." Sheila knew it was time to have a talk with Shaunie.

"Baby, don't get confused. Many girls have sex, not for themselves, but for the boys - to please them so they will stick around. That is not what sex was designed for."

Sheila wiped the sweat from her brow.

Shaunie could hear the lump forming in her mother's throat and like a reciprocal reaction, one formed in her own.

"Sex...is an act for two mature adults who know what love is and want to showcase it in the act. It is not child's play or something to just casually do with any of these little nappy headed boys out here."

Shaunie was as stiff as a board while she looked at her mother and listened to her intense voice.

“There is a little girl inside of all of us.” The lump was fully formed. Sheila’s eyes began to water as she remembered driving her daughter to the clinic after the bathroom episode. “Make sure you don’t let anyone make her grow up too fast.”

Shaunie blinked as she saw a tear fall from her mother’s eyes.

“When you are ready, you will know,” Sheila said and then inhaled as much as she could, realizing she had forgotten to breathe normally.

“Do you understand me?” Sheila said frantically.

Shaunie nodded.

Sheila hoped that her youngest daughter would take what she said, but she knew forcing the issue would only make it escalate. She would revisit the concern when need be, but for the moment, that was all she could take.

“Now you can go finish your homework.” Sheila watched Shaunie as she walked away and up the stairs, carefully taking each step. Sheila tried to gather herself.

“I need a drink,” Sheila said to herself.

***

Sheila paid her sixteen-year-old cousin, Sharita, a high school senior, to watch her kids since Shar was saving to buy a car. Sheila was at the *Kinner’s* hole-in-the-wall bar, miles away from her home in Third Ward, drinking her sorrows away. Six months shy of being laid-off from her EMT job, Sheila had been busy trying to find another job to support her family of three and a half. Her baby daddy was in and out of her life. He was more in than out this course of her life due to her tight grip.

“I found out early on, misery loves company,” Sheila said out of the blue, with a smile. “It may be the only thing that misery loves.” Sheila had had her share of Tequila shots that evening and it was twenty minutes to ten. Luckily, she had found a friend who actually seemed remotely interested in her drunken conversation.

“Isn’t that the truth, mami!” said the twenty-eight year old Latina who was celebrating a victory and felt the least she could do was listen to the sad, lonely lady at the bar. Celestina Rodriguez remembered when she had that same sad look. Two months ago, some random person had listened to her and saved her life. She smiled as she continued to lend her ear to Sheila while staying away from the hard liquor.

Sheila laughed. "She sure knows how to pick her companions, too," Sheila said in between sips. "Like a vulture, she preys on the weak."

"Who you telling?" Celestina said in disbelief. "Believe me; I know exactly what you mean! See my misery is my boss. I love my job, but my boss drains me. She put the damn M in misery. That bitch needs to get laid!"

Sheila laughed. She would take a miserable boss any day over a miserable mom.

"If you ask me, I had no chance," Sheila swallowed. "The odds were against me from the start," the woman listened to Sheila continue. "You can't choose your mom."

The woman chimed in. "Don't beat yourself up. You seem like a good person. You don't have to be a victim of circumstance. Be the mother you need to be for your kids. That's what I do!"

"Thanks," Sheila said, then paused for a moment.

"You know, you probably think I am so weak. As much as I want to, it is hard for me to be a good mother. I just wonder how it is possible," Sheila said.

"A wise person once said, everything you need to know, you can find it in a book," Celestina pushed.

Sheila laughed at the thought since she wasn't one for reading.

"You know, hang in there. Times get hard. But there is possibility all around. I got something for you. Something that may cheer you up. It gave me the boost I needed to deal *with my misery.*

Sheila could see where this was going and she remembered the days she used to roll it up with the best of them.

"Oh sorry, I don't smoke anymore," Sheila, the former wild child expressed.

Celestina had a sense of humor and couldn't help but laugh.

"No. Nothing like that!" she explained. "I'm already crazy! Last time I did that, I wound up next to my boss in bed."

Sheila looked embarrassed. Celestina didn't.

"This is better than any herb. And it gave me the strength and plan to get the hell up out of there sooner than I thought." Celestina couldn't believe that the book gave her the courage to break the unhealthy and degrading relationship she had with her boss.

Minutes later, after a couple of Tequila shots, Sheila found herself by the woman's car in pretty good shape. She wasn't singing drunken karaoke, or standing on tables showing people her past profession. She was cool.

After some digging around, Celestina carefully placed a book in her hands - a microscope and two large pupils illustrated the cover.

"Here you go mami. It's her latest."

Sheila, wondering who "her" was, flipped the book over and the picture of the beautiful black sister's face stared back at her. Sheila saw that the woman wore natural, thin twists in her hair. They were pulled up high in a ponytail, highlighting her European features, and her freckles. PhD was beside her name and the sepia-toned photo that was taken outside in a garden.

The Microscopic View by relationship therapist, Dr. Lynne.

"It's more than a good read," Celestina reassured.

Sheila looked up at the woman who had let her talk her ear off for the past hour.

"Oh no, I don't want to take your copy, I can just pick it up now that I know what book it is."

"No, I got all I needed from it. Your turn."

Sheila smiled. "Thank you...What was your name?"

The women laughed at how they knew each other's business and not each other's name.

"Celestina."

"I'm Sheila."

Celestina reached into her Louis Vuitton to hand her a cute business card that had a woman's silhouette and a pair of scissors.

"You're a beautician, too?" Sheila gushed.

"Yeah!" Celestina said, liking that they had so much in common.

"Where do you work?" Sheila asked, fishing for job openings as soon as she completed her courses.

"Deon's Hair Divas. But, not for long. My cell is on there, so we can keep in touch."

Sheila's heart dropped at the name. *Deon was her boss!*

"What's wrong?" Celestina said while looking at her face.

"Oh, nothing. I blew an interview at *Deon's.* I would kill to be able to work at that salon. Seems like the best opportunity to be taken seriously."

Celestina stood in silence for a moment. Looks could be deceiving. And she was happy to break her deal with the devil.

"Call me and let me know you made it home," Celestina said, wanting to keep the conversation light now.

"Okay," Sheila said with a smile.

"Don't forget," Celestina said.

"Oh and Sheila, *Joy* loves company."

Split Ends

"I have found the paradox,
that if you love until it hurts,
there can be no more hurt, only more love."
– Mother Teresa

The next day, Sheila went to work at the DF Cosmetology School on the South Side of Houston, regretting more and more the day of her "almost" interview. *Who did she think she was?* She never fully fooled with *the Jones'*. Every once in awhile she would think she was somebody and try to do what the *somebodys* did, only to find out that *nobody* cared.

The teenage client that sat in her chair wanted Sheila's identical hair style, minus some of the rainbow colors because of her high school's dress code regulations. Sheila, who was forever experimenting with her own hair, was currently rockin' a multi-colored hate-it-or-love-it, Mohawk. After a few snips and some subtle highlights in her customer's bangs, Sheila scrunched the woman's short razored-bob to create volume. As her hands shaped and the client beamed, all she could think about was *Deon's Hair Divas. So close.* She just wanted to get her foot in the door and if it weren't for her damn shoe in the street, she probably would have at least made it before the door slammed in her face.

As her client marveled at Sheila's work and took a look at the back of her asymmetric style, Sheila tried to convince herself it was for the best. She had a clientele that loved her and would follow her wherever she went. But Sheila kept replaying the words that easily came out of Deon's mouth, "rinky dink." Well, the "rinky dink" shop was packed. She was almost out of beauty school and would only work there until she could find a chair in an upscale salon.

After handing Sheila cash money and giving her a big hug, her client was out of the door, loving her new do. Sheila knew she wasn't worthy of Deon's status, but she wanted to prove something to herself. She remembered the dose of inspiration that had come into her life.

The other night, once her kids were tucked, Sheila had started the book, not thinking that she would have to make herself pull away from it so she could get some sleep. As the pages turned, she felt like she could see herself more clearly. She was starting to like the view.

On her break, Sheila found herself engrossed in Chapter 7 – Breaking the Cycle. Step one, examine insecurity and step two, embrace possibility.

One of her beautician friends, who she usually *girl talked* with on breaks, came in shortly and caught her with her nose stuffed between the pages.

The woman frowned, "What are *you* reading?" looking at Sheila and then at the tabloid mags they normally dove in, which sat ignored on the table.

A bit embarrassed, she murmured, "Oh something that a friend gave me."

The other beautician continued to frown as she read the cover while she warmed up her chicken pot pie. Her co-worker was waiting on Sheila to put it away so she could tell her the latest gossip. But Sheila continued to read.

***

After a long day of standing on her feet and ignoring the beauty shop heat, Sheila was back in effect, on chapter 14 - Seeing is believing. She sat in the long line of cars picking up the car-rider students, waiting on Shaunie to exit. She was almost finished when a car honked at Sheila.

"Oh, sorry," Sheila waved her hand as she moved up to close the space in the line.

***

Later that night after cooking and helping the kids with their homework, Sheila turned her attention to finishing the book. Normally her thoughts were focused on solving the mysteries of *Where's Dro,* but not tonight. He said he was in the studio, but she never heard any music. For the first time, it was not her concern.

Two hours later, Sheila had read every page of the book.

She was never too proud to give credit where credit was due and that book deserved a lot of props. Dr. Lynne had hit the nail right on the head on a number of things and issues. It was beyond self-help. It was a history lesson, it was a bible study, and it was the mother she never had. She had to let her know that this book did have an effect on her, a positive one at that.

She searched the book for contact info and knew that she would call the author first thing in the morning.

***

Before the mother started everyone's day, she got the book and the phone.

As soon as she saw nine digits, she dialed, expecting a voicemail for sure, but a pleasant voice answered instead.

Sheila tried to switch modes from leaving a message to actually talking to a person.

"Hi, I just wanted to leave a message for the author. This book really helped me get some things together in my own head."

"Great to hear. What part of it exactly?"

"The chapter on getting over insecurity in order to see possibility."

"Oh, really! We'll I am glad you called. Why do you feel insecure?"

Confidential

Dr. Lynne was down-to-earth. Sheila couldn't believe that when she called to leave a message, she would end up talking to Dr. Lynne. After a short phone conversation, the author and relationship therapist invited Sheila to come and talk with her at her office, just so she could get some things off her chest.

Sheila wondered if she should tell the doctor everything. This was what therapy was all about, to let it all out. Sheila was new to therapy, but not letting it all out. Sheila had just received a text from her baby-sitting relative after checking on them. Sharita assured her that her babies were okay in her care. She hadn't heard from Dro all day. He had come home around three o'clock in the morning but she played like she was asleep, like she always did.

Dr. Lynne's office was located in the Medical Center area. Her suite was on the second floor of a high rise building. Warm, yet very sleek, similar to what Sheila imagined based on TV shows, but the afro-centric accessories added a unique touch. She took in the rustic hues of red, orange and brown as she sat in the waiting area for only a second when one of the women workers offered her a beverage.

She was handed an ice-cold bottle of water and soon she heard the words "Sheila Roberts, Dr. Lynne is ready to see you."

She was a bit nervous as she didn't expect to meet the author of the book by any means. She had just felt compelled to share her testimony.

When she entered the office, Dr. Lynne was standing at the door to welcome her.

Taller than she had expected, Sheila looked up as they both were about to shake hands. Dr. Lynne could have been a model. She was proportioned to fit the most expensive gowns and suits eloquently. Sheila knew she was forty at the time the book was published, but her youthful glow could easily fool the eye.

Her yellow, freckled face, was absent of make-up and she seemed to purposely omit accessories. She was simple, but her presence was undeniably beautiful. This was bold to Sheila, who wouldn't dare rock the plain look. She never left home without her lashes, her full-fledged face paint and hair that made a statement.

"Sheila, my sister, nice to meet you," she said with an impressed smile that made her eyes crinkle at the sides. "Lynne," she said as she held out her hand.

"It is a pleasure to meet you," Sheila said shaking it back. Dr. Lynne then welcomed her to have a seat.

After sitting on the comfy chaise, Sheila didn't lean back too quickly. She knew this was cliché and wondered if her *real* patients did this.

Sheila looked around her room. It was pretty plain. Nothing flashy, just plants and natural like furniture made of dark stained woods mixed with wicker.

Dr. Lynne thanked her for calling and explained how she had sensed that Sheila needed a spiritual mentor just by her words over the phone.

"I just sense that you are at a turning point and that with the right attitude you can very well have that breakthrough!" the doctor explained.

Sheila blushed. She wanted more than anything to advance.

Soon, Dr. Lynne asked her to start sharing what was on her mind, preferably from the beginning.

"It may be a stretch, but it is the best place to start," Lynne reassured.

Sheila didn't waste any time.

"Dr. Lynne, early on, I had grown accustomed to how shitty my life seemed to be. Excuse my language."

The doctor's eyes crinkled again.

"Call me Lynne."

"Alright," Sheila said, but knew she would find it hard. Sheila continued. "I conditioned myself to deal. It all started with Lisa, my mother. Lisa was an insecure person, who I believe lived to ruin her own daughter's life."

The doctor carefully frowned as she continued to listen.

"I didn't understand her at all. I still try to figure her out, yet, it makes no sense and it takes me back to a place that I can't visit for too long, in fear of getting stuck."

Dr. Lynne nodded her head slowly. Sheila continued after a couple of moments.

"We were two different people. Being a mother was something that I actually wanted to be. I could never stomach the idea that my babies could look at me the way I looked at the woman who gave me life. I know I am not perfect, but I promised myself that I would do my best with my kids."

"Let me ask you a question. Do you think that your mom did the best she could with her children?" asked Lynne.

Sheila scratched her head. She thought long and hard before answering.

"She was fifteen years old and I was her first born. As soon as I was old enough, I took care of the things she didn't want to do. So my childhood was cut short so that she could live her life. She did the playing."

Dr. Lynne listened, not too intently, not too disinterested. Enough to let Sheila continue to feel comfortable sharing. Normally, she had to probe and direct her patients more. Sheila just kept flowing.

"Responsibility, it knew me well. I had a brother and a sister and I had to make sure they got to school on time. My mind was to always, protect Lisa. Make her happy."

Dr. Lynne wrote a note to herself.

"I helped them with their homework. I started cooking early. I remember standing on a chair because I couldn't even see over the stove."

The doctor tilted her head a bit.

"I don't know how I did it, but I did. And I did a good job."

Dr. Lynne listened.

"Sometimes my mother was nice. Most of the time she was sheer evil.

Dr. Lynne spotted a sudden change in Sheila's upbeat mannerisms and made a mental note of it.

"The terror in Lisa's, or my mother's eyes, made me break out in cold sweats." Sheila paused and stared down at the floor.

"The ideas she came up with to torture me, were wicked and unforgivable."

Though empathetic, Dr. Lynne had heard her share of horror stories, so nothing really fazed her.

"Weak. That was what my mother called me when I cried."

The doctor's eyes widened.

"I accepted how powerless I felt and always looked to God to fight my battles. And He did."

The doctor waited to hear what was holding her back.

"My problem though, I always admired the strong. In my mind, they had it made. They didn't have *my* problems."

Dr. Lynne listened to a woman whom she knew had more figured out than she gave herself credit for. She knew her responsibilities, her faults, her limitations. She knew the consequences. Unfortunately, she was stuck in neutral and had a hard time being straightforward about her opinion of her mother's parenting skills. Hopefully, Dr. Lynne could help her find the confidence she needed to stop giving power over to others; hopefully she could help give her the boost by the end of the sessions.

***

The following Monday, Sheila sat back on the sofa a little more than she had the first time. Her mind was somewhere else and Dr. Lynne asked her to explain.

Sheila recalled an earlier conversation with Dro, who had come home unexpectedly, just before she left the house. Instead of the babysitter staying there, Sheila had dropped them at Sharita's before heading to her session.

Dro had asked before she was out the door where she was going. She responded with she was just running errands. Sheila was bad at lying, but she took the chance because she was not willing to share that she was almost late for her second session with Dr. Lynne. She knew that Dro would not take the news of her talking to someone about their life too well, so she decided to not give him the information. She dreaded sharing so much with him, so she rarely did.

"Like last week, I told you I wanted us to focus on the relationships you are in. Tell me about your friends."

Sheila nodded and then a smile spread as she remembered. "They just jealous," she said smiling.

Dr. Lynne watched Sheila's smile carefully.

"That's what Dro used to say about my friends. I had a lot of friends, before the relationship really got serious." Sheila let out a huge sigh. "And my dumb ass held onto those words." Sheila shook her head.

"Who is Dro?"

Sheila smiled. "He is my baby's daddy. We go back to '98. I was in high school. Dro was working on his first album. You see, have you ever heard of underground music?"

Dr. Lynne smiled. "I know a thing or two."

"Well, he is an underground music producer. He works with a lot of artists here. He grew up listening to The Geto Boys, Scarface, UGK and DJ Screw. He had dreams of being the next household name from the south. He decided to go make a demo in 2000 and that was the one I auditioned for. On the set, he just took to me. There were other girls there, but he just took to me. Made me feel special. We clicked. We were cool and we kicked it right away. Everything was going well and then he had to pump the brakes. So many from different labels wanted some of his beats. He was always going to get back to his own thing, but when the money started flowing in, he had to roll with it, you know."

Lynne smiled.

"We got together in 2000. He knew I did hair, I started braiding his. I still do. I got pregnant that year with our first child."

Lynne nodded.

"In the beginning, everything was cool. He had aspirations of launching his own rap album, but there is always something getting in the way. Lately he has been really trippin' because things had been slowing down since 2005, when Houston was on the map."

Lynne shifted a bit in her chair.

"I know he is really feeling like he's the old man in the game, the one that never got his chance."

"Thanks for telling me about him, but tell me more about how your relationship with him affected your friends," Dr. Lynne finally interjected.

"Oh yeah. They weren't jealous. I realize that now. Disappointed, maybe. Jealous, no. Whatever was really there, it was enough to have me."

***

The following week, it was the same story, same question from Dro.

"Where you going?" he taunted her at the door.

Sheila didn't dare say session III with a therapist. Luckily she was able to ease out of the house without too much more conversation.

"Let me ask you this, what do you want Sheila?" Dr. Lynne asked. It was a simple question that sometimes was hard to answer.

"I want my kids to feel loved. I want my husband to love me.

Dr. Lynne nodded as if she had heard the wisest aphorism.

"I haven't had much luck in love. My kid's fathers have always been in love with other people while we were together."

Sheila took a sip of water.

"So what is keeping you in certain relationships where you don't feel loved?" Dr. Lynne asked.

Sheila sat. She wondered. "I guess my kids. I want us to do it for them. Dro and I live together. Common law marriage. At the end of the day, I don't know what it feels like to not have him. That thought scares me. I know that he may not be perfect, but neither am I."

Dr. Lynne took some quick notes on her little pad of paper.

"What examples are you setting for your kids?" the doctor asked.

"We had some good times. Those are the things that I hold on to you know," Sheila said trying to defend her life.

"Is he father material to your children?" the doctor asked casually.

Sheila swallowed the answer.

"Is he husband material?" Lynne threw out.

Sheila seemed a bit stumped on that one, too.

"These are things to honestly think about," the doctor suggested with a reassuring smile.

"Doctor, what is *father material?*" Sheila asked. "What is "husband material?"

"We have our own definition. It is not just a title that someone has. It is being there emotionally, spiritually and physically for someone," Dr. Lynne said.

***

Sheila needed to come home to get the money to pay babysitting Sharita. As she stepped in the front room and closed the door behind her, when she turned around, an object was shoved into her stomach. Dro jammed the object into her stomach even as she struggled to breath and pushed her up against the door.

"Running errands, huh?" he challenged.

Sheila was frantic.

"This look like errands to you?" Dro moved the object that he had so tightly pressed against her stomach up for her to see.

The book that she had gotten from the lady at the bar now sat in her face. She saw the sticky note she had written when she was writing the information, fees, and directions based on their first phone conversation with Dr. Lynne.

Dro took the sticky note off the book and stamped it to her forehead.

"You lying bitch! You seeing a damn shrink!" he shouted.

He once again pushed the yellow paper on her head, making her head hit the door.

He took the book and with all his might threw it across the room, breaking some vases and pictures over by the fireplace, where it landed on the ground.

Sheila was terrified.

"How much you paying her!!? With our fucking money! My money actually 'cause know yo ass ain't got none."

Sheila couldn't speak, she was in shock.

"We both struggling and here you go, throwing our money away on some damn therapy."

Sheila stood in utter shock. It had been awhile since she had seen this side of Dro.

This was the side that made her go into labor early with her Shaunie. This was the side that threw his son down in the cradle when he was crying for his mother. This was the side that had the police knocking at their door and Portia wanting to live with her daddy.

Sheila had promised herself, if that side of Dro returned, she would have to make a phone call.

She called her *other* baby daddy.

Even though, I try to be strong. Even though, I try to move on
Even though, I try to forget. Even though, I try to omit
Even though, I try not to cry. Even though, I try to get by
Even though, I try,
I can't

You try to get the best of me
You don't want to see me happy
You won't let go of me
You just refuse to let me be

But I got news for you
I refuse to let you do
what you try to do to me
It's my time to be happy

GET WITH THE PROGRAM

Kennedy's Herstory

It's the ill-advised televised suicide

They are just waitin', waitin' on us, to finally, finally kill
Ourselves

They are just waitin', amused, at our confused souls because
Souls of black folk, ain't the same no more

We ain't close, we are finally, to the edge
They don't have to watch us jump, they can turn their heads

And they laugh as they walk away
Knowing, we are voluntarily going
downhill

—

How does it feel
to watch someone die
slowly?
They don't even cry
because they don't even know
they are suffering

Yeah, they should,
but there is so much
misunderstood
so much
baggage from the "hood" of hoods
Sister,
Brother,
Mother,
and Father,

the hoods
Loyalty to what? Loyalty to who?
The message just won't simply get through

Less than a picture perfect view, changing the channel
The channel, won't do
There is dead air on every station, you come to
What will the outdated antenna do?

TV Guide can't direct you
Adjust your ears, the static will drown out the tears
That have been cried for many years
By those who ignored their fears, and live the impossible dream
To create what is on screen

Adjust your eyesight
It's not just a screen of black and white
People are doing more than Nick-at-Nite
Nobody wants to cut, *uncut*
All they want to do is bite
Off their

piece of the action
Chasing their own satisfaction
No school house rock to re-run
Learning on Saturday morning
Can't be fun

Replace those
thoughts with what's on the screen
Behind the scenes
there are not enough queens
Relaying messages, and replaying messages
That matter to us

Seeing is believing
That's what's happening
To us

More than a 48 hours mystery
This problem has been going on for centuries
Such vacancy
Love doesn't live here anymore?
The saddest question is

Did it ever though?

We need some law and order
but what we keep getting is, bitch please

There ain't much glory in one life to live
The young is more than restless
The girls are far from golden
The family can't stop feuding
And it's
Putting us all in jeopardy
Or so to speak
The question remains…
What is so entertaining about *Black?*

Full Moon

The clock struck midnight and the sweet sounds of an old Maxwell CD filled the crevices of the humble, yet functional house. It was a house that the home-sick, black and proud, twenty-six year old television news producer, Kennedy James, reluctantly made home. By the end of the current month of November, she would be gladly breaking her lease to return to her hometown of Houston, Texas. The last thing on her mind was breaking the news to her *friend* that had suddenly become a part of the "benefits" category.

What happens in Yorkton, needs to stay in Yorkton, she thought.

With her coal-colored eyes rolling to the back of her head, she rocked back and forth while on top of the twenty-eight year old physical trainer, Conner Scott. As the proud cowboy let his strong hands caress her tight body and silk chocolate skin, Kennedy let her inhibitions go and allowed her toned body to respond to the man who had surprisingly, stimulated her mind early on. Her adrenaline was high as she straddled him and she sped up the tempo.

In awe and delight, his eager sea-blue eyes captured her every move and what dangled before him. They both were alert, yet it still felt like an out of body experience. He was in heaven and *she,* who was supposed to be practicing celibacy, was dreading hell.

Both fitness junkies had met at the country club that Conner worked at. The upscale community was in Basefield, a nicer part of the small town in Yorkton County that Kennedy worked in since graduating from Prairie View A & M University with a degree in Mass Communications. Kennedy despised the Texas town and the small minds that carried on old-fashioned ideas. Luckily, there were a couple of things that made her time there bearable – the work experience she was gaining, the gym, the great outdoors and *the buddy with the sea-blue eyes.*

Conner came in handy, for his mind was far from small. He was something a lot of the men in Kennedy's life weren't – supportive of her dreams and her drive.

To Conner, Kennedy was a breath of fresh air. She would never know how much her presence helped him deal with his proposal gone wrong. In 2006, the year they met, he had just lost his girlfriend of six years in a fatal car crash the day he was going to ask for her hand in marriage. Kennedy was the first woman that took his mind off the tragedy and made him see there was more to life than grieving. Departure still remained a sensitive subject for him, but he was living life, living it to the fullest.

Kennedy was a workaholic on a mission! For the petite woman, who saw life as a calendar that she lived to cross off completed tasks, her motto was *factor in fun when the work was done.* With her journalism background, she had a way of capturing an audience, but an inability to communicate anything other than her career goals. As much as she valued communication, she kept her conversation to a minimum, except when debating.

Kennedy was methodical and adjusted well to the demands and the pressure of the job. She started off reporting for the Yorkton station, but her socially conscious nature led her quickly to move into the production side where she had more control over images. Over time, she had learned to make her blunt and brash personality work for her in her profession in order to please the masses. She censored her straightforwardness, but still struggled to tone down her radical racial justice antics.

For the majority of her life, the former tomboy was most comfortable around males, that was until they started hating her guts because her aggressive, egotistical nature and soaring spirit were hard to tame.

But there was something about Conner that represented *tranquility and fun.* He had a way of making light of things and her issues lighter. She remembered the first time that he interrupted her workout to tell her about how great her form was.

The former high school athlete had learned to stay physically active to function *mentally.* Kennedy kept up her same fitness regimen. She found that her gym membership in the town was a great way to properly release the stress from the job as well as the pent up sexual energy that she thought she could easily suppress, *until tonight.*

She never saw the night's events happening since their relationship progressed gradually. The two innocently worked out together, traveled together, and while doing this, discussed everything under the sun. Kennedy played down the fact that she had found someone she had so many things in common with. They shared some of the same philosophies and dissected the world in parallel ways. Soon, the unconventional liaison made Kennedy nervous to no end, yet it was the forbidden fruit she couldn't resist biting into.

How could this be happening?

She had fought it up into the last moment, but it was beyond her control. She couldn't even imagine what this would do to her past, present and future reputation when she returned to Houston, if anyone found out.

For the first time in her life she did not trust herself or her sound judgment. She needed him to pull out, but it was too late.

Gray Area

The next morning…

Like a sleepwalker, a groggy, open-nose Kennedy was led to the kitchen after hearing the sounds of fresh coffee being brewed. Conner knew just how the caffeine queen liked her coffee - strong. He handed it to her as she stepped into her own kitchen that was foreign to her domestically challenged self. After a whiff of the steaming cup, she opened her eyes fully, thanking God it was Saturday. She would have been at work if it were a weekday because she arrived at the station at 3:30 each morning.

"Bright and shine!" Conner sang doing a goofy dance that normally made her laugh. She gave a half smile.

Conner made his own schedule. He worked various hours and mostly by appointment at the Country Club's Fitness Center.

A hearty southern breakfast was laid out on the kitchen island. Kennedy lived in between both the manicured lawns of the upper class population and the gassy smells of the lower class shacks and trailers.

"This looks so good," Kennedy said, eager to dig in.

Soon they had their plates full of homemade pancakes, sausage, and eggs. The pulp filled orange juice, as bright as the morning sun, filled both of their cups, to the top of the rim. They both picked from one bowl filled with sliced apples, watermelon, cantaloupes and strawberries. After she said grace, they went for it.

"You didn't do all of this yourself, did you?" Kennedy asked enjoying every bite.

"Yes," he said proudly. "Got it from McDonalds and Kroger and laid it out all my myself!"

Kennedy laughed as she gave it a second look. Her eyes settled on Conner who had suddenly changed in his mood. She could no longer see the dimple in his left cheek.

Conner cleared his throat.

"You okay?" Kennedy asked, concerned.

Conner took a deep breath.

"I have been giving this a lot of thought. The more we get to know each other, the more I feel that what we have is special. This may be too early to put this out here, but I want my folks to meet you. To me, it is long overdue!"

Orange juice went down the wrong pipe. Kennedy started coughing.

Conner hopped up, but she tried to fan him away.

"Oh, wow," she finally said, coughing a couple of more times, then clearing her throat.

Conner looked at her with concern.

"You okay?" he asked.

"Yeah, now."

Conner hesitated before returning to the subject.

"After last night, I thought it would be fitting, you know," he said, almost done with his food.

Kennedy couldn't do it. She had never feared anything, but she knew the feeling well now, due to all the questions that formed.

What would people say? Normally she didn't give a damn, but this was different. For months, she had bobbed and weaved around town avoiding people's reactions to the two of them hanging out. Even when they traveled outside of town, she managed to deal with the stares hoping to convey the message that they were on business rather than enjoying each other's company. But meeting the parents would make what they had more official.

Kennedy couldn't look in his eyes so her gaze settled on the mole under his right eye.

"I just think you are a great person and with *us* getting closer, I want my parents to know who I am spending all this time with, especially after last night. I know that you are close to your family as well."

Kennedy felt cheated. She knew that she would want the same thing if it weren't so taboo.

She cringed when she imagined her pro-Black, former Black Panther father meeting the carefree Caucasian Cowboy. Although her new beau had the qualities of what Mr. James pictured as his girl's *Mr. Right,* the pigmentation was way off. Like father like daughter, in his and her eyes, she had just slept with the *enemy,* for goodness sake.

Kennedy didn't even understand how Conner could be so color blind, especially as bright as the morning was.

No one in her family knew about Conner in detail. She had mentioned that she had a personal trainer. She did also mention she hung out with a guy she met at the gym. They figured they were two different people and they assumed there was one other black spot in town.

Miraculously, being with Conner made her feel great. At this moment the idea of moving into a new territory, she felt like a contradiction. A hypocrite. She even saw herself as a lie. That was something Kennedy prided herself on not doing. She wanted to set the record straight. Now was a good time to give Conner the breaking news.

"I have something to tell *you,* Conner."

He was all ears as he sat before a clean plate.

"I am actually moving back home."

Kennedy couldn't look at him.

Conner couldn't believe his ears. The news seemed to drop out of nowhere. He wasn't expecting this. He listened intently for more details. He wasn't satisfied.

"I have been meaning to tell you, but since you brought this up, I feel it is a good time."

Kennedy took a deep breath. Conner wondered if everything was alright with her since her move seemed so sudden.

"As much as I want to meet...your parents...I know that it would not be the best thing to do, with me leaving and all."

Conner looked at her. She looked down at her half-eaten pancakes.

"Why are you going?" suddenly he asked.

"I need to be home," she replied finally looking up, but looking out the window at the beautiful field and bright sun that she envied.

"When were you going to tell me?"

"I just recently decided."

"Did you get a new job?"

"Not exactly," Kennedy said knowing that as soon as she arrived, she would.

Conner looked lost. Kennedy felt so low.

"I really think it is special that you would want me to meet your parents. I would be honored, but timing and circumstance-wise, is it the best thing to do?"

Conner looked relieved as he evaluated what she said. Kennedy was happy to see the look on his face.

"Let me see if I understand. In other words, if you *weren't* leaving you would still want to meet them?" he asked for clarity.

Kennedy gasped.

"Oh yes, of course. If moving wasn't a factor." Kennedy was hoping he understood.

A smile crept upon Conner's face. *There was that cute dimple again.*

Kennedy frowned.

"I got a job offer in Houston, but I declined it because I wanted to stay here with you. But since we feel the same way about each other, I can easily try to get the offer back on the table!"

***

Kennedy punched the dingy boxing bag with all her might. Instead of the country club, she worked out at the local football stadium that had a gym in the field house.

As in sync as she and Conner were, he didn't fit into her plan. Kennedy kicked the mess out of the bag. What they had was the realest thing she had ever felt. It happened without her even knowing it was taking place. She wasn't much of the relationship type, but what they had was effortless – unlike her past relationships she had with *brothers* – brothers who had given her much grief, for being her. Brothers who wasted her time and ultimately hated her for her drive, her ambition. Every moment spent with Conner enriched her life and he happened to be her biggest cheerleader, which she loved.

Kennedy made her way outside to the stadium where she stretched her quads before she did some lunges. Normally, Conner was her workout buddy, but she had to be alone today. As she sprinted up the bleachers, she let out as much steam as she could.

It would have been an easy go if she hadn't slipped up the other night. For the first time, Conner was making things complicated. Since she cared so much about their friendship, it was hard to just let what they have go. It was time to move on, stir things up and make stuff happen. She couldn't do it in Yorkton. She had been in the boondocks long enough, reporting things that had little relevance to her. From soft to hard news, she was fed up with producing newscasts that made very little difference in her life.

Blackoffee was the name of the talk show that meant the world to her. She could see it on the screen! She could almost touch the cup. She could almost taste what filled it.

As Kennedy worked out her tense body, her mind seemed to follow the same idea.

All those long drawn out plans that were drafted after the long girl talks back in the day at Deon's hair salon inspired the show.

No comment

The next morning, holding a cup of freshly brewed coffee, like a creature of habit, Kennedy made her way to her laptop – the one thing that kept her homesick self, connected and in the loop. As she booted up her Mac notebook, her eyes gravitated to the black and white pictures above the desk in her sunlit study, her favorite room in the house. She stared at the pictures on the stark white wall – portraits of Tavis Smiley, Cathy Hughes, Tom Joyner, Susan L. Taylor, and newest edition, Barack Obama. Every person she admired, stared back at her, and there she was, smack dead in the middle. She smiled proudly at her portrait. Seeing was believing and she saw herself amongst the greats.

Kennedy's fingers started to clicking as soon as her laptop allowed.

Web talk had substituted the live beauty shop talk.

Kennedy was doing her own countdown.

She was excited to get back to networking in person with all the movers and shakers. The hustlers and takers. The ritzy and fakers.

Suddenly, Kennedy couldn't believe what she saw on Facebook. She was shocked to see a message from her almost identical twin sister. Kennedy guessed Kyla Withers finally got tired of living in the Stone Ages and actually decided to participate in current technology. Kyla was old-fashioned in every way. She still got her long, unlayered hair pressed. She used *sponge* rollers. She still actually applied lipstick. She wore clip on earrings. She still used curling irons. She still wore cornbread-colored stockings to church.

She was inviting her sister, Kennedy, to Thanksgiving dinner.

Kennedy cringed. *Thanks, but no thanks,* she thought.

Conversation was key to Kennedy's success. But one conversation that stood still in her mind was the one with her twin back in 2005. She remembered it like it happened yesterday – their words brought their relationship to the place it was today. Prior to the talk, the twins had been as tight as the closely knit sweaters Kyla made for her Pomeranian, Butter Scotch *who already had too much fur*. It was a rare day when Kennedy had put her pride aside in order to ask for a favor from her sister, only to find that married life had brought out another side to her twin.

Kennedy ignored the message. She was on a mission that not even her sister could discourage this time.

To be Young, Gifted and Black...By Any Means Necessary

blackoffee
When you wake up in the morning
And you get up out your bed
There's one thing to get you goin'
BlacKoffe,
'Nough said

Refreshing and delightful
Entertaining and insightful
Be sure to get your cup full
BlacKoffee

There's one thing that you need
Your BlacKoffe
To start your day off right
Your BlacKoffee
Get you on your way
To a day early and bright

Trying to avoid Conner was very hard, but she had to do it. She finished waxing the tires of her black 2001 Mustang Coupe. Conner was trying to see her off, but she had worked *around* his schedule.

After wiping down all fours, she stood back to admire her work. Over the years, those wheels had gotten her to many places. She always took great care of her car and she would ride it until the wheels fell off!

Once inside, she sat beside her most-valued traveling companion – her Mac notebook. After buckling up, she put in her favorite Common CD, *Be*. She was ready for the four-hour drive. She had packed up everything in her house, but wasn't bringing it all this particular trip. She would take a little each weekend since she still had two weeks at work and not a lot to move.

Thirty-year-old Bootleg Craig, an old time PV buddy, had room for her in his apartment off the Beltway and Fondren. Craig currently worked at Fryes Electronics and he still happened to attend PV. From 2001 to 2005, Kennedy and Craig were both mass comm. classmates and served as each other's technical support while finishing off projects for broadcast productions. Craig planned on graduating this year. Kennedy hoped this would be his last senior year, especially since some of the requirements changed over the long course of time.

Kennedy had been driving for miles without other cars around. Behind the wheel, she did her best thinking.

First stop, the beauty shop. Catch up with the divas. She had let her former silky bob go natural while being away from Houston, considering she didn't trust the small-town hairdressers to perm her hair. She had grown to like her urban twists and had thought about keeping the look. She doubted Deon did the "natural thing" so she planned on finding a new stylist soon. But she knew to keep in touch and network with Deon regardless of who did her hair.

Second stop, meeting with Mr. Quincy McKnight. Kennedy felt the man had a key to the city, as many properties as he owned. She didn't personally know him, but she planned to snag a meeting with him *to see if she could use some of his venues for the Blackoffee set.*

Third Stop. Downtown strip. Network like there is no tomorrow. Her stack of business cards had remained the same since she left. She was ready for a new pile. She needed to create a new network and restore the old so she could create a buzz for the show.

As the *Be* album came to the last song, Kennedy was approaching one of the main interstates. Even though there were a couple of food chains on the corner, the ride was so smooth and flowing, she kept her pace.

Normally Kennedy had tunnel vision but the thought of Conner divided her focus. She tried to override it with thoughts of how great *Blackoffee* would be once she got it brewing. The thought of the other night made her feel foolish and flushed. While knowing Conner, she had done so well and was so close to keeping her commitment to not engage in any sexual activity prematurely, especially with someone like Conner. This was a commitment she made since her last relationship with JT Hudson. JT was the co-host to most of her shows.

How fast it all happened. How intense it was. Her heart beat sped up at the very thought of the night her and Conner took their relationship to another level, unexpectedly. Suddenly, she was a mile away from entering the next city when Kennedy saw flashing red and blue lights in her back window. It wasn't long before she was joined on the road with another vehicle.

"Fuck!" Kennedy couldn't remember the last time she had gotten a ticket. She wasn't exactly prepared for it either. She thought to herself. *Where did he come from?*

As she reluctantly pulled over, her mind raced.

Was I speeding? She really didn't know. She never paid attention to limits, but to the flow of traffic. Knowing there was no traffic, there was a very good chance she exceeded the limit.

She put the car in park and pulled out her insurance as she sat on the shoulder.

Kennedy watched a short Caucasian male emerge from the driver's seat of the cop car.

Kennedy rolled her eyes as she anticipated bullshit. She told herself she was going to be on her best behavior. She knew her mouth could get her in trouble; it always did.

"Do you have your ID and insurance ma'am?"

"May I ask why I am being stopped?" while she handed both over.

"Your license is obscured by the secondary plates."

"Secondary plates?" Kennedy's eyes rolled to the back of her head. She had a PV alumni frame around her license for years. Then he started asking her questions about whether she had on her contacts?

After she answered, she was written a ticket and given a court date that didn't agree with her plans.

After the cop finally said *good day*, Kennedy was happy to leave the scene. She tried to not let the event trouble her, but it did.

Soon, she realized that the CD had started over awhile ago. Her mind was elsewhere. Not in the mood to hear anything, she just decided to turn it completely off and drove in silence. *Rare.* After a couple of miles, she felt the ride wasn't as smooth as before, literally. Kennedy frowned, knowing something wasn't right with her

Mustang. Her car steering wheel started shaking slightly and the left side of the sports car started to wobble.

"Oh shit. Please, no!"

She knew her tire was going flat, but why?

"I tell ya!" Kennedy said in utter disbelief. "Can a sister get a damn break?"

Kennedy, once again, found herself on the road's shoulder.

The Miss Fix-it, due to being daddy's helper, kneeled down to inspect the wheels she had just waxed. She saw the cause of the jerky ride.

"A nail! One accessory my car didn't need, that was for sure," she said to herself. She had just bought the tires and they were still under warranty.

She always kept a spare. Living out in Texas, as much as people drive, it was wise to. She had actually gone up to the local Wal-Mart to replace hers before she started the trip.

She opened the trunk door. She removed the two boxes she stacked on top of the cardboard that sat on top of the spare. As she finally lifted the plank, Kennedy's heart sank. She didn't see the tire! Her mind started tracing her steps back to find logical reasons why her spare was not in her trunk, but there were none.

She glared at the area the spare tire would have been and then at the flattened one that looked even droopier than before. If she was the crying type, she would've burst into tears. She opened her door and plopped back down in the driver's seat leaving her legs sitting outside the car, feet firmly planted on the cement.

Kennedy reluctantly dialed the road side assistance number that was stored in her phone. They said it would be an hour or two.

"Which one? I mean that is a pretty big gap of time, sir," Kennedy inquired.

They told her that based on the location they couldn't say.

Suddenly a call came through. It was Conner. Kennedy didn't want to answer.

"Hey, how is it going?" he asked.

Kennedy closed her eyes.

"Not too good," she said, trying not to sound too bent out of shape.

"Where are you now?" Conner said checking up on her journey.

Kennedy hesitated.

"I am actually in between Cider Road and Cumbleton."

"So you are making pretty good timing,"

"Was."

"What was that?" he asked.

Kennedy explained the facts.

"Why didn't you call me?"

"I didn't want to bother you. I know you are at work. You would be going out of your way."

"I'm actually not at the Country Club today. I am closer to the Ranch."

Kennedy frowned. She knew the ranch that his family owned was not too far from where she was at that very moment.

"What happened to the spare? I remember you inspected it."

"It's not in the back, otherwise I would've changed it," Kennedy said.

Their conversation was short. Kennedy encouraged him not to worry. The last thing she wanted to do was think about Conner since she had been doing it for the past couple of days.

There weren't a lot of cars passing as Kennedy sat. She counted one every five minutes. The busy body did what she dreaded the most. *Nothing.*

She could actually see the sign that would have marked her exit of the town.

Sitting, waiting, and not knowing when, was killing her. She was bored as hell.

She tried to keep herself occupied, but she was anxious. All she could do was think about where she could have been by now. She knew the highway like the back of her hand even though it was a road less traveled than when she commuted to PV.

She started trying to guess what color the next car would be. *It was that bad.*

After four cars had passed, Kennedy started to surrender more to the thought that she wasn't going anywhere anytime soon.

Questions started popping through her head.

She pulled her portfolio out of her bag.

She reviewed the contents. She knew the words by heart, still she reviewed them knowing that when she met the right people she wanted to make the best impression she could. She was dead serious about the idea, despite the fact that it was rejected by the small town station. She had a reel. None of the news packages on it mattered to her, but she could at least show her skills.

Black issues had been absent from her color pallet since she moved to the station. She felt her passion was denied. Her growth was stunted. And her soul was sick. She did what she could with what she had; limited and outdated equipment and the station's small mind.

She had decided after the election, there was no way in hell she could live there during the Obama Era either. After the election, as her world expanded, in that small town, she could feel the threat of it all closing in on her. The town was somber and was not quick to hide their disappointment with the election results. She ignored as many comments at the job as she could before making the final decision. In that town, she was going nowhere fast.

She had to return to where she once thrived – where her future was promising, where her dreams could not be deferred and where she was dubbed *"the Ambitious Bitch."* She cringed at the thought of the person who said the words. JT *used* to be her best friend. That was until he started to see her differently. "Ambitious Bitch," Kennedy smiled.

Other fish in the sea

Her mind drifted to Conner once more and how it was a trip being with him, one she actually liked taking. He was a release. Fishing, golfing, hiking – *which he called the best exercise*, were activities Kennedy never thought to do.

She remembered the conversation they had while fishing a month ago.

"I want to do a television show that focuses on Black issues. I want a wake up call."

The area was quiet. The two sat on the wooden deck, legs dangling.

"Black issues, eh?" Conner asked as if he needed clarification.

"Yes," Kennedy didn't mind admitting.

"What exactly are Black issues?"

"There is this book, Souls of Black Folk," Kennedy began..

"W.E.B. DuBois." Conner finished.

Kennedy sat, stumped.

"Yeah. Those same issues stand today. Different faces, same issues. Have…you read it?"

Conner nodded.

"For school?" Kennedy wondered.

She remembered how he looked at her as if she had lost her mind.

"No actually, I am an avid reader. It caught my attention, along with other things. Books without limits, is what I call it," Conner explained.

There was a moment of awkward silence.

"Well good for you," Kennedy said.

There was an awkward silence that Kennedy wanted to fill.

"I'm tired of beating around the bush doing stories that don't do anything for that demographic. So, this time around, I am doing things my way. My way or the highway." Kennedy rolled her eyes knowing what was next. She had been down this road before. The road

of idea rejection. The path of non-support from her male counterparts. She expected nothing less.

Conner smiled.

"Even though I know 'your way' probably "singles" out people, I truly hope that you get what you want. You know, you don't hear a lot of women wanting to do the type of stuff you talk about. Pushing for bringing darkness to light. You have my support."

Kennedy looked over at the guy who continued to keep his eyes on her.

"I can't wait to see the finished product. Unless this show is for Black audiences only?"

Before she knew it, she and Conner were off on another adventure. Just a few weeks ago, Kennedy never would have thought she would be hiking on the outskirts of the area.

"Now what is the purpose of hiking again?" Kennedy asked dumbfounded.

"A reason to see you in shorts," Conner said.

Kennedy hit him with a stick she had gotten from him earlier.

Hiking was a good experience until she saw the looks from older white ladies as Conner applied sunblock to her back.

She remembered the whistles as some bikers came up from behind them and passed them.

Kennedy had never focused on nature as much as she did that day, only to avoid eye contact.

Kennedy took in the sights that didn't have eyes to stare back at her.

Kennedy braced herself and focused on the chirping birds that flew above her.

She had never felt so conscious of what others thought. She hated the feeling. She wasn't going to get used to it either; so something had to give, and she knew she had a clue. As their hike came to a close, her leg muscles started to cramp even more producing a sharp pain that made her hop on one leg to the nearest bench.

She remembered the way people had looked as Conner began to massage a cramp out of her thigh. She refused his help.

When Connor stepped away, he took off his shirt to reveal his washboard abs. As she worked to remove the cramp, Kennedy couldn't help but stare. All she had seen lately at work were the beer bellies of the middle-aged producers at the station.

Kennedy looked him up and down. His body was in great shape.

She had to admit, he was cute, *for a white guy.* His wavy, dirty blonde hair. His sea-blue eyes. His dimple. His caring spirit. His support. His silly dance. Him in his cowboy hat.

He made her nervous as nervous could be.

***

Suddenly a blue pick up truck pulled up behind Kennedy's car. Kennedy held her breath and fanned away a bunch of dust that rose from the concrete.

She saw Conner's cowboy boots step down out of the car. "Conner to the rescue!" she said sarcastically standing to her feet.

"Yes, my darling!" he said with a smile. He shut the door and walked to the back of the truck and pulled up a spare.

Kennedy shook her head. As he walked toward her, she couldn't believe he came.

"Thanks!" Kennedy while reaching for the tire.

Conner playfully put the tire behind his back. Kennedy caught a glimpse of his blue eyes that glistened in the sunlight as he looked down at her.

"Hold on woman," Conner said. "Allow me to do the honors. Don't dirty your pretty little hands."

Kennedy stepped back laughing.

"You have done enough," she said. "I really didn't expect you to come out here."

"Anything I can do for the little lady, I will," he explained.

"The problem is, the little lady is a bit on the feisty side," Conner teased.

Kennedy laughed.

Where did you get the spare? Please tell me you didn't buy that.

Conner smiled and let her fuss.

As she finally allowed him to "do the honors" she made herself comfy beside him as he jacked up the car.

She watched his biceps a little more than she wanted to.

As he loosened and removed the lugs, he shook his head.

He handed them to her to hold so she could feel she was being useful.

"What did you do woman? This one's dead," he asked inspecting the tire that ripped to shreds.

Kennedy shrugged.

"Where do you want it?" he asked.

"In my trunk is fine."

After a few seconds, he was back finishing up the tire.

"Oh don't even get me started on the police that made me pull over. *That ole…*" Kennedy stopped herself in time.

"You were stopped prior to this?" he asked as he replaced the old with the new.

"Yes, can you believe it? You probably don't get stopped a lot anyways."

Then suddenly, Kennedy remembered what happened to her spare. When she was getting things together for her trip, she took it out to inspect it in the garage. She received a phone call and went inside her house. After a few moments, she remembered how an unexpected visitor, by the name of Conner, dropped by, moved it out the way, told her that he did, but once she started packing for real, she totally forgot to put it back in, especially since it became hidden when she started stacking boxes up in the garage.

Conner ignored her comment about how many times he was stopped.

"Hey, this may mean, you need to stay put after all," he said instead.

Kennedy couldn't help but laugh.

"Oh yeah, like there is something here for me," she said glibly, looking ahead.

When she looked over at Conner a few seconds later, his eyes were on her like white on rice.

Kennedy swallowed with embarrassment.

"You know what I mean."

"Do I? I thought I did, but apparently, *this* is the truth."

"Oh come on Conner, do you really think what we have is real?" Kennedy frowned.

"Do you really think that it is not?" he challenged.

Kennedy didn't know what to say. She wanted to say the truth, but she knew she had too much to be ashamed of.

"Do you?" he asked again.

"The truth is, I don't know about us," Kennedy said.

Conner shook his head.

"There's so much you don't understand," Kennedy said.

"I think I understand, alright," Conner assured.

Kennedy couldn't stand being stuck in awkwardness with him.

"Let's be real Conner!"

"I thought we were, *Kennedy*. You did say that you were all about 'the truth'. A woman of your word."

She knew he had a point.

"I don't see what you could possibly see in me Conner. Look at us!!!"

He looked at her as if she had lost her mind.

"You know if you got to wonder, then I wonder as well."

Before she knew it, he had tightened her new tire in place and was standing.

He dusted himself off and avoided eye contact with her.

"Have a safe trip," he said.

Kennedy figured it was best this way.

Can and Will

"...the heartache and the hope; the struggle and the progress; the times we were told that we can't, and the people who pressed on with that American creed: Yes we can. At a time when women's voices were silenced and their hopes dismissed, she lived to see them stand up and speak out and reach for the ballot. Yes we can."

**- Remarks of President Barack Obama:
Election Night, November 04, 2008**

Kennedy had had a busy week and she loved every minute of it. She was walking into Bootleg Craig's apartment after midnight. She and her old crony went way back to college days. She was grateful that he let her crash in his pad while she looked for jobs and apartments.

That night, he was busy on his computer uploading something on YouTube. She had gotten so many contacts that Friday night at a mixer at the Red Cat Jazz Café-Downtown; she felt a new rush of energy. It was good reuniting with the women of The National Association of Black Female Music in Entertainment Executives organization. She served as the college rep for the Gulf Coast chapter while at PV.

The past Thursday she enjoyed hanging out at the Breakfast Klub in Mid-town with other avid book readers and gossipers at Nnete's Book Club event. Earlier in the week, she also attended a meeting with Houston Association of Black Journalists at Fox Channel 26.

She had scored a meeting with Quincy McKnight right after Thanksgiving and she knew it would go smoothly.

The *Ambitious Bitch with a plan and a mic in her hand* was back and it was only a matter of time before she did her mic check!

***

Kennedy was going over her plan.

Then her phone rang. It was her sister, Kyla. Kennedy paused. She didn't want to answer it at all but she did without thinking. It was probably one more attempt to get her to join her for Thanksgiving dinner.

"I don't know where you are, but I just wanted you to know about dad. He is in the hospital."

Kennedy gasped.

***

At one time, Kennedy lived with her father while Kyla chose to live with their mom. Her dad understood her; her independent spirit was encouraged there. She learned a lot about taking care of herself under his protective wing. The former activist stood his ground in his community and Kennedy grew up around picket signs and protest lines. Her great aunt had stories to tell about the early days of the civil rights movement when she went into politics, and how their original house was burned to the ground by the KKK. Kennedy's dad rebuilt that house and put some of the ashes in an urn as a testament to the non-stop fight. The family's motto was "What doesn't kill you makes you stronger." The relentless James family kept fighting for what they thought was right, no matter the price.

The apple didn't fall too far from the tree. Kennedy, though a later generation, fought the same fight – all in hopes of making some difference. She knew her history and knew that she couldn't drop the ball.

Kyla met Kennedy in the lobby. They hugged and quickly moved toward their dad's room. The hospital scene was always heart wrenching. The smell was nauseating. As much as Kennedy's mind said look ahead, her eyes gravitated to the insides of the rooms she passed.

"You know he has been asking about you," Kyla said with a smile.

"How is he?"

"He's waiting on you," Kyla assured.

Both women had a unique way of tuning in to others and their suffering, and they felt as if they could help them through it in some way. Kyla always sympathized. Kennedy always had a plan set in motion before she could turn to look away. She remembered when her mother used to visit the elderly to bring fruit baskets and a traveling bible study crew. She and her sister would tag along on her mission to lift the spirits of sick church members. Their mother would give her all to those in need.

There was their dad - old before his time. He suffered from Type 2 Diabetes and he had another episode with his blood sugar. He looked feeble, but with eyes still filled with fire. Kennedy squealed when she saw her favorite guy.

"Kennedy!" her dad said.

They embraced each other, paying little attention to the cords that connected him to the machines. They were his only children and he was so proud of them.

"Daddy, how are you doing?" Kennedy said easing back to take a good look at him. Then she ran her hand over the lines in his face; the lines appeared hard, but represented his tender side.

"They treating you right?" Kennedy asked.

"Oh yeah. I told them they better, or they would have to answer to you."

Kennedy smiled.

"Got that right!"

He smiled.

MORE THAN PUNCTUATION

Kyla's Herstory

This can't be the end.
For we have just begun!
May we continue?

Psalm 1:1-3

Divorce is not an option. The words literally made twenty-six year old, Kyla sick to her stomach as she reached for the blueberry waffles on the top shelf of the supermarket freezer. *The power of language and recalling it.*

It was one week after seeing her father in the hospital and the actual week of Thanksgiving. Her dad felt much better as soon as he saw what seemed to be his favorite twin. Kyla couldn't say the same. She was trying her best to get over the prank call that she had received when someone thought it would be very entertaining to say, *"I was with your husband last night."*

Kyla's *husband* happened to be thirty-five year old Reverend Hilton Withers, the II, the respected preacher of Mt. Gerizim Baptist Church, son of the late great senior who left the church in his eager son's hands.

The etiquette queen found it hard to hold her manners when dealing with the tacky woman on the other line. Unlike her sister, she didn't cuss.

"I beg your pardon," Kyla said in utter shock to the stranger on the phone.

"You heard me!" the irate mystery woman yelled in Kyla's ear.

Hunched over, Kyla moved to the beverage section of Target's grocery area. This was her one stop shop, and today that was a good thing, for she didn't know how long she could travel by foot.

Gaterade.

Next, apple sauce.

Finally bananas.

Her monthly routine. These were the only things she could stomach during *this time of the month.*

Divorce is not an option. Early in their marriage, those same words had taken on a different connotation, becoming the key to her security with Hilton, her husband of four years. Now those same words made her sick to her stomach.

The words alone weren't her problem, but they certainly had a way of adding to her monthly condition from hell. Kyla was trying to beat the visitor that held her captive in her own body.

She had always had a history of menstrual pain, but lately her cramps were *killer.* It was a race against time. She felt the pain coming on stronger. It was right on schedule. Dreadful days ahead. *Thank God I didn't have a job to have to worry about.* Kyla was a housewife that was trying to bear children. She hoped that she would be okay for the holiday that she had planned to celebrate at her house, a nice two story home in Sienna Plantation, a refined community in Missouri City, close to Sugar Land, where their church was located.

Kyla managed to make her way to the checkout aisle, holding a couple of items in a small basket, but unfortunately it seemed that the available registers were on the opposite sides of the huge store. *They always do this!* She made her way down to the long available lines.

In the distance, she saw two figures moving as slowly as she was, but she knew age was their excuse. Though nothing out of the ordinary, the couple caught and held her attention as they moved toward her. All of a sudden, as the pair came closer into her view, her mind abandoned her abdominal pain and suddenly she smiled involuntarily at such a sweet sight. Kyla knew it was rude to stare, but she couldn't help but zero in on the woman's face.

The reassuring ray from the older woman was the same one that had met a crying Kyla twenty years ago on the first day of kindergarten at Rhoades Elementary in Sunnyside, Houston. There stood Mrs. Smith, her absolute favorite teacher. She was the teacher that made *her* want to be a teacher, something she had yet to do, but was always on her mind.

"Mrs. Smith!" Kyla squealed, aware that the woman probably wouldn't remember her.

Both women moved slowly towards one another.

"Is this one of my babies?" the southern belle said in a light, feathery voice.

"I was in your kindergarten class back in '89. My name is"

"Kyla…Kyla James. I know," the woman laughed, a bit insulted.

Kyla stood shocked. She hadn't seen the lady that changed her life since 1991 - when her parents had gotten divorced.

"Well I am now, Kyla *Withers*."

"Congratulations, honey."

Kyla looked over at Mr. Smith who was standing patiently with his wife. Normally, Kyla had a stack of church brochures ready to hand to anyone she came across.

"How has life been treating you, sweetie?" the retired teacher asked.

Kyla stopped to think for a second. "Everything is…fine," Kyla said. "I always wondered about how you were doing. I always wanted our paths to cross along the way. I am glad that I finally saw you."

The two quickly exchanged numbers and hugs and soon they were both going their separate ways.

Psalm 1: 4-6

The day before Thanksgiving came around and Kyla didn't know how she was going to get out of bed. She was beyond weak and with her throwing up left and right, she might as well camp out by the toilet. She had tons of delicious food in the fridge, but couldn't keep any food in her system.

Despite her situation, she didn't have the strength to dial, to talk or to call off Thanksgiving dinner. All she could do was lie in the bed with a heating pad held closely to her skin, hoping that the pain would go away so she could get some sleep.

Her situation with her sister didn't make it any better. Neither did her and her husband's new problem. Then there was also one thing, Kyla couldn't stand – a messy house.

Kennedy didn't seem to want to spend the holiday with her and Kyla knew that their relationship was in a weird place. However, she hoped that they could move forward as they had never fallen out for this long. This was making four years now. All Kyla wanted to do was bury the hatchet.

If anyone should be mad, it should be me, Kyla thought as she remembered the bachelorette party her twin threw for her. If Kyla wasn't a forgiving person, she would have fallen out with Kennedy that very night.

Kyla relived the night of the party from hell.

The summer of 2005…

"Just let your body fly!" Sheila, one of the passion party girls, coached.

The woman hopped up on the shiny, thin stick hanging down from the ceiling.

"Nice," commented Sheila's friend and partner in passion party crime while the party goer slid down. This was Sheila's side hustle. She had a couple more.

Across town, Kyla's bachelorette party members were partying without a care in the world in the hotel suite before hitting the town - all except for the bride-to-be.

"You got to let go," Sheila said to encourage the woman.

"If I let go, I will fall," Ruby, who had an artificial hip, said and the women laughed waiting for their turn.

One by one the attendants, mainly Deon's salon girls, took a stroll down the pole as Sheila shed some light on something she knew about all too well.

In the back of the hotel suite, there was not so much laughter.

"I am too through with you!" Kyla said almost in tears in the kitchen, as she confronted her sister, Kennedy who threw together her racy party.

"You know this would never be my idea of fun!" the shaking bride-to-be said.

Kennedy stood looking at her twin with no emotion - her specialty.

"It's pole dancing for heaven's sake. Are you out of your mind Kennedy?" Kyla cried.

Kennedy thought it was so funny that she was trippin' off her surprise.

"What do I look like?" Kyla was disgusted.

"You just need to chill out. You are about to be a married woman tomorrow. Girl, you are about to be a preacher's wife! I know you are mad, but look at it like this, you will never see one of these babies again," Kennedy said referencing the pole.

"This is my first time seeing one tonight," Kyla screamed.

"I'm sure. So let it be what it is and take it as all fun and games. Get outside yourself for just one day. One day before your whole world changes. Because no matter what you think of this day, you can never relive it. Once you are married, you are married, girl."

Kyla shook her head furiously. She wanted to strangle her sister, but she held back, wondering how her rational twin had become so irrational.

"Having a strip fest is not the best way for me to celebrate. There are other ways. Wholesome ways. Not everyone wants to be bad. You of all people should know what I would have wanted."

"This is not a damn strip fest." Kennedy was glad that she had canceled …the male dancers.

"Well I guess, if you trippin' off of this, you really gonna trip off the cake," she concluded. The 'to have and to hold' illustration wouldn't have probably gone over well with Kyla.

Her sister and she would never see eye to eye anymore. With her preparing for a wedding, she realized this more than ever. In the main room, the fifteen ladies were having a ball being a little naughty. Deon was the last to arrive in her skin-tight denim bodysuit that would have made J Lo go home. She saw that her employees were having a real good time.

Sheila felt her stomach drop when she saw Deon enter the room. Sheila knew all about her from hair mags, but she tried to keep her cool.

"Alright, your turn," said Sheila's partner, the giddy party planner who had been the coordinator for the event, pumped while handing Deon a name tag.

"What do I need a lesson for? Better yet a pole," Deon said eyeing the bar, and not really anything else. She was ready for the after party. She knew they were hitting up the club after this.

The women that knew the diva laughed because they knew she had enough tricks up her sleeve.

As Kyla emerged from the back, Deon could see she was clearly not enjoying herself.

"What's wrong, sweetie?" Deon asked knowing good and well what her problem was. Pole shock.

Kyla couldn't help but laugh. The damage was already done so she just shook her head. She knew what she needed to do.

"Cheer up," Deon said needing to take her own advice.

"Now that the pole kind of jump-started the night, now it is time for a game," Sheila's business partner said as she came out with a bottle of champagne.

Kyla knew the night would continue to get worse.

"The rules are simple. You must drink if the question can be answered with a yes."

As the ladies who had a full glass of Moet formed a circle of chairs, some ladies had already had a couple of sips.

"You must drink if you have had a one night stand," Sheila said.

One brave soul took a sip.

"Snow!!!!" the ladies squealed.

Deon, on the other hand, knew she was not going to play fair on this one. She didn't want all the ladies knowing everything.

"What? The brother was fine!" Snow said defending her sip.

"Cheated," the other lady asked.

Every woman took one, except for Kennedy.

"Stuffed your bra?" Sheila questioned.

Everyone looked at Kennedy.

"I ain't drinkin' to that! It was a padded bra, thank you!"

"Shoplifted," asked the coordinator.

Nobody moved. Deon looked around.

"Y'all know some of you heifers got sticky fingers. Y'all steal from me everyday in some kind of way."

"Went with no underwear?"

Celestina drank to that.

"Nasty!"

"Sex in public places?"

Deon took a sip.

"What, I was young," she wanted to take a sip. Who cares if they knew.

"Smoked weed?"

Too many sipped.

Kyla gasped. She was so disappointed in what she was witnessing.

"Woke up next to a stranger?"

"Don't nobody better drink to that one!" said one of the guest.

The ladies laughed.

For one, the night and early morning seemed to drag on like torture.

"Is this how it feels when the doctors are trying to put you to sleep for surgery and you are still conscious while they dig in?" Kyla asked herself out loud. "You know that is always a fear of mine."

"I think it is. I am certain it is." Kyla just stayed away from the group in a daze; her legs hung from the barstool.

"This may be worse," she said as she swung her legs back and forth.

"My maid of honor did this," Kyla continued.

"My own sister."

"My own twin."

"My own flesh and blood."

Kyla looked around at all the tipsy women who were not listening to a word that left her lips. She knew. She just wanted to vent either way.

Kennedy approached her pouting sister.

"What, you tired of all these games?"

Kyla ignored her sister for as long as she could. Kennedy could see the fumes. Any time her sister started talking to herself, she knew it was bad. Really bad.

"I still can't believe you let these women give me a party. I don't appreciate what you are trying to do. You have no respect for me as your sister and what kind of life I am about to live," Kyla, enraged said.

"Oh really, you still think it's like that?" Kennedy asked coolly.

"You all should be ashamed of yourselves! Bad girls celebrating bad behavior!"

"Look who's talking. You are real judgmental for somebody who's playing innocent," Kennedy challenged.

Kyla swallowed hard. She wasn't the only one sober that night. Seemed like her twin was very alert. So Kyla chose to just keep her cool attitude.

***

As Kyla opened gifts that seemed more like gag, she had figured she had more than enough. The spandex houchie mama dress was a shock, but Kyla gasped at the next gift.

"Nude male playing cards!" Kyla held up the box. "What the heck am I going to do with this?"

"Play solitaire," one of the guest shouted from the back.

Kyla was done with the night's events. She threw down the gift basket.

"Okay ladies, it has been unforgettable. Now I am taking myself off to bed to try and forget.

The women laughed. Kyla was the baby of her family.

"Aww boo, we hope you had a good time though!" Deon said before Kyla escaped, trying to add insult to injury. She liked toying with the weak. Just for the hell of it. It was a habit she never let go of.

"No, not really, but I'm sure you all did. And you can continue to. I just know I am done. Y'all can have this!"

Kyla walked off, curls bouncing with every step.

"Sleep pretty," Deon shouted, hoping Kyla's hair would hold up overnight. She was doing her make-up on the big day and didn't want to have to re-do it if she was crying over hair.

Kyla entered the bedroom and shut the door and locked it behind her.

As she lay down on the cushioned mattress, tears streamed down her face. She couldn't wait to leave the single world behind. She couldn't wait to open her big gift-to-be, her husband. She missed his reassuring voice, and couldn't wait to spend time with him. She felt so blessed God had chosen her for him. She was so grateful she wasn't on the look-out for a man, but instead had been found.

She was scared, but she was more than ready to be his wife. She knew it was going to be a lot of hard-work, but she knew he was so much of what she wanted to work hard for.

Those women couldn't possibly understand what it was like to find true love. True love. They all were in and out of relationships, and bragging about it. She didn't want to be a playette. She didn't need or want those games. She wanted the real deal! To be loved. To be held at night by a man who respected God and then her. She prayed her sisters could find what she had and what God had allowed for her to be taken to a higher level. She closed her eyes and tuned out the noise from the other room with the thoughts of her love, and those thoughts carried her to sleep.

That was then and tonight her wretched thoughts weren't carrying her anywhere.

Maybe I did over-react. To her surprise, Kyla regretted the way she treated her sister at the party. Kennedy was always there for her, especially once a month when she was in dying pain like this. Seemed like that year of her wedding, her cramps became excruciating.

Her husband was supposed to be home later on that night from a minister's conference. He still didn't know her needs, like her sister did. Her sister knew what to pick up from the drug store. Her sister knew what to say to make her feel a little better. Her sister, knew.

Her sister would certainly know what to say about another thing that made her cramps extreme: the thought of another woman *claiming* to have been with her husband.

The voice of the stranger played again in her head, *"I was with your man last night."* Seemed like she was more nauseous now. Knots started to form in her stomach. *Could Hilton really be with another woman?* She never thought she would have to question him. Not *him.* But if he was, she knew *divorce was not an option.* She would have to do whatever she could to keep her man.

Suddenly Kyla couldn't hold it. She threw up all over their bed spread.

***

Thanksgiving didn't happen at the Withers; Kyla, the domestic goddess, was devastated.

As the holidays came to a close, Kyla's daily duties were becoming even more monotonous than the Clear Eyes spokesperson's voice. She got up at the sound of her barking dog, Butter Scotch. The puffy Pomeranian needed to take a leak around 6:30. Kyla ironed Hilton's clothes at 6:45 before he left for work. Breakfast, cooked from scratch, was on the table for her husband by 7:30. She started washing clothes after he left at about 8:00. Then she turned her TV to *Soap Net* where it stayed until he returned home and wanted to watch the news.

As she did the laundry, she normally fixed herself a nice little healthy snack and checked to see if she had everything she needed to create a nice home-cooked dinner later. For fun, she also tried her hand at gardening and had bought a book called *Gardening Basics for Dummies.* She walked the dog, but sometimes he walked her. Then she returned to the house to start on dinner. While she baked, she did some sewing, some knitting. And if she knew Hilton would be away for a long time, like overnight, she did the unthinkable: she went to the back of her closet, pulled out an old gym bag, pulled out a spandex, houchie mama dress, a gift from her infamous bachelorette party, and did re-enactments of Beyonce videos. The dress fit her like a glove.

Lately, Beyonce wasn't enough. Kyla was ready to try something else. She wanted to make money. She was a homebody, but she hated being alone in the big two-story house that was a gift from their church. Hilton was always off mending souls, but she needed him to tend to her needs as well.

Grass is always greener

"Butter Scotch, no!" Kyla screamed as she yanked the dog away from the bush he tried to mark.

"Bad dog. That is not our yard!"

Kyla continued down the street, deciding to take another route in the neighborhood and change up her usual pattern. She wanted to see what the other lawns looked like since she was realizing that her thumb was not so green.

After seeing one lawn after another, Kyla felt ashamed. The lawns, as a whole, were so well-manicured that she felt embarrassed for even trying. *Maybe I should just try things in the backyard to get the hang of it.*

Suddenly, Kyla heard loud barking that seemed to come from a dog two times Butter Scotch's size.

Fluffy Butter Scotch shot forward like a jack rabbit on crack. Kyla hadn't been holding his lease too tightly and he got away from her grasp.

"Butter Scotch!" Kyla hissed. She looked around to make sure she wasn't making a scene. Then Kyla ran after the dog whose bark was bigger than his bite. She could hear chains rattling against the wooden fence.

"Oh no!" Kyla thought as she saw her little dog find a slight opening and disappear behind the fence.

"No!"

A man emerged from his house. He had been in the middle of shaving because he had white crème aligning the frame of his face when he went outside to see what all the fuss was about.

All he could see was the behind of a woman as she peered into the little hole in the fence that he re-nailed several times before. Kyla continued to peep through the hole that the fluff puff plopped through. She pleaded with him to return to her, but the little dog moved closer to the bull dog that eagerly waited on the little dog to step a few steps closer.

"Excuse me Ma'am, I…" he said while standing behind her.

Kyla screamed out of shock when she heard a voice!

She turned around quickly to see who the voice belonged to, only to scream again when she saw a man who looked like he had rabies.

"Ma'am, I was trying to help you. Please." The man said rushing toward her.

Kyla felt her knees locking, and then she blacked out...

Psalm 2:1-3

"Butter Scotch," the words escaped from Kyla's mouth when she saw her furry pet through her foggy vision. The little dog was sitting before her on the couch of the man who caused her to faint.

The man was relieved to see that the woman was only unconscious for a brief time.

Suddenly Kyla started to make out other things. Butter Scotch was being held by the individual she had seen before she fell.

Kyla couldn't make out his face but could see that, free from shaving crème, it was a very nice one.

"Oh my God, where am I?" Kyla said starting to sit up from the couch.

"You fainted outside, so I brought you in here until you…"

Kyla knew her dog seemed very calm because he was letting the stranger hold him without any problems.

Why doesn't he do that for me?

Kyla looked around the room. It was similar to her own house floorplan wise, but just a one story.

"I caught you before you fell," he said. "I put some water there for you, too," Berry Judd said, pointing to the tall glass on a nearby table.

"I'm Berry," he said warmly.

"I'm Kyla," she said politely.

"So I'm not the only Black person in the neighborhood," Berry said.

Kyla laughed.

"You have a nice little dog," he said looking at the top of the dog's head. Butter Scotch looked up at him.

Kyla laughed at the dog in Berry's hands and shook her head.

"I'm still mad at you," she said with a smile to her dog, whose eyes finally settled on her.

The dog barked.

Berry laughed.

"Thanks for getting him for me, he was about to be your dog's dinner."

"Jacks is not your average bull dog," Berry said.

Kyla laughed. "Yeah, he's a bull, for Christ Sakes."

Kyla's eyes scanned the room. She saw many plaques on his shelf. There were framed documents that read *Texas Educator Certificate*. She saw several pictures of him with teenagers. Several books – mainly non-fiction titles.

Kyla perked up.

"How long have you taught?"

"This is my fifth year."

Kyla was impressed. She didn't know too many younger, nicely-groomed Black male teachers. She remembered not having any when she was in school.

"What subject?"

"All. I teach AVID students."

"Is that something new? I don't know what that is."

"It is a program that helps high school students in a number of ways."

Kyla shook her head.

"You know that is so funny. I just saw one of the teachers who inspired me to teach."

"You are an educator also," Berry asked.

"Oh, no. I always wanted to," Kyla cleared up.

"Well…it's never too late," he said.

Kyla's eyes rolled to the top of her head.

"If only I knew where to start. It's funny. In college, I majored in English. I had planned to get my certification while in school, but some other things popped up. Kyla held up her left hand.

Long ago, Berry noticed a woman who was as adorable as a newborn baby. And the big rock on the woman's hand.

"You know there are all types of avenues that you can take advantage of in order to become certified. In fact, one of my first students came to visit me before the holidays. He just graduated from college and he enrolled in an Alternative Certification Program."

Berry was willing to give her more info on the program, as well as a contact number for the guy so that if she had any questions, she would be able to contact him.

"What a blessing," Kyla said after thinking about how she had just prayed about direction.

All of a sudden, her energy level seemed to rise as the idea of putting her English Degree to use was put out there.

Once Kyla got back on her feet, Berry walked her and her dog out.

Berry had tried to drive her back home, but Kyla insisted on walking.

She couldn't help but notice his beautiful landscaping.

"Who did your yard?"

"Actually, I did," Berry said surprised at how excited she was about what she saw.

"When do you find the time?" Kyla asked, knowing teaching was a grueling job.

"Right after work, every day, I come out here and do something to clear my head. You should see my back yard!"

Kyla didn't even hesitate.

***

The two and Butter Scotch walked back through the house and out the back door while his dog stayed under control at the very sight of him.

Kyla was amazed at how their backyards could be so different.

They stood on the deck that Berry had built himself when he first moved in. Kyla's eyes panned the wide yard. There was a hammock stretched between two trees.

"Come see the gardens." At this time of day, the back was so much cooler than the front yard.

Kyla moved with Berry. She inspected the vegetable patches and flowers that surrounded them.

She saw some things that were new to her.

"What is this?"

"Oh," Berry hesitated. "Those are some special herbs."

Kyla left that one alone for many reasons.

"You do a lot of partying back here?"

"No actually, I am more of a homebody.

"Me too!" she said.

"I live for the summers. Get to really enjoy this," he said. " I can't wait!"

"I have been trying to plant for the longest. I have been trying to keep my grass green. It's so hot this November."

Berry started asking her about what fertilizer she used and a couple of other things, but he soon realized that she was clueless.

"I'll take a look at your yard and you let me know what kind of landscaping you want. We can go from there."

Kyla smiled. "I have a lot to learn."

Berry's face mirrored hers.

***

As Kyla and Butter Scotch walked home, Kyla felt like she had fallen into a good thing. She decided she would focus on her two goals: first, she would start substitute teaching at the local high school for the English Department, and second she'd plant seeds to grow into a beautiful garden of her own.

Lesson Plans

Kyla was called to sub for a 9th grade English teacher. She was more than ready for work that early morning. It felt good to have somewhere to go at the start of the day. She was actually excited about the experience she would gain, even though Hilton felt she was putting herself in danger.

As she entered the school, she walked through the lobby to find the front office.

She felt like she was passing through giants. *What are they feeding these kids?*

Many were socializing while some were actually in the same zone she used to be in while in school – *the get to class on time* zone. This was a small percent.

Finally, she approached the check-in desk to sign in. She was covering Mrs. Brownton's freshman class.

The receptionist was about to hand her a badge and the sub folder with all the plans, when suddenly a thirty-something Asian woman came in, pulling her rolling tote behind her. The woman smiled slightly as she parked her carry all in the middle of the room. Kyla noticed it was full of manila folders.

Both Kyla and the receptionist's eyes were glued to the lady.

"Yes, Mrs. Lan," the receptionist said.

The woman had a mild and meek voice, but she managed to say. "I'm leaving."

The woman behind the desk froze.

"What? I don't understand. Leaving…" She looked stumped. "The sign-out sheet is on the other desk."

The lady stood there. "No, I am gone. I am not coming back."

"Wait a minute, Mrs. Lan, you can't just leave like that."

"I'm sorry," Mrs. Lan said.

The woman behind the desk sat in shock.

Kyla tried not to be rude, but even she couldn't help but stare at the woman who eventually walked out the door, leaving her basket of manila folders there.

Moments later, the lady behind the desk regained enough composure to hand Kyla her badge and the sub folder.

Kyla graciously took the items and tried her best to not add to the untimely moment with any unnecessary banter. She left to find the classroom. The school was a bit of a maze, but eventually she found Mrs. Brownton's name outside the door.

School. It used to be one of her favorite places. She had been a great student. Conduct was never an issue. She was president of the Student Council. She graduated in the top ten percentile of her class. She was on the drill team, ballet was her specialty, and she had never earned a demerit in her life. She was even a part of the Home Ec Club, known for her baking skills.

Kyla unlocked the door. As she walked in, she tried to ignore the blemishes on the wall, but her OCD nature made it difficult. Mrs. Brownton wasn't too tidy either. Kyla had to stop her impulse to organize. She stood and stared at the desk for about a minute or two before sitting down. She couldn't help herself. She started straightening up the area, knowing that Mrs. Brownton would appreciate it later. She figured during her lunch break she would get to those cluttered shelves.

She finally found a seat at the desk and opened up the folder to find the bell schedule as well as lesson plans for the day. They were pretty basic. The students were working out of a standardized booklet. She couldn't wait to sub when she would do more than babysit.

Kyla smiled as the kids began to trickle in. Many were laughing and carrying on conversations with one another. Some, with sleep in their eyes, managed to make their way to their seats. Kyla made her way to the door. A lot of the guys made comments when they saw their sub. Kyla's disapproving look stopped most from continuing. She noticed some of the girls with attitudes and she wished she could just wipe that frown off their faces. She was delighted that many kids met her with a smile though. She liked their parents already.

As soon as the bell sounded, Kyla found a bunch of eyes on her.

The television announcements started as she began to introduce herself. The kids thought that this was funny for some reason.

After the announcements were finished, the television went blank.

Some of the kids laughed at her last name.

"Are you married, Miss?" asked one of the boys.

"You see that big ass ring on her finger, fool," said the girl who set beside the boy.

Kyla's mouth dropped open.

For the rest of the day Kyla's mouth kept dropping open. If she had a dime for how many inappropriate things that were said, she would be able to feed a million starving children a day. She was already paying to feed one.

***

It was only first period and a calm, yet stressed Kyla was ready to strangle someone. Just in a matter of seconds, her blood pressure rose. She was a simple woman who liked rules. She followed them well. She knew them by heart. She valued obedience. It baffled her that she had repeated herself a number of times yet got the same results. She really wanted to teach, but wondered if she could deal with unladylike behavior and far from *gentle* men on a regular basis.

Kyla decided that her goal for the rest of the day was to not let the kids make her lose her religion. She had a career to start. She knew that if she stayed focused on *Him*, she would not get detoured by "them."

QUEEN D SYNDROME

Deon's Herstory

**"Diva is the female version of a hustler…
If you ain't gettin' money, you ain't got nothing for me."
-Beyonce**

Diva,
***I am Sasha Fierce* album**

Spotlight

"I have a theory. When you first meet a man, and you think it is love, imagine that person broke, constipated and with a STD. If you can still *want* to be with him, it very well might be love," one of the clients said to the salon women.

"All three things together or separate?" one customer asked for clarity.

The women laughed.

As the women conversed, Deon passed a picture in her studio that always caught her eye, no matter how many times she saw it. It was a picture of her outside the salon, standing there posing as she cut the ribbon. Though it was over a decade ago, she remembered it like it was yesterday - the opening of *Deon's Hair Divas* salon. Normally, she wiggled with excitement every time she thought of the day.

Deon's parents, Josie, a beautician and Russ, a doctor, were the first out of their family to move out of The Boot and to the Lone Star State more than 25 years ago. In her new home of Houston, Josie had put her heart and soul into making women feel and look beautiful with healthy hair. Later, she opened up the salon in Third Ward.

Almost a decade later, Deon's salon was more high profile and what Josie could only dream about. Her salon was set in a very exciting part of the city with a number of radio and television stations, boutiques, shopping centers and the famous Reliant Stadium a couple of miles away. For Deon, her focus was to hire diversely-skilled hair technicians that matched the highly diverse atmosphere. She did just that.

Lately, the salon wasn't enough. Deon craved something more than the spotlight.

Girl Talk

At Deon's salon, the women were already addicted to the *BlacKoffee* show Kennedy had created and it had only been on for three Saturdays. Deon was excited that Kennedy had asked her to be on one of the shows that focused on entrepreneurship that was scheduled for January.

So far, Kennedy's show was taped at various locations around Houston and broadcast on the city access channel. The local 8'o clock morning show was their caffeine fix for the day and it *got the salon talking again.*

"Dating Games We Play" was the topic of the show.

"Many may say that today's black relationships are in trouble," said Kennedy.

As Deon watched for a moment, she had to admit that she was proud of her client, but she was not interested in hearing anything about relationships at the moment.

"Many of us don't know how to maintain a strong relationship that can weather the storm. Today we are exploring the ways to build stronger relationships within.

With her first book, *LOVEBLACKLOVE:* T*he Ultimate Guide for Black Couples,* this amazing author is challenging us to now look deeper within with *Microscopic View,* her new book. Please welcome Dr. Lynne Parker to the show."

On the screen, the women watched as woman after woman asked the doctor for love advice. And the salon women were busy giving their own expertise.

"Honey let me tell you, loving a Black Man can be hard," said a married client.

'Girl, *finding* a Black man can be harder," said one of the single clients.

"Not just *any* Black man, a *good* man, that can be impossible," one of the customers said.

"Not to mention, one that is available," Ruby said.

"An available, good man, that doesn't prefer men," said another client.

The women laughed.

***

Deon needed a cigarette break. Ruby caught her drift and met her outside in the back.

"Mother Nature looks like she couldn't make up her moody mind today," Deon's veteran stylist, Ruby observed before lighting up her cigarette.

It was now 8:30 in the morning and both stylists were on their routine smoke break.

"Looks like the devil is about to beat his wife," old-school, Ruby joked, looking up at the pouting sky. Little drops of rain started to cry down from the hot, shiny heavens.

"Oh, looks like he is whooping her ass, now," predicted Ruby, as the rain increased.

Deon slowly exhaled the smoke from her cigarette, creating a small fog that expanded into a circle and faded away.

"Am I talking to myself?" Ruby guessed, after monitoring Deon's disengaged eyes that were looking somewhere off in the distance which Ruby found strange since they were surrounded by dumpsters.

Deon had slipped out of her self-absorbed character for a moment. She finally realized Ruby had been moving her mouth and was possibly saying things to her in between puffs.

"What?" Deon declared trying to catch up, but figured if she didn't get it, she wasn't trippin'.

"Oh nothing. I rather know what's on your mind, the way you were looking and all," Ruby insisted now intrigued for details.

Usually not one to reveal or share, Deon was at a different point in her life. She needed answers. If she *did* share, Ruby was always her best bet. Ruby's unflinching loyalty and dedication to Deon was apparent to everyone who knew both of them. She had been there during Deon's rise and had been an integral part of her current success.

"Get this, girl," said the former beauty pageant girl, who weighed herself three times a day. The other day, I was just picking up my dry cleaning. When I was walking out the front door, this guy was walking in and," Deon's eyes widened as she shook her head while she remembered him.

"Was he *that* fine?" Ruby asked anxiously.

"You know, I really don't even remember how the man looked. I just remember how he...smelled."

Ruby cringed.

Deon laughed. "Nothing like that. He smelled like someone I found irresistible *and he felt the same about me*," Deon's eyes widened as she tried her best to be modest. It was hard.

"*Ohhh,* I see," Ruby said.

"All it took was a whiff of that cologne and it alone sent me back!" Deon said.

When it sent her back, it sent her *back* to her undergrad days at the University of Houston. It was where she laid the foundation for her business.

The nostalgic moment also sent exhilarating graphic details to her mind. There they were, the two exhibitionists underneath the bleachers. Her back began to itch as she remembered the stinging strips of grass that rubbed up against her body as the man who wore that same scent did as well.

Football practice was over and all the other players were long gone. Till this day, she still wondered how she ended up underneath him and remembered nothing else mattered at the time – not even the dewy, humid air that stuck her freshly-permed hair to her face. At moments like this, which were routine, all she valued was how perfectly their bodies stuck together in the moisture of it all.

After college, they walked away and went their separate ways without even a single thought. She wanted to know if they could ever pick up where they left off.

"I had to keep walking even though my knees got weak," Deon determined from her senses.

"Ohh, he had it like that?" Ruby asked.

Deon nodded. "Yes!" Deon could not imagine who was getting what she used to get on the regular – he was very giving.

"The real question is, what happened to this guy and why y'all not together now? Ruby asked.

Deon stood still for a moment.

"How did he get away?" Ruby continued.

"And that's the thing. I really don't know. I remember one day, we were fucking like animals and then just like that, we weren't. Then again, we were so young, too," Deon concluded. "I remember we never even talked about it either."

"So where is he now? Is he married? Taken? What?" Ruby inquired.

"That is why I want to talk about it now," Deon concluded.

Window Shopping

Deon parked her Mercedes securely in the packed Galleria Mall garage with no intention of getting her hair touched by the possessive dampness. The wedding she had been dreading was finally near. Autumn volunteered to help find a gift and Deon was relieved. The high maintenance, head honcho was on a mission - to treat herself to some jazzy outfits for the upcoming wedding events as well as get the bride a couple of things – a bachelorette party gift and a wedding gift. Two heads were better than one, she figured. Snagging two ensembles for two events was going to be a piece of cake. Unfortunately, she hadn't felt that way about her other responsibility. Deon had put off the gift picking until she just couldn't any longer. Shopping for other people was a chore, so that was where Autumn came in. She knew her niece would find something functional for the bride-to-be.

"Alright, I'll meet you back here in an hour and a half." Deon eyed her niece. "Sharp, Autumn. Your watch works right?" Deon started but didn't finish due to the look on Autumn's face.

"Hey watch your tone! I am doing you a favor!" Autumn said.

Deon was shocked. Autumn was really trying to stick up for herself now-a-days.

Deon fixed her lips to say something she wasn't comfortable with. "I apologize."

***

Deon was ready to take the mall by storm. Since the stylist had a knack for shopping, it was a sport that she easily excelled in while some were left in the fashion trenches stumbling through an obstacle course.

As the two split up, Deon couldn't believe she was one of the last girlfriends standing without a jewel to rock on her ring finger.

Deon went searching for that desirable dress to sport at the wedding and preferably a cute blouse and mini for the bachelorette party. She had planned to take pleasure in both events. Whatever she found had to make not only a new statement, but make her feel a hell of a lot better! Despite her new plot, she was pissed about her relationship status and her age, but it was time to step up to the challenge. She was approaching a monumental time in her life. She wanted to have the marriage thing happen by the age of thirty and for good reason. If things didn't materialize within the next month, she wouldn't be a happy camper. Anyone who knew Deon, knew that she got what she wanted. That was that; otherwise, the world suffered.

Deon was approaching Saks 5th Ave. As she strutted closer to the store, all eyes were on her. Different groups of men made double takes while she whisked past. She smiled at none and laughed at many. If it had been just a day ago, she would have taken the stares poorly. Now she had a bit of a sense of humor about it. *Just a bit.* She still was repulsed. To *think* they actually thought they had a chance with her? Deon DeVaulle - a woman far from ordinary. She still thought it was a trip. *Was this what turning thirty meant?* As a woman increased in age, the quality of men decreased? A sad truth that Deon planned to alter fast.

Even though she put no pressure on herself to meet men, especially at malls, she knew that even in her social circle of the power elite of Houston, the pool of single men was shrinking. That was not even considering the ones she could actually see herself with. The thought was more excruciating than the pain she felt from her Manolo pumps. Approaching the Big 3 0 was causing her to trip out. So many good men in her past didn't seem all that then. She confidently let em' go in hopes of securing better. The logic behind it all – she didn't want to settle for less. She figured it would only get better, so why go for the bronze or silver when you really want the gold? She was certainly starting to feel like she missed the mark with that theory. But after the smell of a stranger, Q was back on her radar and smelling like a grand idea.

As Deon strolled through the store, she looked for something to catch her eye. Q was a valuable asset and she regretted that she cut her losses so soon in the game. They, together, could grow their two empires. Together, they made a great team. She bit her lips at the enticing thought.

She was single and knew that he was unattached, too. If they had a chance to start up where they left off, who knew what would be? The timing had not been right then, but she had an inkling, it was appropriate now more than ever. She was thinking of the master plan and once it was executed, she knew she would have her man.

Reassurance came to her when she thought of their silly pact they had made years ago. It was simply a joke, but it had been decided with such conviction! By the age of thirty if either party was not tied down or with the love of their life, they would come back to one another. Imagine.

Deon smiled and walked with a new direction. She felt that there might have been a reason she hadn't settled for any old moe joe. And why hadn't Quincy publicly settled down?

This was their time.

later…

Autumn could see that Deon, who was walking back with two shopping bags, seemed to be in a great mood. The two came face to face at the elevators at exactly the appointed time.

Deon could see that Autumn had a nicely wrapped box in her hand, so she wasn't the least concerned about what was inside.

"I found exactly what I was looking for," Deon bragged.

Autumn was proud that she had checked the couple's registry and bought some things that they wanted while staying within Deon's hundred dollar budget.

***

Churches made Deon itch. She was the last bridesmaid and she walked down the aisle in the hideous canary yellow gown with a tan sash that she had stuffed her top in. Deon was wearing along with the wedding party, her least favorite hairstyle (after the Jheri Curl.) Deon panned those who were attending the well-awaited wedding while holding her breath. There were several U of H classmates, but her eyes were open for one in particular. The exceptional weather allowed the guests to sit outside in the Castle Gardens.

Deon finally made it to her place with the other bridesmaids. Her job was almost done, she thought as she tried to settle down. To go with the bride's 50s Glam theme, she had done her far-from-favored finger waves for the wedding party. As much as she hated doing the particular style, the truth was, she would rather do that than to stand there in another wedding. She was retiring. This *was* her last one; a sentimental moment for the far-from-syrupy woman. Deon's spirits sank as she realized that Quincy didn't seem to be there.

THE BLACK WIDOW

Nadia's Herstory

I'm fighting! Each and every day
I'm fighting! Fighting to make a way
I'm fighting! For everything I have
I'm fighting! I'm fighting!

I'm fighting, constantly fighting with
my own state of mind
Visions of what I want and need
seem to collide

Dealing with me,
takes a lot of courage inside
Dealing so deeply,
to put all my pride aside
Dealing with the pain,
I don't want you to see
means dealing with the secrets,
that deal with keeping me

Pushing Buttons

A strange feeling came over Nadia as she stood in the pitch-black night of her front door stoop.

Moments earlier, she had pulled up to the two story home, quite delirious. She normally worked a later shift at Memorial Hospital in Boston, but her supervisor let her off early because of her migraine. She was also working as a waitress to pay her way through nursing school and she was almost finished, that is if Frank, her bank teller husband, didn't jack up their finances with all these different plans and ventures he proposed.

Nadia was drawn to mysteries, yet there were none in her mundane marriage. Frank was unapologetically predictable. At first, this was necessary for her to break away from her sporadic home life. After fulfilling both her domestic and professional duties, she grew tired of Frank and was looking for an escape route. She resented that he was clingy and didn't grant her enough space, and that he was around without a real purpose. Frank was a materialistic, impulsive shopper, something she despised. Nadia gave up on trying to keep him grounded. The very sight of him made her look away. For their union existed miraculously. The days were long, redundant and draining.

While on the road, she had missed every light due to being stuck behind two slow U-Haul trucks. *What idiot would be moving at this time of night?* She was finally able to arrive at her destination. As she sat in the driveway, she could imagine sinking into the plush cushions of her and Franks' king size bed. She hoped he was already knocked out. She sat in her Honda Accord pressing down on the button to the garage door opener; she pressed so hard she almost sprained her thumb. Teasingly, the button lit but did not fulfill its purpose; therefore, her car, that wore the words *wash me* quite often, sat in front of the house and not beside her husband's spotless, waxed Chevy truck.

She swung open the door of her dingy sedan. After slamming the door to it, she stormed to the front door of their residence, ignoring the snow. The front porch sensor light was not on so she had to fumble in the raven atmosphere with her keys, trying to feel for the right one and the right fit a little longer than she expected. She beat on the door for the third time, just in case Frank didn't hear her the first couple of times. He was known to leave her hanging because he could get so wrapped up in plotting his pipe dream schemes. *This is ridiculous!* She was unsuccessful with every try and became more and more upset that she was so close.

She turned to see if anyone was watching. The coast was as clear as it could be. Nadia intentionally dropped her keys and picked them up along with the spare key she had fit between one of the brick steps. She quickly and finally unlocked the house door.

Nadia paused and counted to ten before reacting. This was something she felt ridiculous doing, but it actually had spared other's lives.

Every light seemed to be on in the house she had decorated on a budget. She didn't even want to imagine the light bill. But she calculated it in her head. She was good with numbers and predictions.

The counting didn't help one bit.

"Frank!" Nadia snapped while she slammed the door behind her rattling, picture frames of their wedding on the wall. "Are you out of your pea brain mind!" She was fuming as she threw the keys in a bowl that sat on the table that stood in the entryway. She would be damned if he played the stupid role, his specialty. Nadia, herself, played many roles, and she didn't appreciate the type cast.

As she moved throughout the house, she didn't hear the answer she wanted and didn't expect it.

He would always laugh and just deal. No real reaction. Just like a machine, he worked, cranking out his prediction of his greatness. She wondered how great he really saw himself. She swung open the garage door. She found his car there and the reason the garage didn't come up.

"Frank! What is with locking the garage?" Nadia frowned.

Nadia stood in a heavy silence. She accepted that Frank, supposedly her better half, was not there. *This must be a holiday,* she suddenly realized as the thought of not dealing with Frank gave her more energy.

Nadia left the thoughts of his whereabouts at the garage door as she closed it and walked back into the house.

As she double checked to make sure she was locked in, she punched in the code for the alarm. Nadia almost yelled out her husband's name once more, for kicks, but decided to save her breath and energy as she turned off some of the lights downstairs instead. It was 10:45 PM. Nadia kicked off her ugly hospital shoes and let them stay by the front door after making her rounds. She started taking off her scrubs as she headed upstairs. She just wanted to take a nice, warm bath. The bed was calling her.

This was a Twilight Zone moment for her. There was always someone around, working her nerves. Frank. Frank's family. Frank's friends. Frank's clients. Tonight, she would be able to get that peace and quiet. When she walked up to their master bedroom, she started to hear the sound of music playing lowly. It was on a slow jams station.

Nadia frowned as her mood went from eased to intense. *I know I turned that stereo off and certainly wasn't playing slow jams.* As Nadia walked over to the music, she hit the power button once more. Women's intuition had her on edge. As much as she wanted to jump in the shower and then the bed, she felt like sleep wasn't coming any time soon.

He has a lot of explaining to do! Nadia found an empty phone charger stand. Her head snapped around to see if she could spot the cordless phone. Ready to get to the bottom of it so she could finally rest, she quickly pressed the page button. If she could just quiet the noise, the beeping, the beeping under the bed.

Nadia let out a loud sigh when she knelt down on the carpet to take a look under the bed that sat high. She quickly stuck her hand under the frame that held up the king size mattress and patted her hand around, feeling for the phone that still beeped at the same monotonous tone that she despised.

After a few times of sweeping her hand over the grainy carpet, Nadia frowned when she felt a stale dampness in the low, bumpy threads. She slowly pulled back her hand and her eyes blinked hysterically at what she saw. Dripping wet, and covered with bright red blood, Nadia gasped.

Instinctively, she jumped back away from the bed crashing into the wall. At the moment, the pain was unfelt as springs of pressure seemed to shoot up and down her spine.

She was overcome with a feeling she could not handle as the sound of the phone beeping still continued. Nadia refused to move. *Women's intuition played a number in her head.* As she took her other hand to cover the side of her neck that ached, in her heart, she couldn't stand the thought of seeing anymore. At that very moment, even though she pushed it away, she realized why she had felt a sense of anxiety that whole day. Now she was certain something had gone terribly wrong in their house while she was gone. Paralyzed with emotion, all she could do was sit on the bedroom floor.

Nadia couldn't budge. As her blood ran cold, she started to process what else she had felt when she reached underneath their bed. It didn't make sense at the time, but now it did. The cold, clamminess of lifeless skin is what her hand touched.

She had to call 911 but she couldn't reach under the bed anymore to grab the beeping phone. All the other phones were downstairs. After realizing she was experiencing this by herself, Nadia started screaming hysterically. Trembling, she made her way out of the room on her knees leaving a trail of red handprints behind her as she crawled. As she approached the hallway that led to the stairs, Nadia eased up enough and grabbed on to the rail. Her hand seemed to stick to the wooden rail. She found her footing and placed one foot at a time in front of the other making her way down the steep stairs. She misjudged them.

Before she knew it, she was tumbling down the sharp steps like a gymnast during her floor exercise, Nadia crashed to the bottom of the stairs. Her head slammed into the entryway tile.

***

"No! No! Not again!" Nadia tossed around violently in her hard twin-size bed that sat in the center of the small, run-down Houston apartment room. She screamed so loudly, she was sure her noisy neighbors could hear. She turned and jerked trying to fight herself awake, but she couldn't. Like a broken record, the words kept replaying *"Look at your husband."* It was a sight she could not witness. Her leg got caught in the sheets causing her to eventually fall to the cold, hard cement floor of her bedroom. The cruel fall released her from her recurrent vision. Rising to her knees, she didn't know what was worse; her dream or her reality. A part of her bed cover was still wrapped around her leg and she made an effort to untangle herself, but it felt as if her heart was about to jump out of her chest! Once unloosed, soaking wet, she ran to the bathroom and splashed cold water on her face. She stripped off the soggy t-shirt and took a cool, wet towel and placed it over her hot skin. She looked and felt like a total wreck. *She was.* Her bloodshot eyes stared back at her in a disowning way.

Nadia wished it would go away! But it was never gone! It was the only thing that kept her at night, holding her tightly. Even when she tried to let it go, it stayed. In that sense, she was not alone.

"I cannot go on like this," she pleaded, not knowing if she even heard herself in her small box of an apartment.

It was one of the same nightmares that haunted her sleepless nights since she left Boston on a one-way ticket to Houston in search of a new life. It replaced the other ones. So now she didn't have a choice. Nadia refused to close her eyes, in fear of sleep. That was nothing new. Who was she trying to fool?

Bite Me

As Quincy lay back in 25 year-old lingerie model, Alyssa Nishell's hotel bed, his eyes bulged in astonishment. He groaned as he could feel the prickly, thorny legs creeping along his paralyzed body. Their fangs began to clasp with certainty, ready to stab and inject their poison.

He frowned as the tiny, but vigorous creatures continued to tiptoe in on the treacherous torture. Quincy was a strong man, but neither his mind nor his strangled body could escape the sticky threads weaving around him with a vengeance. To try to squeeze out of the mess would take every ounce of effort he did not have! Quincy made his last attempt to move his body, but with all dismay, not even the sound of his yell escaped his mouth. Defeat somberly began to chill his body, but Quincy was not ready to surrender! He violently shook himself awake only to find he hadn't been sleep for long. It was 4 o' clock in the morning and Alyssa was still lying beside him in the same position, sound asleep. He covered her bare body with the ivory white sheet that formerly hung off the edge of her bed.

***

Later that morning, the sun peeped through the hotel suite's blinds, illuminating Alyssa's animal-print thong that had been tossed on the floor beside the mess of a bed. She had checked into the Westin Galleria that evening and was anxious to reunite with Quincy who was at the moment, hopping out the shower feeling refreshed and rejuvenated. Alyssa, in town for only a week, was in Houston for business. A modeling gig. She loved staying in the hotel that was connected to the Galleria Mall, which carried the world's upscale stores and boutiques and high-end brands. She hadn't planned on sleeping in, but she was knocked out.

Quincy had a long day of business and pleasure ahead of him. Last night had been gratifying though. Seeing Alyssa again was always entertaining. For him, the evening began with the playboy hosting a very grown and sexy party at Club SINtinel, a downtown club that he, along with his paternal and frat brothers, had recently opened. Immediately, after leaving one of urban Houston's new hotspot a little earlier than the others, he topped off his night with visiting his *friend* whose face was buried in the plush, pillows. Alyssa Nishell came to her door with a pout that did very little to hide her eagerness to see him and a robe that didn't disclose her curves. He knew he had left the party for a good reason.

Alyssa, along with many other booty calls, knew just how to spoil Quincy with plenty of attention and affection. From girls buying his lunch in grade school and young women fighting other young women to wear his letterman in high school, today as a man one month shy of his 30th b-day, nothing had changed much. For he was as spoiled as ever. The fact of the matter was Quincy was always told by his mom, his charm would be his blessing and his curse. His philosophy was, you had to care in order to get caught. He had never cared for a woman, not even his mother. Not after what she did, or better yet, who she was.

Quincy dried off his chiseled chest admiring his naturally built physique that for a bonus feature, he shaped and sculpted at the gym. He was the whole package. The man that made women from all walks of life drool like dogs when he stepped on the scene. He cracked the door open a bit to look over at the 5 foot 8 model, lying there. He figured what he had going for him, it was certainly not a curse.

Cool, but not committed, Alyssa unconsciously knew the deal and she was always *down*, always. That night wasn't any different, Quincy thought as he smirked arrogantly at himself in the mirror. He noticed his Blackberry's blinking red light. He had a couple of text messages he hadn't opened.

He scrambled through the ignored. Many were from the boys, plotting out the next go round.

Some were alerts from his business e-mail and were messages left by clients.

Then there was one text message that made him do a double take. He recognized the number right away even though it had been years since he had seen it.

Deon had called and left her call back number.

Quincy's eyes widened as his mind wondered what she could possibly want, calling him. It wasn't everyday that they talked. In fact, they had fallen out of contact and he didn't even know the latest concerning her. So it must be something big.

There was some interest there, but not enough to fit the call into his schedule at that very moment. He would have to hit her back if he had the chance. He needed to be on his way and that was the way it was.

Quincy slid on his crème slacks and turned his attention back to wrapping up his time with Alyssa. Alyssa was a cool girl and they stayed in the shallow end of the pool. It just wasn't like him to get caught up emotionally into deep levels with the girls he shared his bed with. He knew some guys were unaware of how over-flooded they let their pools get, but it just wasn't in his nature to drown in those waters. Surprisingly, so many of his boys came to him for advice, but he knew he was far from and expert in relationships. He was an expert in moving and shaking. He buttoned up his baby blue Kenneth Cole collar shirt that complimented his silky smooth, deep cocoa skin. It was time to get a move on.

For the finishing touches, Quincy sprayed just a touch of cologne on his neck. Instantly, Quincy's eyes bucked from the reaction.

"DAMN!" he howled, and the bottle dropped from his hands and crashed to the ground. Quincy clinched his teeth as he grabbed his neck. He held his neck for a good minute before uncovering it.

Repulsed at the sight on his near perfect body. An unrecognizable spot accessorized his smooth skin.

Alyssa, in the other room, took a deep breath inhaling a smell she associated with ecstasy. A smile spread across her face.

"Shit!" behind closed bathroom doors, Quincy, grunted while looking at the bottle he had just purchased that past weekend; it was scattered in little pieces on the bathroom floor. He took one of the clean towels and catered to the liquid. He hoped Alyssa was still sound asleep, long enough for him to disappear. He didn't like dealing with the morning after drama, not even for the bodacious bombshell. To him, aside from how they were packaged, inside women were all the same - they wanted to drain you dry.

The towel was now drenched in his scent. The pieces of the bottle were in the trash.

Quincy washed his hands and then turned to take a closer look at the…blemish.

Though repulsed, Quincy managed to snap out of it when he could hear Alyssa's slight shifts in the bed that creaked at every movement. He needed to have been gone. He popped his collar and like a thief in the night, smoothly managed to tiptoe through the hotel room and out the door. Soon he was in the parking lot and then securely in the driver's seat.

First up, he was off to meet with one of his clients who was interested in purchasing a home in the rebirth of the Third Ward District.

***

As Quincy pulled his red Hummer up to a red light, he was met with laughter on the other end of the phone line.

"You need to get that checked out man. It could be poisonous!" said his frat brother Kile Elliot, who was lanky and had no rhythm. Kile Elliot was as silly as silly could be.

"Dawg, it felt like my flesh was on fire!" Quincy said into his Bluetooth as irritated skin still throbbed. So mortified at the sight of the bright red hideous mark, Quincy took his tenth double take since leaving Alyssa's. The sight of the mark made him feel annoyed all over again.

"I mean I know I have an affect on women, but I don't remember Alyssa biting me or anything like that," said the pretty boy. Besides, last night was one of the calmer nights," he boasted as he couldn't help to continue to glare at the fleshy wound.

Quincy shivered. He wanted to rip off his shirt and scratch the skin that itched like crazy underneath the fabric.

As he tried to ignore his tingling body, all he heard on the other end was laughter. Repulsed, he realized looking at his neck did absolutely nothing to relieve the stinging sensation.

"You know I'm used to pain, but damn! This shit is different," the former high school and college star quarterback said. He had endured several injuries, but the bite was making him irritable. He couldn't quite put his finger on it.

"How did shortie react?" the buppy asked, doing his best *cool* impression.

"Please, I wasn't even trying to fool with her this morning. She wouldn't have been able to do anything," Quincy answered referring to the dependent woman.

Regardless, Quincy knew he had done well exiting and not waking Alyssa because the last thing he wanted to hear was her *nagging.*

"Oh and get this, guess who called me?" Quincy said.

"Who?" Kile Elliot inquired.

Quincy couldn't help but smile…"Double D."

"What!!!" Kile Elliot laughed.

"Yeah, man," Quincy said, liking the reaction.

He tried to suddenly change his tune.

"What her bourgeois ass want?" Kile Elliot said casually. This was another example of how his genuine efforts seemed to not matter. He tried everything in his power to get her attention, but nothing ever seemed to work, not like it did for his boy, Q.

"I don't know. I saw it…this morning." Quincy thought.

"Whatever it is, I bet it's gonna be good. Where she been hiding? I remember she used to be in the mix," Kile Elliot asked.

Quincy sat for a moment.

"Yeah, that was back in the day. It's been a minute man," Quincy said thinking about their college days at U of H. He had the biggest crush on her.

"I thought you two were gonna be together, homie, didn't you?" Kile Elliot kept laughing, happy that this was not the case. Hoping that it wouldn't be the case soon. Wondering if he had a chance.

Quincy chuckled at the thought, not quite sure how he felt about bringing up past predictions.

"Oh, we were together all right…" Quincy started.

Kile Elliot cleared his throat dramatically.

"But back to this neck bite...what you gonna do about that?" Kile Elliot quickly said changing the subject reluctantly remembering how Quincy was the chosen one and Kile Elliot was overlooked.

"Man..." Quincy didn't know what to say. "As soon as I get out of this meeting, I need to do something."

After getting off the phone with his brother who couldn't seem to stop chuckling, during the remainder of the ride to the location, Quincy attempted to ignore the bite on his neck and the voice of his mother in his head by pumping his favorite old-school joint, *Joy and Pain,* by Maze and Frankie Beverly. As he rolled down Highway 59, he thought to himself, all *these damn women.*

Like a ritual, colorful nights like the past, led to visions of his mother, Marie. It was an image Quincy just couldn't shake. All he ever wanted to do was make her happy, but he knew no man could ever do that. Outside of his successful career, he knew his mother's expectation for him at his age and *he knew he was* nowhere close to achieving it. He handled his career like he handled the ladies – by carefully having his hands in many places. But anyone who really knew him knew it was so much more to him than his exterior. Few knew the real story. That was the way he liked it.

By the minute, the stinging seemed to sharpen! It was an itch that couldn't be scratched. Quincy turned up the speakers of his 360 and drowned himself in the music by singing with Frankie *"Joy, and pain. It's like sunshine, and rain!"* If only he could permanently drown out all the voices of irritating women in his life, in his head.

***

As the nail tech started Deon's manicure, Deon felt like a desperate school girl waiting on the call, on acknowledgement, and far from the Queen D she was. Quincy had not returned *her* call. Her mind wandered: *Maybe...should have...left a message. Maybe he didn't have the number anymore and thought it was some random person. Maybe it got lost...in all the other numbers. That is probably what it was,* she thought as she got her cuticles cut at an upscale spa in Rice Village.

She was going to once again step outside of herself and do something she wasn't too proud of.

Deon started to dial the number with her free hand and all she got was his voicemail.

She used to get all access.

She wanted to get this handled now. While she had the nerve. It wasn't every day that she put herself out there. In fact, it wasn't any day. This, in her book, called for desperate measures. Time was ticking. Her 30th birthday was in a month. She needed to go for what she wanted, because truth of the matter, she *got* it. She wanted Q back in her life.

In My Head

Months ago, when Nadia first got to Houston from Boston, the doctor had asked, what was stressing her out and Nadia knew that her *whole life* was the answer. The fact that it continued even after she moved, stressed her out even more. She remembered it like it were yesterday, but it was actually five years ago when she had said good-bye to Boston and hello to Houston. Her first job was at Johnny's Steakhouse and she learned that she could say good-bye to Boston, but Boston didn't quite say bye to her.

Even when she squeezed them shut, the lights shot like bullets to her eyes. Every sound in the noisy kitchen blared like sirens ten times louder into her ears. Nadia Master's 5 feet 6, one hundred and twenty-five pound body, grew heavier by the second! She stood with her eyes shut and her hands covering her sensitive ears. Losing her balance, Nadia stumbled back to the wall, crumbling slowly to the cold tile floor. As she sat huddled over while still in distress, she tried to massage her throbbing temples as she rocked herself back and forth, but the pain was excruciating! There were so many places she would rather be. Outside of her body was one of them. The unbearable aching made her forget entirely where she was. Two minutes later, once she remembered, it didn't surprise her that none of her "Johnny's Steakhouse" co-workers noticed her sitting all balled up in the back, on the kitchen floor, in between the two freezers just waiting for the massive storm in her head to pass. Nadia hadn't had a migraine this severe since she was a little girl!

A dizzy Nadia wrestled with the idea of how could she get herself out of the mess she seemed to always be in. She knew she had to get it together before Dan saw her like this! But the manager was the least of her worries. She couldn't believe that she was acting in such a way, better yet, reacting. She had promised herself to never let anyone intimidate her again! She had done well, until two skeletons from her closet sat waiting on her to return to their table.

With her eyes opening slightly, Nadia managed to stand up. Slowly, she made her way over to the nearest sink. After splashing the ice-cold water on her face, she proceeded to cleanse her hands with the employee soap. While taking several deep breaths, Nadia was relieved to feel a little better as she dried off her damp palms. Without thinking, she shook her head in disbelief, but quickly regretted it when the slight gesture almost sent back her chronic headache. She stood still for a moment as she realized, no matter how fast she ran, and Lord knows she could run fast, her past was right on her tail! Tonight wasn't any different.

As she returned to two smirk-filled faces looking her up and down - two former college classmates of her Frank, Nadia wished she were bringing the bill instead of drinks.

As Nadia avoided eye contact, all she could think about was how it was just her luck. "Of all the places in the world, I would see these two jokers from Boston," she thought as she sat the drinks on the coasters.

"Finally," snapped Holly, Nadia's former bridesmaid, while swinging her blonde hair. "Thought you'd never return. We are ready to order."

Nadia tried hard, very hard to keep her attitude under the radar as she whipped out her order pad and pen from her pocket but she couldn't stand the sight of Holly. To just be in the presence of someone who smiled in your face as they stabbed your back was hard to bear!

"Okay, what will it be for you two this evening?" Nadia said attempting to sound pleasant as she looked directly into her beady brown eyes.

Holly eyed her closely as her forehead wrinkled.

Nadia felt the hot room closing in on her by the second as they continued to stare.

"If I weren't mistaken, you didn't seem too thrilled to see us, Nadia," stated Holly.

Nadia looked at Holly and then at Cameron, who sat across from her with the same permanent smirk Nadia yearned to slap off his face! She could tell he loved every minute of the reunion.

"Well you know how it is, you are mistaken," Nadia replied coolly trying to remain on her best behavior as she remembered such a helpless study buddy Holly was throughout Intro to Psych, Observation and Recording of Mental Health, Abnormal Psychology and all the

other undergrad classes they took together. Nadia had helped Holly immensely with studying the different mental disorders and medical terms for upcoming tests. Nadia fumed inside! How dare Holly even come at anyone like that with her poor judgment of character! All Nadia could think of was anyone who even thought about dating snake-eyed Cameron needed to get her head examined!

"Besides, I wouldn't want you two to starve on my account," Nadia answered quickly.

The two looked at each other slowly.

"Funny you mention starve. Looks like you've dropped a couple of pounds. I guess all those legal issues have really taken their toll," Holly figured as she continued to look her up and down with her jumpy eyes. "As they would."

As if she really cared, Nadia thought as her heartbeat began to tap faster than her pen against the blank order pad.

"Especially, with all those people watching! I know it was stressful. We know how you can't stand being the center of attention. Yet the center is where you always seem to stand," she continued.

"Like you didn't help make it that way" is what Nadia really wanted to say but she figured she would leave her personal issues at the door. "If only Holly would too," Nadia wished. Even though Cameron hadn't said anything, his presence was enough to add to the smoke-filled room.

"Holly, she probably wants to forget? And that she did a great job doing. Your memory come back yet hun?" Cameron asked in his best concerned voice. He and Nadia were not the best of friends considering Cameron hated Frank's guts. Before Nadia had met Frank, Cameron had pursued her in college. Nadia always took Cameron as not being interested in women, yet that was who he dated. There were several things about Cameron that rubbed Nadia the wrong way. She couldn't get over the fact that she didn't feel comfortable around him, and still didn't. Cameron reminded her of many men she ran away from.

Nadia smiled and shook her head. "These days, I am doing just fine, thank you. Besides, it's been almost a year since we all have seen each other and you can imagine how much that has helped me. Out of sight, out of mind," Nadia said, surprised she even said it.

The couple frowned, as the passive aggressive woman continued.

"You know Nadia, I really don't get where all this hostility is coming from," Holly snapped pointing her finger at her.

Nadia knew that she did! She felt insulted that Holly continued to lie in her face.

"Well, you know Miss Masters has always been hard as hell to read," Cameron diagnosed closing his menu.

"Yeah, even to us. And we are well on our way to becoming doctors." The two laughed at themselves enjoying the sound.

Nadia gulped as she felt her empty stomach drop as they went on and on about how they had just started med school.

"As long as I've known her and even after all the psych classes, you would think she wouldn't be such a big mystery," Cameron said with a laugh that made Nadia's skin crawl. "It's really cute, but I'm sure it can get old fast to others."

Holly gave Cameron a cutting look before returning it to Nadia.

"Like they say, I guess you never really know a person," Cameron concluded slowly.

The undertones were blaring bright. Nadia would rather both just say what they really wanted to say, that Nadia murdered her husband. But they would never give Nadia the satisfaction. Instead they would examine her like she was a mental patient in a psych ward!

"Are you two ready to order, or do you need me to come back?" Nadia pressed out through her tight lips.

"Oh no, we wouldn't want to lose you again, we are ready," Holly said closing her menu.

"Impossible," was all Nadia could think. As she took the menus back to the kitchen, she tried hard to catch her breath but as she punched the orders into the machines she wanted so badly to punch them! So they were on their way to being doctors! "Poor patients," was all she could think. As Nadia poked at the touch screen, she thought about how she would have been well on her way to becoming one! She wanted to help protect the children from evil adults. "If only someone was there for me," she thought. "If it weren't for Frank and the money issues that came with him, maybe I would be okay." But like her life, anything she wanted, had a definite way of reversing. It was going to be a long night

and it was going to take a miracle to keep her from whooping those devils upside the head with their menus!

Nadia came to wonder, with friends like that, who needed enemies? On the path to success, out of nowhere, Nadia had come up on a detour, one that frustrated her more and more. After graduating, she felt stuck in a place she could not quite get out of. She wanted to be moving on with her life. She tried to convince herself that she would be back on track in no time. She just had to keep her cool, which was going to take another miracle!

As Nadia scrambled in the back, the duo impatiently waited at the table amused by the evening.

"Frank didn't deserve to die like that! He was a good man," Cameron said.

"You didn't even like Frank!" Holly said sharply.

"He still didn't deserve that!" Cameron said looking around the restaurant.

Holly thought to herself: Yeah, Frank deserved me, but you will do.

"May he rest in peace?" Cameron said looking directly in Holly's eyes.

Nadia still couldn't manage to gain her full composure. It killed her to know that she was letting two losers get to her. To think, she counseled Holly for years because she couldn't handle her own problems. Nadia, being faced with the biggest crisis of her own life, knew others would ridicule her. She imagined Cameron, but not Holly, jumping on the bandwagon. Just the thought of their faces adorned with fake smiles and insincere concern made Nadia hotter than the dishes she placed on the tray.

Returning to the table, she just knew she had to get through the night!

"Here you go," Nadia said as she placed the heaviest order on the table.

"I didn't order this!" Holly announced sharply, as if insulted.

Nadia took a better look at the plate of barbeque chicken realizing she had typed in the wrong order all together.

"I ordered ribs," she continued. "Barbequed ribs!"

Nadia wanted to let Holly have it! The demeaning tone in her voice cut her like a knife. Nadia already had a lot of emotions welling up inside of her, over twenty years of emotions she couldn't quite explain. But all she could do was just stand there as Holly kept going on and on and on about how she specifically made her order clear, but her voice eventually faded off as Nadia's vision began to blur.

Her body, once again felt very heavy. She felt unstable as her heart started to pump harder. She was losing her balance, again!

"I am really sorry about that. I will get that taken care of," Nadia managed to utter while removing the plate from the table to place it back on the unleveled tray. But before she could move, Holly's voice got not only her attention, but also everyone's in the restaurant.

"AHHHHH!" Holly hollered with pain as she shot up out of her seat. Nadia's hand let the steaming hot plate of chili knock over into her lap and on her cashmere pantsuit.

"What is wrong with you?" Cameron instigated gathering together napkins as fast as he could while Holly stood in tears as the remains of the chili burned her thighs.

Nadia couldn't do anything but stand there looking at the red sauce drip down Holly's leg. The sight was even more alarming to Nadia. It was as if she was watching a calmer reenactment of a nightmare she knew all too well!

Dan, the manager, was the first to rush over, but Nadia did not notice at all. All she could do was look at the bloody red stains from the sauce. Moments after Dan apologized, trying to make everything alright, Nadia knew that, of course, nothing was.

She could run, but could she hide?

She was in Houston, but her mind was all over the place. She was trying to track down so much, it was starting to take its toll. Nadia sat stiff as a board as the cold stethoscope sat on her tender chest.

"Breath in," Dr. Pates began in her thick middle-eastern accent.

Nadia took a deep breath as she clenched her teeth in the arctic room.

"Breath out," the physician suggested.

Nadia released her breath, but there was still an aching cramp caught in the center of her chest hindering her ability to breathe liberally.

"Sounds pretty good. Any known heart problems?"

Nadia looked down at her bitter hands as she tried to stretch them to add life back into them.

"Not that I know of," Nadia answered while still wondering.

Nadia not knowing much about her parents, except for their first names, seemed to make *everything* so much more complicated, even simply filling out forms for her medical history.

Even though Nadia worked with nurses, she didn't feel comfortable sharing her problems with them.

"That's okay; you are doing the right thing by taking even more precaution. If you continue to feel uneasiness in your chest, any pain, please do not hesitate to call me," Pates said reassuringly.

Nadia nodded with little emotion. She just needed medication to make the ghost disappear.

"It can be a number of things. If you're under a lot of stress, it could be anxiety, but we can look into it even more if the problems persist."

Nadia tried to take a deep breath. She could still feel the catch in her chest. She could only carry out short ones in the cold office.

"I thank you for coming in today. I am going to give you a couple of samples for anxiety," the doctor said walking to the cabinet.

"But continue to pay attention to how you feel, and if your heart beat continues to feel irregular, please come back in for more tests," she said handing her a bag that crackled with the sound of plastic packages. I also put some samples in here to help your insomnia. Did you have any more questions?"

"No, I think that is it," Nadia said knowing she did, but doubting a doctor could answer.

"Okay, Mrs. Masters. Stop stressing." Dr. Pates smiled. "Take it easy. You are too young and too beautiful to be strained!"

She left Nadia to dress.

Stop stressing, Nadia laughed. *If only it were that easy.*

After Frank's death, she needed to escape. Anti-depressants didn't quite do the trick. She had been here before. So much was suggested. Therapy didn't seem to be something she could see herself sitting through. She knew all the terms bi-polar, manic depressive, described her cycle of moods, but deep down she knew she wasn't there. *It was just that protecting secrets* was crazier than she thought. She needed to find a safe way to release them.

Nadia decided to try and follow the doctor's orders, just for the time being and take the remainder of the day to do something she enjoyed for a change. She worked at a personal care home and the owner of the elderly home had given her the day off. She remembered getting a flyer for an art gallery/coffee shop. *If anything mattered to her, it was art.*

Pure Illusion

I can see you watching me
Not sure of what it means
Leading me to feel something
I can't quite explain

I look into your eyes
not sure of what it means
Just that they are trying to
tell me something

I know one thing for sure
and that's when our eyes meet
I feel connected with you
Close to you, special to you,
complete

Through your eyes lies mystery
A clear explanation I can not yet see
But through my heart I do believe
that through your eyes I see

Quincy hasn't put himself out there as being tied down to anyone. Deon tried to reason with herself. She knew from articles that he was still an eligible bachelor; *believe it or not.* She smiled imagining why and how that status could be put to an end.

Even though they were out of touch, Deon was confident that her touch still had an effect on him as much as his had on her. She wanted to test the waters. She was sure that the timing was now right for them and their current status would be enough to sort out their formerly complex relationship: a relationship that was enough to strip a rich and fertile forest of its roots then freeze it over seconds later. She was hoping they both had cooled off since then and now were more of a moderate temperature.

As an undergrad studying Business Management, both Deon and Quincy displayed such promising potential as individuals, and as a duo. Both graduated at the top of their class. To the last day, both vied for that top position. Deon graduated with a small fraction of a point ahead. On graduation day, she remembered turning around and sticking her tongue out at Quincy. She thought he would give her that smile, the way he always did right after her childish antics, but he didn't. She convinced herself that she didn't care. At the time, she, easily bored, childishly wanted to replace his ass, and settled on the idea of seeing what else was out there, topping the charts.

They thought they were grown then, but they were adults now! *A lil too adult*, for Deon. She tuned out her ticking biological clock and the vision of a timeline without marriage date. Who knows what could be? They were both living up to their potential, that was for sure. They needed to talk. Deon kept reciting three questions over and over again in her head – 1.Why didn't you smile back? 2. What happened to us? And 3. When can we get back together? They had a lot of catching up to do and not a lot of time to do it if this love connection needed to be made.

She was happy to finally get a response from him. They were going to do a late lunch at one of his establishments. She knew she wanted to meet with him so the sparks could fly again. *What a pair we are.* Deon got excited at the idea. How convenient were her thoughts, impulsive her motives. What a faultless time to let what had been what she saw as a high-quality investment come full circle, if he was game. *He needed to be!* Even though that was years ago, their bond was so strong, she felt it needed to be reactivated.

***

Tall, chocolate and too fine for words, Quincy abruptly stopped stirring his steaming coffee. Across from him, suited up in a two-piece Chanel number, Deon DeVaulle sat with her eyes unusually open wide, piercing through the strands of her thick bangs, trying to meet his detached gaze. She knew it was an unlikely reunion for the two, she held her breath, barely on the edge of her seat, waiting to hear his answer in the artsy coffee shop, which sat hidden behind the edgy art exhibit hall, the shop's main attraction.

The woman who was a *business* woman first and beauty empress second had a lot of work ahead, but she sat waiting. Waiting and waiting to hear what she wanted. Waiting for him to proceed with what could be "good news" for her! She could hear her

Blackberry vibrating violently against her M.A.C, NW20 Studio Fix compact in her Coach bag that sat in the empty seat beside her. She tapped her Prada stilettos, subconsciously hoping that they would produce a more rapid response from Quincy. Deon knew it was a call she *needed* to answer, but she knew that she *wanted* an answer from the distracted male that sat in front of her more.

As she anticipated his rich and sensual voice, to her dismay, Quincy left her with silence. Her astonished eyes watched the abruptly frozen man become mysteriously taken aback by his discovery and lost in its findings. *Never* had he seen a work of art so rich in composition, so unique in design and so perfect in execution. Fascinated and intrigued, Quincy admired the flawless, well-sculpted structure. He couldn't control the urge to examine *every* detail, *every* line and *every* curve up close and personally!

Deon and Quincy sat on the farthest end of the shop. But with tunnel vision, Quincy singled out Nadia Elaine Masters in the stark white exhibit hall across the way. She stood like a sentinel directly in front of the narrow doorless opening that connected the dim shop to the bright hall. Nadia couldn't budge because of shock. The artist somehow happened to capture a moment so real. It was a flash so vivid and personal; her misty eyes remained glued to the depiction. To Nadia, it proved to be utterly breathtaking to her that paint could produce *her* reality!

Not knowing quite how to feel about the awe-inspiring piece, she frowned as she continued to study each and every inch of the canvas. *There was no way that this could look so accurate,* she thought to herself.

As Quincy continued to spy on the coca brown-skinned beauty from across the way, he knew it was not only her well-crafted stature that mesmerized him nor her long, thick, chocolate mane that showcased her sharp, yet tender facial features. No, it was simply the fact that there was more to this woman than *what met the eye.*

The ladies loved and wanted Houston's Most Eligible Bachelor to leave his bachelor ways behind. Quincy knew what he wanted - this woman who possessed more than beauty. She had an aura he couldn't deny then or now. He remembered her and the way she moved. It had been a couple of months ago since October's

Masquerade Ball, but it was as vivid as yesterday. He spotted her amongst all the regular honies at the sophisticated Halloween party. The distinctive way she moved on the dance floor at the SINtinel kept his attention. Even though she wore a mask that night, like all the other guests, he was sure that this was the same woman. Her mystique was driving him then and now as he remembered the way she moved. As she stood *still,* Quincy's thoughts moved rapidly.

Suddenly, Nadia's thoughts were interrupted as a chill slithered down her upright spine. She shivered as the feeling of being taken in crept upon her.

She blinked for the first time in minutes; coming back to the moment she realized how long she had been there in the popular mid-Downtown gallery "Renazance Lounge." *Too long,* echoed in her brain. Nadia looked at her watch in disbelief. She had let a whole eight minutes go by without even feeling it! Nadia swallowed hard and a heavy sensation came over her. She had just stopped by the gallery to clear her mind and she definitely *did*, maybe a little too much. Her thoughts raced and her heart jumped around in her chest. She turned away from the painting that she now saw as silly and obscure, in order to get an idea of what was going on around her. There were several people networking and doing their own thing, but she knew that feeling of someone watching her all too well.

The sensation lingered; she hid her embarrassment. She took one more look at the canvas then coolly gathered her wits as she eyed the nearest exit.

A few feet away, Deon's vanilla skin was now as crimson as the poppy color of her shoes that she tapped furiously on the slate floor. Her eyes were still fixed on Quincy. For her, enough was enough! Her untouched coffee and patience grew colder by the second. Everything was going at a steady pace. She and Quincy were actually getting somewhere and in seconds, things had come to a hasty stop - a stop that left her panting. She wanted her damn answer. She wanted them to get back to being *them* again, in 2009. Unfortunately, it was the perceived Nubian Queen that stood so close, yet so far away, that was on Quincy's mind, now! He yearned to reach out and touch Nadia. He knew he had to make a move, fast.

Deon frowned once again at Quincy, not knowing how to describe the expression on his usually aloof face!

"What are you looking at?" she snapped, whipping her silky long ebony tresses around, not sure of what to focus on in the crowded hall across the way. She was not going to sit in this state of confusion with him any longer.

Quincy's eyes widened at the thought. *A masterpiece!*

He answered to himself as he involuntarily left Deon more than mind-boggled at the table as he went after the stranger he wanted to become more familiar with. Soon a crowd started to form in front of the picture that caught Nadia's eye.

After swiftly maneuvering himself through the zigzag pattern of tables, chairs and people like the agile football player he had been on the field, in a matter of seconds Quincy stepped into the exhibit hall. To his dismay, the woman was *nowhere* in sight. He frowned as he gazed out the clear glass doors at both ends of the hall. Puzzled at how she had gotten away so fast, again, Quincy stood searching all possibilities but still, no visual trace of her. It was as if she vanished into thin air. Not even close to being satisfied, he desperately turned to face the art piece, the one she was immersed in, as if it would offer some clue to one of the many questions that had now tackled his mind. Quincy knew what he saw, but he was not sure what he was looking for. What she had gotten from the painting he would not know. *It was just a painting.* In fact, Quincy quickly figured he had seen better. Whatever it was, at that very moment, Quincy was determined and convinced that it wouldn't be long before, like the painting, he would be holding Nadia's attention; better yet, holding her inside the captivating embrace that so many women desired - like the one he left behind.

A wicked smile crept upon Quincy's face. They would meet again. And the next time, he wasn't letting her get away!

Venom

Deon sat fuming as she sat alone at the table. Too embarrassed to replay the thoughts even in her own head, she chose to look at her phone. She couldn't concentrate. It was just something to do until she could gather her composure.

"What the hell was that?" she shook her head, dumbfounded then looked around to see if anyone saw.

"Did he forget? He must have forgotten!" she asked out loud.

Deon didn't realize she was *talking to herself.*

He must be still mad at me, she figured.

She called Ruby on speed dial. While the phone rang she was still talking to herself.

Who the hell was that? She needed to find out fast and she would.

She wanted her answer.

She wanted her man.

When Ruby answered, she hung up the phone. She realized she didn't want her to know what happened. She was too ashamed.

How things played out didn't make any sense to her whatsoever. Deon sure did get a good look at her, the woman that stood there.

There had to be another approach, she thought to herself.

Moving the bitch out of the way was one, she concluded.

***

One week later,

It was payday.

Christmas was around the corner and Nadia had no one in particular to buy presents for.

Laying low was the goal in Houston and it had its benefits. But it was something about the month of December that made her feel *low.* Her current job as a caretaker at a personal care home was a modest one. She worked for a week and was off the next. She had a favorite among the senile women. Nadia loved the charming Mrs. White, also known as Mama B.

Dealing with Mama B took her mind off her worries. Then there was the fact that the woman was always getting into something in the house. Nadia thought about what Mama B would like for Christmas. She, too, was a hard one to figure out. She had been a giver and those were the hardest people to buy for because they didn't allow themselves to receive.

Going to the bank brought back memories. She continued holding an account with Wells Fargo, the bank that her husband had worked at. He was good at counting money and spending it as fast as he counted. *Good for nothing… marriage. Down the drain,* she thought.

This time, she could control her own, everything. She could live below her means. Saving up her money, she wanted to purchase a house. New or previously owned. She still debated. She had been doing her homework, reading up on the single woman's guide to buying a house while the patients at the care home were asleep.

It was time in her life to hold back from playing a role and actually start being the real her. She wanted to do something that would mean the world to her. Some people wanted marriage. Some people wanted careers. Nadia always needed shelter, a place of her own. A place she could call home.

Like pop-up books, Nadia watched new communities in Houston being built left and right. An avid admirer, Nadia was making it a habit to check out each and every one of those communities on her days off. She would fill up at the gas station by her apartment complex, ignore the whistles of men passing by and go from community to community, collecting booklets filled with floor plans. The chameleon crafted her next master plan.

She wanted something small, maybe a one-story.

Nadia valued the nice get-a-way feel as she entered what appeared to be a modest community right outside the busy city. Nadia recognized the *McKnight Homes* logo as she drove up to the community that sat off of 288. She had seen commercials.

There were five, far from cookie-cutter model homes that complimented each other. The row of houses welcomed her with the idea of comfort, more so than some of the other homes in the same price range. She could see herself instantly living on the street for one very reason. The homes looked like updated replicas of Rose Street, the street she had first lived on as a child in Houston with her foster care mother. Rose Street was also a street Sheila lived on years ago.

Those were the days she actually was safe. Those were the days she slept tight, underneath her quilt that her guardian made just for her.

Nadia figured she was just going to browse the homes, no strings attached.

The models all had traditional style fronts. Earth-toned paneling mixed with brick. As she approached the first house, she noticed the house was named the "The Elaine." She did a double take. *What a coincidence,* she thought. The house had her name on it. She walked through the office that was connected to the home.

"Hello," she said making her presence known.

There was no answer, so Nadia proceeded.

Nadia was anxious to view the inside of the cute, red brick model home. The unlocked door made a beeping sound when she opened it. She was pleasantly surprised. She expected to see a more traditional home and got a more contemporary feel. The smell of cinnamon spices filled her nose as she stood in the gallery-styled entryway. She adored the hard wood floors that bounced the slightest sound off of them. *Imagine coming home to this every day.*

She eyed the two grand art pieces that faced each other as they aligned the two parallel walls in the foyer. One was a renaissance portrait of a knight and the other was of a regal woman.

Then her eyes got ahead of themselves and panned what lay before her. The fairly open floor plan allowed her to peak at the spacious formals ahead. The layout looked nothing like the home she stayed in with her guardian. She finally closed the door, eager to discover more of what the house had to offer.

Removing all decorative things, the house was amazing because of the aesthetically-pleasing architecture. Her eyes drifted up to the high asymmetric ceilings once she stepped into the den. She then took in the various elements, in no particular order. She was in love.

Nadia saw the house as her own personal space. She became territorial with the ideas that popped in her head. She wanted to scratch the surface a bit. The space was vaguely decorated, similar to the pad of a bachelor. But Nadia saw what she would do with the innovative space to make it more complete. She would kill to add some finishing touches to the model home. The safe, monochromatic creamy color scheme didn't serve the space well. She knew that the room would come alive even more with a splash of more vibrant colors and if some metallics were thrown in to give it more of an art deco feel.

Nothing moved her like art did. Walking forward, she gawked at the great bone structure, the archways. The rounded corners added European dimension to the space and the different sculpted items that embellished the area.

Her apartment only gave her so much to work with, she thought.

A house. She shook her head. A home. Better yet, *a hiding place.*

As much as the house had, it was a major component. *Her.*

Swiftly, yet sometimes staggering, she continued to move along the living area and kitchen. Finally she reached the destination she was more concerned with – the hall of bedrooms positioned in the back of the house. There were three doors.

She peaked in each staged room that led to the end of the hallway.

Nadia knew that the French doors at the end led into the master. Without thinking, she opened them with authority and stood taking in the view at the room that awaited her.

The first thing that caught her sleepy eye, was the lush queen size bed that was directly in front of the entrance - set up high, regal like a throne in the middle of the room. Nadia, at that moment did not want to have to go home. She could just…stay there. She could just flip off her shoes, climb into the cushion, bring the day to an end right then and there and worry about the rest later. She actually thought about how the realtor would just have to call the police on the strange woman who took a nap in the model home. She tickled herself at the thought of the headlines. Wouldn't be the first time she made news. But it would be a more light-hearted piece this time around.

Nadia walked forward, trying to keep a logical mind as the bed cushions called her. She stood at the foot of the bed, still fighting the idea that seemed like the brightest at the moment. She ran her hand slowly over the soft, silky cool comforter. *So nice.*

Nadia's forehead crinkled.

There was room for so much.

She felt ridiculous. She frowned at the thought of how much she would risk just to catch some zzzzs. She did the best she could to curve her appetite and finally turned away from the main attraction.

Nadia finally noticed the rest of the room. The room had a nice view. Over to the left, there was a patio set by the window that gave the view of the backyard. Nadia saw something on the table that struck a chord. She decided to walk on over to the chessboard that sat as the centerpiece. *It's been awhile.* She needed to brush up on her skills, that was for sure. Get back in the game for old times' sake. She had defeated her share of opponents in the past. She had a funny feeling that soon she would have some more playing to do. Her hunches were always right, unfortunately.

Nadia smiled as she recalled the rules of the game.

She knew the Queen was the most powerful. She could move.

The King *could make the moves*, but he was ...limited, making him subject to...attack. Then, the game is...over.

Then there was the Knight, who had many advantages. He couldn't be limited as much as the other pieces. As much as he could block, he could still be limited.

After a few moments of playing back past games, Nadia somehow gravitated back to the one thing she wanted the most right now: comfort.

As she stood facing the bed, suddenly another recurrent feeling came over her. Out of instinct, she quickly looked up in the mirror that hung above the bed. She found what gave her that feeling. A smooth Billy Dee character, leaning coolly against the door watched the woman he recognized. From the back. He knew they would meet again. He also knew, this time, he wasn't letting her gracefully dash away.

Nadia slowly turned her body around to see if the reflection rang true. Then their eyes met and locked tightly, held in place like tight handcuffs on a criminal. A thousand emotions ran through them both, simultaneously, as they stood motionless in each other's presence. *There were no masks this time.* And this gave a whole new dimension to the intensity. Nadia knew that this time, she had nowhere to run, and certainly nowhere to hide. She wasn't sure why her gut had her in protection mode, but it did and she already had a plan, a plan that she lived by. If someone came at her in the wrong way, she was prepared to *hit and run. And last but not least, worry about the rest later.*

"If it isn't the blessing in disguise. We meet again," Quincy said, standing as she watched an alluring smile spread across his million-dollar face. The grin didn't melt the perilously-tense energy that surrounded them. "You still owe me a dance!"

"Oh my," Nadia said covering her heart as all the color drained from her face. *He actually remembered her* from the Masquerade Ball in October. Suddenly she looked at one flirty night of fun, as another possibly, big mistake in the long run. She leaned her weight against the bed. He suddenly looked apologetic, but she read the pleasure he hid.

"You okay?" Quincy said starting to move forward to comfort her. He was stopped by a hand gesture that said, *stay over there.*

"Sure," Nadia said, closing her eyes as she cleared her throat. She allowed herself to sit back further on the thick bed. Quincy's light smirk faded into a concerned expression as he saw her still holding her hand over her chest.

"I didn't know anyone was behind me." Then suddenly she snapped. "What are you doing here?" Nadia asked as her hand quickly went to her hip.

Quincy started to chuckle. "Well, I sort of own the place."

"Unh, Unh," shaking her head in disbelief, Nadia said looking around.

"Uh huh," Quincy said mocking her childlike tone.

"I don't think we formally met at the club. Quincy McKnight."

Nadia blinked and then realized his hand was held out. Such straightforward gestures seemed so multifaceted in her world. So Nadia returned his handshake and forced her teeth to show.

"They call me a lot of things," she said determined to keep her distance.

A couple of guesses filled his head as he waited for her name.

"Did you have fun that night?" he was curious to know how her Halloween turned out.

Nadia laughed and once again didn't respond.

"You certainly were moving like you did," Quincy said.

Nadia shot him a sinister look. The energy that was present between them was as passionate as it was that night on the dance floor. Nadia knew she needed to leave.

Quincy quickly changed the subject.

"I didn't even ask you were you finding everything okay?" he finally said.

Quincy rarely worked in his communities. Today, one of the sellers had called in sick and he was relieving the one that was there so they could go to lunch. He wasn't too happy about it earlier, but once he saw the striking woman on the monitor in his office when he returned from showing one of the model homes on the farther end, it was a lovely idea.

Quincy smiled, knowing that they would see each other again, but never did he expect under these circumstances. *Three times the charm,* he figured.

Nadia didn't want to even know what lay behind his mask. She stood and walked around the other part of the room, opposite of the window, looking at things a second and third time to avoid eye contact.

Quincy's eyes stuck on her, watching the way she moved around.

"I hope I didn't startle you," he said.

"Is that what you wanted to do?" Nadia snapped her head to look at Quincy.

Quincy did like her reactions.

"Clearly not," he said.

"Why do I not believe that?"

"Can I help it if you ignore me?" Quincy asked. "This was not the first time."

"I had been calling out to you, but it was as if you didn't hear me!" Quincy thought back on it amusingly.

Even though Quincy wondered just how oblivious the woman was, he certainly didn't have to wonder about how stunning she really was. There was always something standing in the way of them and he enjoyed seeing her without a mask and a picture blocking his view.

Even though Nadia had walked into the master bath, she still felt him, though he stood in another room. The moment their eyes locked, his presence was stirringly strong and it alerted her senses to the point that slumber slipped her mind long ago. She was wide awake.

As she emerged from viewing the bath, she looked over at the man with the undeniable smile. She returned to standing in front of the bed. Nadia took in his deep, chocolate eyes, mysterious yet sincere, letting them penetrate hers deeply before turning away.

Quincy studied her and the way her energy seemed to intensify.

"Sure? What about you?" Nadia stared for a moment before her eyes moved over to the chess board. She knew she took the easy way out. She begged for it to take the spotlight instead of her.

Quincy looked in the same direction. All he could do was wonder what was going on in that mind of hers.

Nadia walked slowly over to the chessboard.

He surprisingly chose to come closer to her, so near that she could smell his endearing scent.

She wondered how well he could read body language.

While facing the natural light from the window, she tilted her head up to look up at him.

All Quincy could think about was how, unlike the many who wore club lights as their most valued accessory, she was even more striking in broad daylight.

Nadia, who was melting inside, hated to admit what she felt.

Nadia tried to retrace what happened. *She went into the house, in a room then this man appeared. She didn't hear him, or anyone, for that matter. She was slippin'.*

Nadia frowned then removed emotion from her face altogether, her specialty when need-be.

"I never got your name," Quincy said coolly as Nadia blankly looked.

"I never gave it." Nadia laughed. Quincy stood speechless.

"Mr. McKnight, I must be on my way," Nadia said turning to face him, who blocked the door.

"Well, did you see anything you liked?" Quincy had been so sidetracked that he didn't even give her the usual McKnight Homes spin.

Nadia eyed him. "Yes, I did…But…"

"But what," Quincy eyes widened at the word.

"It may not be for me," Nadia said.

"How do you know?" he pressed.

Nadia watched him come closer as he awaited her words.

"Women's intuition," she concluded.

"What exactly are you looking for?" His eyes urged her to stay.

"That's the thing, at the moment, I don't need to be looking, really."

Quincy nodded. "Yeah, most people look for what they want."

"Most people do."

Quincy wondered what made her…*her*. There was never enough time.

"Well whatever I can do to assist you, just let me know." He pulled out his card and handed it to her. "We have a lot of…models. So maybe if one day, when you are ready," *there was that smile again,* "I can help you find the right one."

Nadia nodded and she actually believed he would. That was the scary part.

Nadia shifted around him.

"Well…it has certainly been a pleasure finally meeting you," he paused looking disappointed.

Nadia smiled to hide hers.

"It was nice talking to you," she couldn't believe she actually meant it.

Quincy looked as though he actually blushed. He turned his face a bit. When he turned back more composed, a frown sat on her face.

"Oh my, looks like something bit the mess out of you,"

Quincy remembered the mark that he had hidden so well. All of sudden that feeling returned.

Nadia suddenly raised her hand to his neck. Gently, she touched the area around the bite mark.

"Let me see."

Quincy turned his head a bit. Her touch was soft and it helped relieve the burning.

"I think I have something for that."

***

Quincy walked over to the chessboard. He stood, studied it for a moment. He was a very precise, well-thought-out man. Every chess player knew that control of the center was important in the game and boy he could feel a good game coming on. He knew his piece. He thought out potential moves he would make, potential positions. He knew it wasn't smart to touch until you were certain you wanted to play it. Any wrong move could mean the beginning of the end… He wasn't resigning anytime soon. He knew what he wanted to capture.

"Did you see the rest of the homes?"

"Maybe another time. Besides, I really like this one."

"Yeah, the Elaine is a favorite of mine as well."

"We ask all visitors to sign our mailing list."

Nadia reluctantly followed him to the office she had passed through.

He gave her a card to fill out.

She wrote her first and last name and cell phone number.

There were other questions she briefly answered out of common courtesy.

"Nadia." He looked up and nodded. "That is fitting."

"My thoughts exactly," Nadia responded.

"Thanks for dropping by," he said.

Nadia smiled.

"Beautiful home," she said.

Before Nadia headed out the door, Quincy, with his eyes still on the board asked, "You play chess?" Quincy waited on an answer he felt he already knew.

Nadia answered without any thought. "No," she said with a flirty half-smile.

"Do you?" she asked.

Quincy laughed.

"No," he said. "Just wondering,"

"Have a good day,"

As Nadia walked out of the office, she couldn't help but smile. She knew for sure that she would not be making the first move.

He watched her walk away from the glass door. When she was out of view, he stared at the card she had filled out. *Nadia Masters.*

Black Christmas

While out doing some holiday shopping, Nadia was mad at herself for entertaining the thought of Quincy McKnight in her life. Outside of the house, everything seemed more real. He didn't fit into her real life and she certainly couldn't fit into his.

She knew just what she wanted to get Mama B for Christmas, and she was headed to get it in the department store when suddenly she was interrupted.

"Hey, girl!" a person called out to Nadia from behind.

While her eyes rolled up to the top of her head, reluctantly, Nadia turned to face her phase two of hell.

A vibrant, dimpled-face woman with an edgy Mohawk stood smiling back with excitement holding an armful of sleeveless tank tops.

"Remember me?" she asked.

How could I forget, you knocked the shit out of me, is what Nadia thought.

It was that girl who tackled her on Main Street. *She just didn't give up.*

Nadia needed Sheila to disappear. They had both grown up together in Sunnyside, Houston, casual playmates that lived on the opposite sides of the same block. Nadia's guardian and Sheila's grandmother were best friends and it just sort of trickled down, but the two didn't have the same fate. After Nadia's guardian passed, she moved to Boston.

"I am so sorry about the street collision!" Sheila said.

"It is really okay," Nadia insisted for the thousandth time.

"It is good that I ran into you again. Let me make it up to you."

Nadia blinked.

"I'm fine really." Nadia tried not to snap, but her blood pressure was rising.

"I'm a beautician. Let me do your hair, for free. Your hair is gorgeous. But with some shaping up, get some of the dead ends off and put in a good conditioner, I'm sure you will love it for the holidays."

Nadia thought about it for the moment. More than likely, no one would even be seeing her for the holidays. She probably would be working during Christmas to keep her mind *off* of the holidays.

"I don't think so," Nadia said frankly.

"Look, I will pay you."

Nadia was as confused as she looked.

"Money is the last thing that motivates me," Nadia said insulted.

"Look, here's the deal. I got another chance to do something that means the world to me. The only thing is…I am in need of a hair model."

Nadia knew the look in Sheila's eyes all too well - the look of desperation.

"If you do this for me, I will leave you alone."

Nice thought, Nadia thought. She knew it was a risk. Sheila made her nervous because there was a possibility that she wasn't as dumb as she looked. Nadia knew Sheila hadn't seen her in years, and somehow she remembered her enough to see that little girl's face in her now.

Hours later, Nadia was walking into a lavish salon with Sheila regretting every part of it.

Sheila was all smiles, but the women of the salon weren't. Sheila walked her to the back of the establishment.

A woman with jet black hair and heavy eye make-up looked up at them both.

"I found my hair model, I'm ready," Sheila squealed.

It was something about the way Deon looked at Nadia that made her feel like she had made a mistake feeling sorry for Sheila. Deon smiled at her.

"You can use my chair," Deon said.

Something came over Nadia and she acted on it.

"You know what, can you do a mean cut?" Nadia asked.

Sheila's eyes bulged. "Yeah, that's my specialty, but on you? Your hair is past your shoulders. I was just going to shape you up."

"Yeah, but I have been wanting a new look for so long."

The two women looked at her and then at each other.

Rubik's Cubes

Back at her apartment, Nadia liked looking in the mirror to see someone she didn't recognize. She liked the edgy hair that Sheila seemed to whip into shape. Suddenly her phone rang.

Nadia wondered. No one ever called her.

"Hello," she said.

"Hello, may I speak to Miss Masters?"

"This is she."

"Happy Holidays!"

Nadia rolled her eyes waiting for a cue to hang up.

"Who is this?"

There was a chuckle on the other line.

"Here at McKnight Homes, we have some specials going on for the month of December and you are the first person on my list to call. I thought you may want to know about them so I decided to personally call and invite you to come check them out."

Nadia recognized the voice and suddenly she felt jumpy.

As she stood in the mirror, Nadia didn't even realize the expression on her face was actually one of happiness. As many looks as this chameleon had, she had never seen herself this way. Without hair to hide behind and the personas that came with it, she was exposed.

***

Quincy's mouth made a perfect O when Nadia stepped into his office. His heart was beating faster than he liked to admit.

Nadia acted as if nothing was different as she stood looking at his awkward expression.

"Hey, I thought you were going to show me some of these deals," she announced trying to have something to look at rather than his face. She couldn't let him see her reaction to his eyes on her.

Quincy shook his head. "Please excuse me, I am sorry, but…"

Nadia waited. She waited for the words she wanted to hear. She waited for the expression she wanted to see.

"You look even more striking!" he finally said.

Nadia frowned. Those were not them.

"What?" she asked.

Quincy stepped away from the office desk, walked around, to come closer.

"I really dig your new look."

"Really?" Nadia asked feeling clueless.

"Yeah," Quincy said without hesitation. "I mean you were beautiful with long hair, but you can really see your gorgeous features now.

Nadia didn't know what to say.

"What made you just up and cut it?"

"It's so hot in Houston," Nadia offered, refusing to go into detail.

"I take it you are not a native," he said walking around her as though she was an exhibit in a museum.

"I'm from up north," she said rigidly.

Minutes later, after Nadia maneuvered the conversation back to the initial purpose, she gladly held the packet that Quincy had put together for her as they walked to the rest of the houses.

"I brought you some ointment," Nadia said handing him a box of crème as they stood at the front porch of the *LeBlanc* model.

Quincy smiled. "That is actually sweet of you. Thank you."

He looked over at her again.

"So you're not made of *all* steel."

***

Nadia didn't remember any of the houses she viewed after the *Elaine*. Her mind was made up as they returned to the office to give her an estimate and projection based on her income.

As Quincy, a numbers man, clicked away on the computer calculator, there was a postcard that caught Nadia's attention. Nadia picked up the card and stared at the photo. She wondered could the water be that clear. Could the colors be that bright? All she had ever seen was smog, foggy water in Houston and bland, snow backdrops in Boston. This picture was perfect to her, too good to be true. Paradise. She always wondered what it was like to have a smooth getaway.

"Beautiful, huh?" Quincy inquired as he plugged in the last numbers.

"An understatement," Nadia answered, somewhat in a trance.

"Last time I was there, I bought some really nice artwork from one of the locals," Quincy said. He was about to mention that one of the pictures she was so immersed in was one of them, but he wanted to move the conversation in a different direction.

"Ever been?" he asked casually.

"No, always wanted to go," Nadia said without thinking. Her budget never allowed her to think of such things, let alone act on them.

Once finished with the projections, Quincy printed out a copy that Nadia could take.

He went over a couple of things that she had inquired about and in no time, Nadia had an idea of how her life could be; owning her own home would be like having her own slice of paradise.

***

Two days after, Quincy anxiously called Nadia.

"Do you have time to look over the material?" he asked Nadia.

Nadia replied that she did.

"Did you have any questions?"

She didn't and said she would hold onto the info when the time came for her to buy.

"Are you going to be in town for Christmas or are you spending time with the family up north?" Quincy asked. Nadia thought about what she wanted to say.

"I actually don't have any plans. I may work the holiday shift at my job."

"Where do you work?"

"At a personal care home for the elderly."

"Oh. That spoils it," he said.

"Spoils what?" she asked, cluelessly.
"Your Christmas gift."

One love

Nadia couldn't remember the last time she felt butterflies in her stomach. It was one day before the holiday, a holiday she had learned to dread. She had given Mama B her Christmas present early- a record player to play her classics. Mama B encouraged Nadia to go on the vacation she happened to mention while in her presence.

"This is certainly not your average Christmas," Nadia said as she stepped off the island transit that took the tourists from Montego Bay to the exotic White Sands Resort.

"I am certainly not your average guy," Quincy exclaimed while making sure the lady safely stepped onto the sand. He was sure he was making a good impression on the woman he saw as complex yet beautiful beyond measure.

All Nadia could think of was *Can this be real?* The scenery and the sincerity of the company were surreal. She didn't trust her own eyes or the butterflies.

"I have never seen colors at their brightest." Nadia gushed as she took in the view of the turquoise water and palm trees while her sandals left shoe prints in the sand. It looks just like the postcard," she said as the driver drove off.

Quincy was delighted in her response, one free from her usual cynicism. For it truly contrasted her routine wisecracks and deliberate jabs at his ego; he knew he was getting somewhere, slowly, but surely. Quincy knew the mysterious lady was hard to impress, but from the sound of things, he knew he had done well so far. He planned to continue.

Nadia felt surprisingly serene. The right amount of sun and wind touched her skin, like she was right at home in the exotic paradise and its 80-degree weather. Aside from the outside, on the inside, she was feeling more naughty than nice as she thought of her travel partner. Flying off on a whim with practically a stranger, a sexy one at that, was out of character. *This was nothing new.* She could blame it on Mrs. White. The woman urged her to go and live a little. Nadia always listened to her elders.

Nadia usually ran away from risks. But when she had to risk it all, she succeeded. When necessary, she played out parodies so well that Oscar statues bowed for her. Not so much into the arts as much as she was a science and even sci-fi girl, her acting skills were superb. The innate abilities came more from survival than they did from theater training. As a child moving around so much, and conditioning herself to deal with the various tests of being a foster child, she learned many truths and her mind stored many things in order for her to not be eaten alive. She knew how to use people to get what she needed. She knew how to disappear before they even knew what hit them.

But this time, her acting skills weren't up to par and in a sense, she didn't want them to be. She didn't know what role to play, and what thing to say to Quincy. All she knew was that she liked the way he made her feel. It was realer than any Aretha song and the feeling was long overdue. From the start, their strong attraction was hard to deny, but over just a short period of time, their bodies had seemed to have this unspoken communication. She felt guilty about actually wanting to hear what their body language said.

She was not going to let her feelings get in the way; they never had in the past. She knew the game. But she was playing a game of her own. She wanted to test the waters in this exotic place, just to make up for all her years of hell on Earth.

Thrilled with being hidden away from all the attention he drew from Houston women, she was at ease and was not the least bit concerned about the fast pace in which Quincy and she were moving. Going with the flow was her plan and she hoped that Quincy got her drift.

Quincy looked at how Nadia seemed to fit in amongst all the beautiful things as they started to follow the crowd along the trail to the resort. The eye candy was unbelievable.

"Two days in paradise," he said. He had a ton of activities the two could experience together for their stay. For now, he just enjoyed the stroll to the hotel he had handpicked for a reason.

***

After the two checked in, put up their luggage, washed up and changed into something more suitable for touring, they happily returned to the sands for the latter part of Christmas Eve.

There were several stops and little markets that grabbed the eye. It was like being a kid in the candy shop, zigzagging along the way.

Quincy noticed a man with cotton hair who sat behind the table of delicious fruits.

"You want anything?" Quincy asked Nadia.

"Oh, no. Thank you," she said quickly, eyeing the beautiful jewel-tone beads.

Quincy noticed Nadia.

"I do," he said and they stopped at the table full of carts of fruit. Quincy bought some bananas and coconuts.

Across the way, Nadia's eyes widened when she saw the most exotic and unique beads and stones hanging on jewelry stands.

She felt like a child again. With her grandmother, finding different treasures.

After buying his fruit, Quincy started to walk toward the cart that Nadia seemed to be curious about.

"These are so pretty!" Nadia said, picking up some of the stones.

The color combos were enticing. Not only were there green, black and yellow necklaces, but some of the jet black and red stones matched one of her outfits she planned to wear.

***

Nadia didn't expect to be wearing some of the jewels she had just admired, but Quincy insisted on draping her neck with the delicate treasures. He also bought a hand-crafted jewelry box to store them in. Though not much of a material girl, Nadia surely liked the way the stones felt on her skin, and she really liked the person who bought them for her.

"Thank you," she said for the hundredth time, still brushing her hand over the smooth, cool surfaces. She had tried to refuse the jewelry, especially because of the price set for them, but he was persistent.

"It's my treat," Quincy said. "Just call it your Christmas Eve gift." He had a Christmas gift waiting in the hotel and hoped that his surprise would go over well with the special woman who had seemed to appear in his life.

As the two continued to stroll, there wasn't much talking, but their senses were at attention.

Nadia wet her lips at the smell of jerk chicken.

"Lunch break?" Nadia hinted.

"Yeah, it's about that time," he agreed.

Moments later, as the two carried their heavy plates over to the nearest bench, the aroma of spices were so intoxicating the pair couldn't even wait to sit down. They couldn't open the plastic that enclosed the utensils fast enough, as they settled down and ate, facing the band. Nadia envied the barefoot kids kicking up sand and chasing each other.

"Are kids supposed to be at the resort?" she asked.

Quincy looked over at her perturbed face.

"I take it you aren't too fond of the little ones."

Nadia laughed. "I'm just out of my element."

"Your element, huh. There is so much that I want to learn about you."

Quincy studied Nadia's wicked expression trying to figure it out.

He liked that she didn't react to him like most women. She held back a lot and all that did was make him want her more. Never one to back down from a challenge, Quincy enjoyed that she presented one he had not yet figured out - a code he had not yet cracked. Nadia was worth his time he planned to put in.

"I'm not that interesting of a person," Nadia said. "Trust me."

He could see through the almost perfectly crafted protective layers she had built, and he could see a person he actually enjoyed being around.

"Since you are one big mystery to me, answer me this. For a man that could literally have everything he wanted, why would you be sitting here with me? Why are we here, on Christmas Eve?

Quincy knew she was almost right.

"Chemistry is not man-made. Can't be bought either. I remember the first time I saw you, I felt something. Every time I am around you, I know that it is something there. Something you can't get just because you want to have it. To tell you the truth, I am not sure what has drawn us together. But I don't believe in coincidences. You meet people for a reason. I'm interested in getting to know you. All that and you are kind of easy on the eyes," he explained.

Nadia allowed herself to laugh.

"You ain't too bad yourself." Nadia felt corny, but she let the words slip right out.

It actually was simpler than she expected, yet Nadia was having a hard time trying to figure out which role to play. None of the old ones seemed suitable for this new script.

In such a short time for Quincy, Nadia had brought more smiles to his face than the average pageant girl on her competition night. He knew that those layers she had would soon be peeled off if he played his cards right. But it was more than just a game.

When Quincy and Nadia had finally made it back to the resort to freshen up before going out to the Christmas Eve Party, they worked around each other well, respecting each other's space and privacy without much effort.

As Nadia stepped out of the stone-tiled bathroom shower, she shook her head in awe. It was so mesmerizing being in such a lovely environment - from everything to the outside to the inside. She had never been exposed to such picturesque things, natural and man-made.

To Nadia, the beach house had an interior that was out of this world. She picked up her purse and met Quincy in the foyer. The beautiful paintings of flowers, trees, and birds set one's mind at ease.

"Hey, gorgeous," Quincy said, admiring how stunning she looked in her red flowing dress. The onyx and red jewelry that were bought earlier were the perfect accent.

Nadia felt her temperature rise at the sight of Quincy. There was a sense of panic that swept her the very moment their eyes locked, but Quincy's smile seemed sincere and it reassured her that the best person for her to be tonight was herself.

"Are you ready, my lady?" he asked taking in the alluring view.

Nadia let her eyes cover all the bases. Quincy looked irresistible.

"Yes," Nadia said keeping it simple.

"Well, off we go." Quincy said as they linked their arms.

The two strolled through the long terrace trimmed in colorful wood. Against her skin, Nadia could feel Quincy's goose bumps on *her own* arms.

The formerly blue and white sky was now navy with hints of silver. The bright palm trees wrestled; the turquoise sea now glistened under the moonlight.

Quincy could hear the echo of live music on the farther part of the island.

Remembering the way she moved on the dance floor to the dance hall song the night of the masquerade ball, he gently tugged Nadia's hand tighter wanting to recreate those moments in Jamaica.

"Let's go check it out," he said, walking toward the sounds of the island.

Nadia was game; she let herself be pulled by the enthused man. She could feel the beat of the Christmas songs that were remixed with an island twist. The sounds led them through what seemed to be a festival.

All types of couples were enjoying themselves, but Nadia and Quincy didn't notice. They were so tuned in to each other, nothing else seemed to exist.

The music was so amazing and its rhythm kept them deep in the trance that had taken over them the moment they locked eyes. As they reached the dance floor, Quincy pulled out his hand to Nadia, who accepted him leading her along. Soon they were both in the groove. On the dance floor, they were in sync with one another and oblivious to their surroundings. Nadia's nerves were all over the place when she was close to Quincy, while they seemed to sway in the same smooth style. Somehow, she found herself awfully close to him. They rocked and rocked and she rolled and rolled. There was something exhilarating this time with not having any masks. Same moves, nothing to hide behind. Others took notice of the two.

Couldn't take their eyes off the electric couple whose sparks flew higher than cloud nine. After some dining, dancing, and drinking, the two wanted to wind down.

When they returned to the lodges, Nadia realized she couldn't remember the last time that she had had this much fun. She had never been so happy in her life.

Quincy was hoping his surprise would go well, tomorrow.

"You take the bed. I can sleep over here," he insisted in making sure she felt comfortable.

***

After emerging from the restroom in an oversized t-shirt, Nadia climbed into the big fluffy bed, cautious of her every movement. She looked at the couch that Quincy threw a pillow on.

Quincy, aware of his every move, began to take off his shirt, never meeting Nadia's eyes. Nadia took in his look through a squinted gaze. The very sight of his chest made Nadia weak all over. He headed to the shower.

How the hell am I going to sleep with him around? It's bad enough my ass can't sleep as it is, she thought.

She laid in the bed long enough to know that her restless energy needed to get from beneath the covers. She needed some fresh air so she headed out to the balcony.

Nadia wasn't sure what she wanted. She wanted Quincy then and there, but she felt too much. So many emotions she had pushed way in the back of her mind were having a field day within her body. She knew this place was paradise, but she didn't want to lose her mind here.

Quincy could hear the soothing sounds of the ocean's song as he came from the shower. Soon he was joining her out on the terrace that overlooked the sparkling water that glistened under moonlight. To see it in this light painted an even more fascinating picture.

Nadia got lost in the stars above and the waves below. To see their story unfolding at that very moment was satisfying. She looked back at him and lifted her head up.

Mistletoe, unassumingly, hung over their heads. Both fighting temptation, seemed to notice it at the same time.

Both laughed.

She didn't need mistletoe to tell her what to do. She looked back at the ocean with a menacing look on her face.

"I am tired of all the bull shit," she thought to herself. She wanted him then and there. She didn't want to think about tomorrow. She didn't want to worry about when they returned. She just wanted to act on the rush, act on the feelings that were foreign to her usually numb life.

Nadia turned to face Quincy and looked into his eyes. He returned the same action, looking into the depth of the windows to her soul, and witnessing a vulnerability he had always seen and wanted to protect. His smile was sincere and alluring. She had never felt so special; he kept his undivided attention on her. The messages were sent subliminally. The way he looked at her as he gently touched her face set her on fire. She was convinced they were the only two in the world and that was a nice feeling. Quincy softly ran his hands through her silky short hair, then softly tilted her head back. He began to kiss the front of her neck, which sent shivers all over Nadia's body.

She didn't pull back or push away, but she let herself be very receptive. He kissed and caressed her neck with his lips until Nadia couldn't take anymore teasing.

Soon, Quincy gripped her tiny waist and pressed both their firm bodies together as they glowed under the moonlight.

With the sea as their audience, Quincy enveloped her inside his steel arms and held her tight. Suddenly Nadia knew what security felt like. She lingered in his strong embrace. Something new and something she wanted to get used to.

***

Nadia could feel a hand on both her thighs as her legs were being slowly stretched apart. She was half asleep, but she tried to squeeze them shut but his hands were so strong as he snapped them back open. Nadia struggled to see through the darkness. She could only feel him as he climbed on top of her, disregarding her discomfort. He continued to hold her legs apart as he pushed his way inside of her.

"No!" she cried but he covered her mouth with his sweaty palm, smothering her as he continued to enter her.

Nadia's eyes bucked. She had never felt so much pain. She cried a muffled scream. She tried to push him off of her, but his body was so heavy and the pain was so deep inside. She was beyond mortified as she could feel her insides ripping apart with no consideration. She screamed, but no one heard her.

His sweat dripped in her face as he pounded away inside of her like a mad man taking delight in her torturous screams. Her body was tired. She tried to create enough energy to push him again or gather up enough breath to scream, but she felt suffocated with pain and pressure. Nadia closed her eyes wishing it would end.

***

"No! No!" Nadia continued to wail as the sharp, twitch of pain increased.

Quincy tried to shake her, but Nadia hit him violently in the face. He looked at the woman he earlier wanted to protect. She was very fervent, irate even. Her eyes were glued shut as tears streamed down her face and she had hit him so hard, he was seeing stars.

Quincy frantically tried to wake her up, but she now started to punch him with all her might, hitting him mostly in the ribs. He used more of his upper body strength, but he still was careful to not to hurt her. She was so aggressive he couldn't quite get a hold of her long enough to try to save her from the vision.

He backed off a little as she tangled herself up in the sheets twisting herself around like a snake in water, fighting the air for moments at a time.

"Nadia!" Quincy said gently. "Please, wake up!"

"Leave me alone or I'll kill you!" she screamed and cried hysterically.

Quincy continued to try to revive her from her nightmare, for he didn't recognize the woman he so adored for her coolness and composure.

"Nadia, wake up, you are having a bad dream."

Nadia eventually opened her eyes to only see her second nightmare, a mortified man staring back at her as though he had seen the devil. Nadia didn't know what had happened, but she knew enough that she was beyond embarrassed. Tears started to stream down her face and she remained without words as she curled herself into a ball.

Quincy touched her. She was soaking wet.

"It's okay. I'm here. I will protect you." Quincy wanted to be heard, understood and taken seriously.

Nadia continued to cry as Quincy lifted her into his arms. He had never imagined seeing her like this and it was a sight he wished to never have to witness again. He could only imagine what would bring her to this point and wanted to do everything in his power to eliminate that force.

"You don't have to be scared," he reassured.

Suddenly Nadia's whimpering lessened and she opened her eyes wider to look at Quincy.

"You had a nightmare. A really bad one."

Nadia stared into space.

"Just relax, it's all over now."

Nadia was still trembling from her vision and now she was ashamed of how she must have looked.

After thirty minutes of lying in Quincy's arms, Nadia's heartbeat returned to a normal pace. The dream seemed so real, as it always did. Quincy sat in silence, still troubled by her scream. It echoed in his ears and was tormenting his heart.

He would hold her all night if she needed. He preferred.

To Nadia, Quincy's body felt so strong up against hers. She allowed herself to let go and soak up his strength.

"I couldn't sleep, either. It's the adrenaline, of being somewhere else," he informed.

He could tell Nadia was still in a different world. He just continued to hold her until she stopped trembling, hoping that she would return to *this one*.

Nadia had never slept so peacefully.

***

When Nadia woke, it was to one of the most amazing pictures she had ever seen. She wiped her eyes to make sure her mind wasn't playing tricks on her. As she sat up in the bed, directly at the edge of the foot of the bed was a charming framed masterpiece. The same picture she stood for minutes enthralled in, sat with a big red ribbon wrapped around it and a big red bow that screamed *remove me soon.*

Nadia stumbled out of the bed in the Jamaican hotel and slowly walked over to the picture. Kneeling behind it with a smile on his face, was Quincy.

"Merry Christmas," he said, finally standing.

***

Later that Christmas Day, on the plane, Nadia sat beside the man who had showered her with unimaginable things and showed her another side of herself. Leaving Jamaica had Nadia wrapped in mixed emotions. Quincy had been the perfect and most thoughtful gentleman, yet she regretted it. There were *feelings* involved. Ones she couldn't escape. She knew the vacation was over. The idea of the two of them being together was impossible. She abandoned the idea of playing that game. She knew how Quincy saw her through his eyes. He saw her at her worst last night. She would have to mask the shame and play another game to get things back to where they needed to be in order for her to move on.

*Sin*tinel

Deon had planned to go way out for her 30th on January 3rd, but as the New Year rolled around, she, instead, sat staring at the flame from the candlestick shaped in the number. Being as fly as she was at thirty was not enough icing on the uneaten marble cake that was designed as a sleek, 50s style blow dryer!

Houston's finest were out to see and be seen in the arena style mini dome but tonight was no ordinary night at Club SINtinel. The unique club that was known for its artsy, elaborate settings, was normally a place where two types of people met. Houston's well-dressed, well-educated, heavy-hitting entrepreneurs came to network with those who considered themselves deep, renaissance brothers and sisters. Nights consisted of spoken word Tuesday, live band Wednesday, Zydeco Thursday and Talent night Friday. Saturdays, the club could be rented out for concerts and things of that nature, but this Saturday, Club SINtinel was just a straight up party! The divas at the salon had taken the task of planning a surprise birthday bash for Deon and rented out the VIP section.

Deon sank back into the retro-burgundy leather pin-cushioned booths in the midst of the high energy and smoky atmosphere. *Am I having hot flashes?* Deon thought. Deon wanted to act on the words *it's my party (and I'll cry if I want to.)* She usually craved attention, any kind, but tonight, it was the last thing she wanted. Especially in *his* club.

As Quincy strolled through the club coolly, swagger and all, her heart sank.

Son of a bitch! Deon thought. She was still fuming. Still pouting. Still in the same state of shock as she was the day that he was distracted by the picture observer in the coffee shop weeks ago.

***

As he surveyed the club, Quincy was hoping that his invitation would not be ignored. He had invited Nadia, urging her to get out of the house for a bit and check out the flourishing club. Some of his frat brothers were in town.

"Q, this all you?" Junior, a mailman already gone postal, said to Quincy while looking at all the people at the club.

"Got some help from my friends," he said, looking around the club at the different guys that had unique jobs and carried them out so well, it didn't look like they were working. Quincy always had a knack for finding everyone's specialties and strengths and knew how to set up a collaborative success through delegation.

JT Hudson, wearing long sandy dreads, a shirt that wrote, "I love my Black People" and a digital camera around his neck snapped away, capturing the livest party people and the coolest club posers.

JT was like the little brother in more ways than one – through their frat and just through mentorship. JT was a big dreamer, known for taking the easy route. After graduating from PV with a Mass Comm degree, his idea of going to film school entailed sitting at home watching the director's commentaries on DVDs. That was then. This was now and after Quincy took him under his wing, within a year, he had finally settled on photography as his profession and it suited him rather nicely. It allowed him to work with his big brother and other great minds in building Club SINtinel into what it was today!

When JT found he could work and play hard as a photographer, he was now emerging as a household name around the city! JT knew he had Quincy to thank. Working under his business name, *Focused Man*, had JT snapping away and allowed him to rent a nice condo overlooking the city.

Then there was Kile Elliot, rarely seen and rarely heard. The two frat brothers met at a Greek party. He knew how to connect the dots. Known simply as Elliot, this right-hand man shied away from the limelight, but bridged a lot of networking gaps in Houston. He started out at PV, studying computer science, pledged undergrad and transferred to U of H to take care of his ailing mother for the remainder of his underclass years. Kile Elliot was a "technical guy" and was quickly building websites for the frat and young entrepreneurs. He was cool, but he was a nerd and everybody knew it and respected it. Quincy admired that; his mind was out of this world.

There were others floating around enjoying life in the club, but these were the other two points in his pyramid. Q came to these two before coming to anyone else with the idea of making his ultimate childhood dream a reality - opening up a club. Real Estate supplied the capital, but the club was his heart – bringing an array of people together to have a good time.

Being around so many people from his past, present and future, was a cool feeling for Quincy. As he walked around, checking up on everyone, his mind was still on a certain someone who he wished would roll through.

"This is 21 and up right?" said Junior, who reappeared. The bald, hefty brother was sporting a dark brown Sean John sweatsuit with yellow trim. He was an old head in Q's organization with the same young mind he had years ago.

Quincy eyed him, cautiously scared to answer. "Yeah, but don't get carried away, now Mr. Engaged."

***

As the club quieted to wish the birthday girl many more, Deon continued to sit staring in space, making Ruby frown. Deon had been in a daze the whole evening and it was unlike her. The women of the shop were now more aware of her strange behavior.

"What are you waiting on?" Ruby nudged her boss and pointed to the uncut cake.

Deon finally blew out the waxed two digits that stood like a stranded passenger waving to be rescued on a deserted island.

Moments later, Ruby, with a beer in hand, started saying something to Junior that made him laugh. She had been sitting with the fellas as the other stylists were out on the floor.

Deon was out of it. She tried to get herself to be more upbeat, but she was shaking inside. She couldn't even do what she did best, *brag.*

Suddenly, there was a sight that caught her eye. The woman that she could strangle with her bare hands appeared at the door.

Deon cut her eyes at the woman who stood solo, looking coolly around the club before proceeding.

As he held his half-sipped drink, Quincy stood up straighter and coolly straightened his tie at the sight of the woman. With his free hand, he brushed his black and white pinstriped suit and re-tipped his fedora.

***

Nadia stood taking in the atmosphere. Once again, Mama B was to blame. Before leaving her shift at the personal care home, she and her favorite patient had a lil pow wow. The resilient woman pushed the young lady to seize the moment, live a little, have a little fun and dare not turn down the man's invite. Nadia tried to persuade her that it wasn't a good idea - that she wasn't a club person, that this man had many women he probably invited, that she shied away from too much attention and that the club, this particular club, everyone was watching everyone -- but the woman wouldn't hear it. Nadia couldn't see Quincy, but she could feel him. She tried to keep her cool, but whenever Quincy's eyes fell on her, there was something that took over her.

***

Like a train wreck, Deon couldn't help but watch what she knew was tragedy before her eyes. A combustion of flames. A collision of heat. Her worst nightmare was about to replay - again.

She watched a man she could hardly recognize light up at the sight of a mediocre woman. Yes, she was cute, but no she *was not* Deon. This was *her* party and she had *nothing* to celebrate. Quincy had to be getting back at her for 'ole times. Earlier, Deon entered the club in blindfolds. When they were lifted, there were many happy faces, many hugs and kisses from people who had come out to party *in the name of Deon!* There were so many reunions. None seemed to matter because *he* just stood and smiled once she sat at the table he had sectioned off for her and her Divas. Quincy maybe mouthed *happy birthday* or something of that nature, but nothing more. Just a mediocre moment.

She was going to have to extinguish the flames. It was not going to be pretty.

***

This was the club Quincy casually talked about, Nadia thought. It must have taken a lot of thought and magic, she figured to carry out so many things successfully at such a young age.

Nadia fell in love with the exquisite place at every glance. She took in the grand atmosphere and the energy that was bouncing off the gleaming, white walls.

***

Quincy remained cool as Nadia surveyed the room.

Nadia snapped back to the party once she felt his hand brush her arm.

"I'm not letting you pass me by," Quincy said.

Nadia giggled.

"So caught up in the ambiance. Look at this! You never cease to amaze me. This place is really nice," Nadia said.

Round, white, cloth-covered tables circled the entire nightclub. Glowing small, white, round vases sat in the center of each, creating a luminous, flowing futuristic illusion. In contrast, the dark, chocolate booths that curved around the tables half way, created an undeniable retro vibe.

Two tall, white Romanian columns stood evenly around the club and vintage draperies elegantly decorated the space between each column.

"Thank you so much for coming out. I know this is not your scene. I wanted to see you again, especially since you have been ignoring me."

A reggae beat started to form as the two stood peering into each other's eyes, forgetting their audience.

***

Kennedy was loving being back in Houston. She had her business cards floating and was making things happen on the dance floor. Things were back in tune. And she was promoting her show that had been receiving rave reviews. Then a flash caught her off guard. The light made her stop dead in her tracks. Seeing him and his camera threw her off completely. It had been some years since she had faced the one guy who put her in the "bitch" box.

As JT stood looking at her, Kennedy figured it was going to take all her willpower to stay refined and professional to keep the *bitch from boxing.*

Instead she gave him a smile and a business card with the logo that read, *Ambitious Bitch Productions.*

***

Deon had to get up. Her Gucci dress was too cute to be seen only from the top. She was out of shock. She wanted a word with the man who owed her a conversation and an apology, even though he was flirting with the woman who kept dropping in. Deon was too fly to make a scene.

Who did he think he was, *rejecting her?* They had too much history. She didn't want to have to go to extreme measures, but she knew exactly what she was going to do to make the situation right for her. *Make Nadia history.*

I got something for her ass. Deon relished in the thought that *she knew Nadia's dark secret.*

I got something for his ass, she thought as she took a sip and strutted around in the club.

Deon had done anything and everything known to man and woman. Nowadays, she was ready to do the unimaginable. The settling down thing. She didn't want to settle for less, either. She wanted Quincy.

As soon as Nadia went to the ladies room, Deon caught up with Quincy. She needed to talk to him, alone. Then she would deal with Nadia.

"Hey stranger," she said, eyeing the lips she couldn't wait to be reacquainted with. She settled for a hug that felt more sibling-like. She was tired of feeling the sense of uneasiness in someone she was more than familiar with. He was a sudden stranger without real conviction. He wouldn't let her have it. For any length of time.

"Can I talk to you for a moment, in private?" Deon asked.

To get away from the noise, the two walked up to one of the offices upstairs. Reluctantly, Quincy gave her his undivided attention.

"What is going on?" he asked.

Quincy looked confused.

"You know, I went to great lengths for us to come together and chat for a little bit," Deon recalled.

Quincy stood there.

"What the hell is wrong with you? Quincy, what has gotten into you?"

She was tired of being denied access.

Quincy watched her glass eyes melt.

This version of Deon worried him. He knew she had some drinks in her system and hoped that she could get it together, emotionally, before they returned to her party.

"So what is it about her pussy that has you so strung out?"

Quincy shook his head, offended.

Quincy thought he heard the words slip out, but he knew it was rare, very rare that they escaped Deon's mouth. She had gone too far.

"You can't have everything *you* want," he said.

"Look who's talking! Look who the fuck want to act like that doesn't apply to them."

"Look, what we had, we don't have anymore. Don't try to make something out of nothing, Deon."

"I know what this is. You couldn't even handle me!" Deon shouted.

"I knew I could have you *any which way, any day.*" Quincy said calmly. "I didn't want to."

"Fuck you, Q!"

Quincy was about to leave. As he headed out the door, Deon continued.

"Your ass has always been in competition with me. You want women that ain't got shit going on for themselves. Your ass want to shine so damn much you scared of anyone else's light. So you pick up these old rags to riches broads, or project hoes or mass murderers and shit and turn them into your lovers!"

"Cause they needy ass women looking for a damn meal ticket, or in your case, the next victim."

Quincy stopped in his tracks, with his back turned to Deon.

She was still talking.

"I remember the first time you looked at me, before you knew I saw you wanted me. I remember the first time I let you fuck me. You loved every minute of it! Someone who can do stuff in bed that even makes your experienced ass blush."

"I never loved you," he said turning around to face her.

Deon was speechless.

Quincy continued. "What we had was less than love."

"You know you don't believe that," Deon said.

Quincy shook his head at her.

"But you take your charity case," she continued.

"Have a nice life. Have fun finding what you want!" Quincy said turning back around before he walked away for good.

"You have fun running like a lil bitch! Cause your little girlfriend you took to Jamaica has a couple of reasons to make you."

Quincy stopped in his tracks once more. After a couple of seconds, he walked off. Deon knew she had to go to Plan B.

Deon had seen Nadia go into the ladies room earlier and she had gotten her cell number from Sheila. She decided that tonight would be the perfect opportunity to let her know her past was not so private after all. All she needed to do was expose the new girl's dirty little secret. *If she couldn't have Q, she certainly wasn't letting Nadia get him.*

***

As Quincy returned to the dance floor, he searched for five minutes before texting Nadia. She was nowhere to be found. While in the middle of his message, Quincy, along with the other party goers, heard a sound that stopped the party instantly.

Suddenly there was a shrieking sound. The sight of a woman tumbling down the stairs made many people's hair stand up.

As Deon crashed to the bottom of the stairs, screams of terror filled the club.

There was blood on the dance floor! *A lot of it.*

PhDepressed

Dr. Lynne's Herstory

Patience Love-n-U

September 19, 2008

Dear Dr. Lynne
I have always focused on love, but what if love doesn't love me?
Sincerely,
Ready for a change

Dear Ready for a Change,
How is your relationship with yourself? So many times, we focus on outwardly love. Are you putting in half the time and effort to nourish the relationship with *you*? Get centered. Get to know what your heart and soul desires. You will attract what you need when you are the best of who you are. Try it.
Dr. Lynne

***

November 23, 2008

Hello Dr. Lynne,
I gave up my life to be a wife and I am mortified that my picture-perfect marriage is falling apart. I feel in my heart that my husband is not being faithful. I am too embarrassed to prove it. I don't know what to do.
Sincerely,
Down and Desperate Housewife

Dear Down and Desperate Housewife,
You have got to pick yourself back up and face the truth sooner or later. You have to be a big girl and talk to the man that vowed to cherish you *and only you f*or the rest of your lives. You need answers now in order to determine what you have to do later. Living a lie is not really living at all. Also, try getting out of the house sometimes. Maybe get a day job. It may add some spice to your own life and make him realize all that he needs is at home.
Dr. Lynne

***

November 23, 2008

Dr. Lynne,
I am not ready to settle down. I have a plan that is still not executed. I have many guy friends that have been there for me and then they turn on me right when I need them, as a friend. I feel guy's love for me, turns into hate. When has *drive* every been a bad thing? I am tired of being hated on because they can't accept my ambition.
Public Enemy #1

Dear Public Enemy #1,
Don't fret. You are who you are. Stay strong. Stay focused on your goals and your plan. Make no apologies. When it is time for you to settle down, don't settle for less. The man who deserves *you* will love you at your best - that includes your drive. The right guy won't feel threatened by your ambition, but instead he will value it. In fact, being with the person who deserves you will help drive you in the right direction.
Dr. Lynne

***

December 20, 2009

Dr. Lynne,
I have heard this happen throughout the years. I have seen it from afar. But this has never happened to me! A man, that used to be mine, rejected *me.* I don't know what has gotten into him! Now is the best time for us to be together. It makes perfect sense.
Too Cute to be Shocked

Dear Too Cute to be Shocked,
It may make perfect sense to you, but though you and this guy may have had something, you can't possibly say he used to be *yours.* I am sure you are a beautiful person, but beauty is in the eye of the beholder. You can't make another person see things the way you do. Stay beautiful, and maybe set your sights on other things, like eating some slices of humble pie – *no offense my sister.*
Dr. Lynne

***

December 27, 2009

Dear Miss Lynne,
This guy makes me feel I can be me. Like I can take off the mask with him. I have never felt like this before, so alive. When we are alone, everything is fine. But I can not risk my private life for his public one. I am so afraid my past skeletons will ruin what we have.
Scared to feel

Dear Scared to feel,
You can't run your whole life - away from things that make you feel uncomfortable. In actuality, there is nothing to fear, so face it. Everyone has a past, but there are two types of people in the world: those who embrace their past faults and learn from them and then those who let their past run them into a tragic future.

Is the life that you are losing worth the great life that you could have? Could you be letting fear cheat you out of something special? Forget what you are hiding from, for this could be a blessing in disguise.
Dr. Lynne

Dr. Lynne checked her website blogs daily. She also checked it throughout the day, delighted to reach out to her sisters, nationwide. She focused on answering each and every e-mail or blog, etc. She had patients, but she knew if she could help those who couldn't come and sit on her couch, in some way through the web, she would.

Traditional Psychiatric Therapy was still a taboo subject in the black community and she knew that through the web, things didn't have the same stigma. She helped whoever, whenever and however she could. That is what she knew she was put on this earth to do.

Recapture

Once,
there
was
a love so strong
No whipping could burn it

Once
there
was
a passion so deep
No soul could be sold

Treachery couldn't sell out this love
For faith kept it
Above
the danger

Once relentless
Now senseless
Love

Did it
Runaway
Too
Or did it not make it through
The underground
Passage?
Or was it scattered, to never be heard of again?
Now, in the new Broken-Promise Land,
where sandwiches are filled with
Salmonella poison

It's up to you to

Name it
Reclaim it
Have faith in it
Again!
Recapture the love
Share what is and has always been within

At the Shrine of the Black Madonna bookstore in South Park, Houston, several ladies watched a screen that projected one-by-one, random women walking into unknown booby traps. The crowd cringed as a middle-aged cook on her own show, carefully cut potatoes and somehow, her finger. Then a poised ballerina gracefully leaps towards the left and then leaps right off the stage. Many women covered their mouths to keep from laughing. Then a little son is shooting a toy in the direction away from him and his mother. Somehow the spinning dart hits the mother in the nose, knocking the skin off. Then there was a professional woman walking the busy streets of Downtown, Houston and somehow she trips on her on two feet.

Forty year old, Dr. Lynne observed the different reactions to the montage. She had a habit of gathering snippets of info in order to see the whole story. She had been deaf for the first ten years of her life and it made her a keen observer. She read people better than they read themselves for a number of reasons. Today, she stood as the professional she always wanted to be, yet her job made it easy for her to live in quiet desperation.

It was early February, and Dr. Lynne's annual book tour *Me, Myself and my Sisters - where is "the hood?"* highlighted her new book *A Microscopic View through the Two "I"s* and had covered 10 cities. Houston was her last stop. Her hometown was where she had ended her tours over the past seven years. To sum her up, she was a dedicated, yet somber, sorority girl who knew what it meant to over extend herself to others.

With not a wrinkle, nor a gray strand present to prove the grueling years of studying psychology, she didn't see herself change much physically, but emotionally, she was at a point of where her moods would swing so much, not even her own expertise and logic could calm them. One thing that hadn't changed was the fact that she was a killjoy to those who knew her well, while being a Godsend to those who briefly ran across her words.

Early on, she led a privileged life. Having the finer things, not to mention a live-in nanny, led Lynne to feel guilty for the silver spoon placed in her mouth and anxious to feed others with more than empathy. Quiet by nature and quite withdrawn by circumstance, as a child she had read a lot and as an adult she did the same.

"How many people have insurance in here?" Dr. Lynne said addressing the crowd.

Practically everyone's hand raised.

"Who covers you, your home, and your car? What policy or plans do you trust?

There were many examples given from the crowd.

"We want the best protection, right? I mean, even if we can't afford the best, we know who the best companies are. When it comes to our health, our home, our car, we look for a quality plan, otherwise what is the point of having it? Not having insurance is the biggest and most fatal risk to take," the author said to the women who held a copy of her book.

"Think back on the last time you had a freak accident; the last time you were left stumped. You didn't see it coming. Once it came, you still didn't see how. And not to mention, it hurt; either of pain or of embarrassment," Dr. Lynne said at the seminar.

In their chairs, the women were cognitively taking a trip back.

"My last book was *LOVEBLACKLOVE*. In *Microscopic View,* I refer to the two Is (eyes) of love. The first "I" is for "Insurance." The second "I" stands for "Inventory." Both of these things prepare you for a relationship and should be set up *beforehand.*

Many women made notes or flipped through their books.

"As women, we can protect our property, but think nothing of properly protecting our hearts. So many sisters suffer from a broken spirit and they may not even know it. We *endure* versus *ensure* protection." In a fitted crème cashmere top, tan pleated slacks, and a gold raw silk scarf draping her right shoulder, Dr. Lynne stood in front of the packed crowd at the afrocentric bookstore that featured the hottest author's book tours. She coolly paced from one side of the stage to the other looking into the eyes of her fans and critics, both the same.

Autumn stared at the big microscope that was the center of the enlarged book cover that stood behind the author. Kennedy took pictures of the event while in the crowd.

"I listen to women, all day long, cry their poor little hearts out because when a storm hits, or when a collision occurred, they didn't have any coverage. When you decide on an insurance policy for your health or property, you are expecting that accidents can happen. It is the same thing with love. Fortunately, with love, we have warnings that eliminate the freak accidents that can occur with property and even health. We know women's intuition is not a joke, but why are there so many women laughing?

Many women stopped their natural smiles, which made Dr. Lynne smirk.

"Red flags are presented to you in enough time for you to brace yourselves; but by ignoring those signals, soon you may be blinded by what you think love is and in too deep to really see it may not even be love at all."

So many women nodded, knowing the feeling of seeing what they ignored revealed anyway.

"It's okay to love. But love is not a freak accident. It doesn't just knock you out. "

There were many women who nodded.

"On my website blogs, I answer millions of e-mails from women all over the world who want to know *how and why*. Most start like this, *Dear Dr. Lynne, I met this guy…* "

Dr. Lynne could spot the guilty from their expressions.

"Then, of course, the individualized drama starts."

Many women smiled.

"One thing that they all have in common is the ability to ignore signs that give them the answers. It kills me that I spent years in school just to tell women stuff they already knew!"

Many giggled.

"Honestly, I just point out the red flags that women refused to acknowledge," she said.

"Even *after* this, I am sure I am going to hear from some of you who are smiling and nodding," she informed.

She took a sip of water.

"Question: Can you rationalize your love gone wrong? I'll let you think about it," she concluded. "Write down what you think happened."

Lynne gave the women a moment to jot down what they saw as factors before resuming.

"I hear so much, *I don't know Dr. Lynne. He just appeared out of thin air and before I knew it…*I was pregnant. My credit was jacked up. I had moved in. He had moved in. He hit me. *Whatever."*

She scanned the audience.

"There are a whole lot of *before I knew its,* aren't there?" The Dr. smiled as the women nodded, telling on themselves.

"Since you couldn't rationalize it, it stayed wrong or got worse. Therefore, you are without a healing plan, and instead, headed for a tragic ending."

So many women held the personal experience in their own head as the speaker continued.

"Leave room for mistakes. Nothing is perfect. No one is. Therefore, relationships aren't. So leave room for a good healing plan."

"Ladies, when your relationships go wrong, what do you do?"

Many women shared their own testimonies of how they reacted to disappointment.

"Make a vow to heal vs. kill," Dr. Lynne urged. "What you ladies shared were all common reactions but they only make matters worse. You need to allow yourself to deal with the reality that it *didn't work out* and give yourself permission to heal so you can be in better shape for what will work out."

Many women looked hopeful.

"Now this is where self evaluation comes in," Dr. Lynne said.

"Anyone worked in retail?" the doctor asked.

Many women raised their hands, including Autumn.

"So you know when you are preparing for a big sale: TAX free weekend, Red Apple, Christmas Sales *all in* October; you know the managers and staff take inventory. It is a must!

Autumn nodded.

"Before the store is ransacked by people who want to take advantage of the goods, the store already knows what was supposed to be there in order for them to fully access what they can count as *gain and loss.*"

She took a sip of water before continuing.

"We know there are all types of people that are coming to get what they can get; some people will use their hard earned cash for the goods while some will lie, cheat and steal."

The doctor paused as she surveyed the audience.

"For some of you literal ladies, I am by no means trying to compare love to prostitution, but I am just simply saying *just know what you have to offer or not offer before the store is open.*"

Many conservative audience members finally smiled.

"Second 'I' is for inventory! You need to take inventory before even getting yourself in a relationship."

Autumn laughed as she took note of what she planned to do for the new year.

"It takes some time and a microscopic view to really get an inside look before the *public views;* what they want or could pass on."

"Let's be real with ourselves, ladies. Once again, freak accidents happen in life, but not in love. We have got to do better with being able to avoid trouble by getting into healthier relationships, not so called *freak accidents.*"

"So to my sisters, get your insurance and inventory!"

After her speech, the Q&A session went on and on and finally it was time for the actual autographing portion. Dr. Lynne never knew what to expect.

Lynne took a sip of water as a short, thick woman approached the table in a jazzy number. Lynne gasped. She always wondered how Sheila was doing since she just dropped out of contact with her.

Sheila smiled proudly at a woman who had taken the time out to mentor her during a low period.

"How has life been treating you?" Dr. Lynne asked excited to hear the answer.

"Been going through a lot," Sheila shared with a smile.

"Why haven't you called me!?" Lynne said a bit offended.

Sheila shook her head.

"I have been out of pocket, but I am still focused. I ended a very unhealthy relationship so I can make the others healthier…Chapter 7," Sheila referenced.

Lynne stood up to hug her.

"It was so good to see you!" they both said as they parted ways.

Sheila never imagined the author answering her phone call months ago.

After about nine people, Autumn finally reached the table. The author looked up at the young lady who looked like a modern hippy and smiled warmly. She remembered when she used to wear her hair like that. Wild and crinkly and all over the place, like fire. Now she kept her unruly tresses in twists that were pulled back in a ponytail, easier to maintain – but still relentless from root to tip.

"Hello my sister, how are you!" Lynne greeted.

"Really great," Autumn said, empowered.

"And what is your name?"

"Autumn."

Autumn watched how the author wrote. Her handwriting was so unconventional.

"I am really excited to read this. I have read a lot of great stuff on your blog." It normally took Autumn a day to read a whole book. They both exchanged kind words then Autumn was off.

Towards the end of the line, Lynne took another sip of water. A nice looking man in his early twenties approached the table. His suit was crisp and untainted; he looked like he was on a job interview.

Dr. Lynne smiled proudly at the distinguished young brother, protectively holding his hardcover book in his left hand.

She met him with a warm smile, being grateful to have such a broad fan base. She knew she was truly blessed to reach so many different types of people.

"How do you do, Doctor?"

"Fine, just fine. Thank you, and how are you?"

"Grateful to be here. I really enjoyed this," he said looking around for a second. It's very inspiring to be around so many, great minds. The possibilities are endless," Malcolm said.

"Well, I am happy to hear that you did get something out of this," she said.

She caught a look.

"And who do I make this out to?" she said reaching for the book and opening it.

"Your future husband," the man said.

Lynne's eyes bucked as he looked up at him. She looked around to make sure her publicist, assistant or just other book fans didn't hear the comment she least expected. She didn't need that kind of press. Her smile faded as she held her pen in hand, waiting for a real identification.

The man could see he had clearly upset her, but he still stood behind his statement.

"Malcolm, Malcolm Taylor," the boy announced. *"The third."*

She swallowed her true reaction and chose to slowly write his name inside the book. Finally she recovered a bit.

"How …cute," Dr. Lynne managed to say while feeling far from flattered.

Malcolm didn't flinch in the midst of it all. Lynne had always looked younger than her age, but she knew the guy had to have been aware that she could have had a son his age.

"Honey, you are like half my age," she threw out there.

"Half, plus 5 years," Malcolm corrected lacking the sense of humor he needed to lighten this moment.

"We'll I'm sure there is a long line of 25 year old women looking for you, since you seem like *such a good catch."*

"That may be, but I am also wise enough to know that in this life, there are a few things that you know for sure. I have been a fan of yours for quite some time. When I read your books, I know for sure that you are the one. I don't think age is a factor and from what I have read, neither do you. You have said it yourself, in your books."

Malcolm started reciting some of her thoughts, in and out of context.

Dr. Lynne closed the book, holding back her comments because she knew how long the line remained. This kid just wasn't giving up the apparition on making his intentions a reality.

"Well thank you for thinking so highly of me." Lynne said, wanting to look around for a hidden camera set up to embarrass her. Her publicist, with a worried look on her face, made her way back to author. Her assistant brought her more water to sip on.

Malcolm's smile faded and for the first time he looked unsure. She could see in his eyes that this was not a joke to him. This kid was dead serious. After handing him the autographed copy, she held out her hand to shake his.

"Thank you so much, Malcolm."

Malcolm nodded, stopped to look at her once more and finally walked away.

Words, if only they were that simple, she thought. She didn't know what to make of the encounter.

That was one thing about book signings. The "out of this world" conversations came with the territory. A lot of times, that is where she met a lot of her future patients. Though she hated to admit it, she wanted to hear more from this Malcolm, III. He left more than an impression. He left her mind wanting more snippets so she could form the whole picture.

Silly me, tricks are for kids!

Dr. Lynne went back to her undergrad alma mater, Prairie View A&M to visit and be the guest speaker for her sorority's seminar on Physical and Mental Health. She saw a familiar face among the crowd. After many hugs and talks that followed the seminar, the familiar face made his way to her as well.

"You may not remember me from…"

"How can I forget *Malcolm, III*? Good to see you again," she said, turning his handshake into a hug.

One thing Lynne had was a good sense of humor. In her profession, it was wise to keep it.

"I hope you weren't offended by my comment at your book signing," Malcolm said. "I do apologize."

"Well I must admit, it did take me by surprise," she said. "I accept your apology. You know there is nothing wrong with expressing yourself, and I do appreciate your thoughts."

"It's just that I really admire you and your choices that you have made. I have followed your career over the past seven years. I am receiving my master's degree in psychology here at Prairie View, just as you did. I plan to model the next steps off of what you did as well."

"Wow," the doctor said.

"Yes, as I get ready to work on my PhD, I was seeking mentors. Since I am already such a student of your work, I was wondering if you wouldn't mind being my mentor."

"Since I can't be your wife, right?" she said smiling.

Malcolm didn't laugh. He always wanted to be taken seriously. *Always.*

Even though she knew better, she took him up on his offer. It was quite ridiculous, she thought. *She could see the headlines now:* all things *Cougar* came to mind.

***

Hotel Lynne was always open. Lynne's residence's three guest rooms were filled with family who were having hard times. She needed people around her at all times. She hated being alone.

Back at her cozy, yet spacious home near the Medical Center, Lynne googled the young man on her laptop. She needed to do a background check. He was very active in his community. There were articles written about him for his school paper. He had written some articles that were published in different journals. She was actually impressed with his insight that must have come from being well-read and naturally in tune with the world.

She knew he had his head on straight. What did he need her for? She chuckled at the thought of him at the book signing.

Where were you in my twenties, she laughed. She couldn't find many men with the same mindset as hers. Many of her male counterparts had lost their luster. She had just gotten out of a four-year relationship with a man in her profession who she thought had no zest for life.

Then there were the others. Dr. Lynne met guys all the time, but her women's intuition, her *best friend and worst enemy*, didn't let them stay in her life too long. Red flags hit her in the face before she could even give the guys a chance.

Instinct made her love journey a lonely one.

***

What turned out to be a mentor meeting turned out to be more of a physical than Dr. Lynne expected. *Did she feel ashamed or exhilarated?* Her body desired his touch and he read her mind. She tried to act like the more mature adult, but behind the closed doors of her office, she reverted to a school girl's state of mind with his head buried under her skirt. As Malcolm's tongue explored her lips, in an instant, Dr. Lynne questioned everything she stood for.

How was she going to make sense of this?

***

Returning to work, she couldn't look at her patients the same way. There was a certain humbleness in her eyes that suggested she had gone through a change. That sofa that her patients sat on didn't seem as foreign or far away as it once did.

FORCES OF NATURE

The Story of the Elements that be

I pray for the mind of an artist
It can be delicate and
It can be excruciatingly raw
Its pinch is unforgiving

Those who don't understand, tip-toe around it
Trying not to set off,
The ticking time bomb it is
The sharp knife that punctures,

It sometimes plays up and sometimes plays down
And because of this,
Nobody wants to pick it for their team

Ambiguous, it is
Simple, it's not
I pray for the mind of an artist

Hendrix hadn't been able to sleep because his mind was held hostage by a certain someone. In the wee hours of the morning, Hendrix found himself brushing off dusty keyboard keys. He sat stiffly in front of one of the many instruments he could play. This was the one he knew and loved, but it had been shoved in his closet since Hurricane Rita.

It had been years since he stroked the keys. The sound came with so much pain. Sitting there, on the bench, he laughed at himself and the way he had given her his heart. He remembered why he had to leave the keys alone. As he closed his eyes, his mind went to a place his heart had never left.

The notes dangled in his mind as the song flowed through his fingers playing out the melody effortlessly. He didn't understand then, but after being out of the situation, he had an epiphany.

A montage of memories panned around in his head. He remembered when he first saw Autumn walk into English I Composition. He sat up straighter even though it didn't matter. Autumn didn't even realize he was in her class until fall final exams when he built up enough courage to invite her to the Spring Musical Showcase event.

He smiled as he remembered how her face lit up at the mention of music. He remembered the butterflies he felt when he looked out at the audience before the show started. Autumn was one of the first people there that night. After all of his classmates played their solo pieces, they gathered in the reception hall to greet their friends and family. Autumn deliberately stayed after for refreshments and found Hendrix to tell him the funniest story he had ever heard.

"*You were the one.* Practicing in Room 105 in Hobart!" like a detective finally cracking the case, with satisfaction, Autumn gushed. Hendrix blushed then and he blushed now as he sat.

The rest was history.

Suddenly he could hear footsteps of the twenty-five year old Martinique Boudreaux emerging from the bedroom.

"Baby, I can't sleep with all that noise," she said.

Hendrix stopped playing, but kept facing forward.

"Please come back to bed. Do you know what time it is?" his girlfriend pleaded.

***

That same morning, Autumn reached and grabbed two things from the nightstand. She slept with a pen and pad beside her. This was one of those desperate moments she needed to clear her head. It was still dark outside, so she turned on the lamp beside her. She ignored the clutter and focused on the blank space before her. She allowed herself to get lost in a world fairly old to her - she got lost, in order to be found.

Lord, I need you so bad right now
To help me get over the past right now
To deal with the real of the here and now
Because I know now, I know now

Yes, there will be storms outside
But cloudy skies won't pour on my pride
Thunder and lightning won't shake my peace
On this journey to a brand old me

I'm ready to start this journey
It's been calling me
From the very start

Like a bird
I'll fly away
I'll follow my heart

Journey

Everybody's got something to say
But I don't care anymore
Just woke up one day
And I don't share anymore

No one said it would be easy
But I'm on my way
To a new life ahead,
Miles away

Places to go, things to do,
People to see
But the one thing I'm searching for the most
Is me

As I go traveling down this dusty road
Now is the time
To let my new life unfold

Autumn hesitated as the adorable five year old girl stood with a soft, white teddy bear in her hands. She held the bear as tight as the stuffed animal held a red stuffed heart.

How did that get out here? Autumn wondered while looking at the Valentine's Day gift that had been given to her by Hendrix their sophomore year in college.

The girl's big brown eyes looked like they would water if she couldn't have it. The girl's mother asked how much did Autumn want for it. A bittersweet smile formed on her face. After some hesitation, she finally spoke.

"I can't put a price on that one," she finally said.

Autumn slowly kneeled down to the girl so they could be eye to eye.

"Now that is a very special bear. I want you to have it, but I need you to promise me one thing."

The girl listened intently.

"Please take special care of it."

The girl eagerly agreed and gave Autumn a hug. After they embraced, the little girl told Autumn thank you.

Her mother gladly gave her the cash for the items she and her daughter had collected in a short amount of time.

Autumn was doing some early, much-needed spring cleaning. She had de-cluttered her bedroom and moved a number of items outside – if only she had taken inventory. Having a yard sale seemed like a bright idea until she found out that the high of the day was a blazing 101 degrees, but Autumn wasn't letting the blazing heat stop her from purging. Her pack rat days were over and she was ready to make room for the new!

It was late March, but she was determined to take more control of her life and make 2009 an unforgettable year as a whole. Maybe it was the Hurricane, maybe it was the Dr. Lynne book tour, maybe it was just *time;* whatever prompted the event, she was grateful and determined to move forward, move on and move out. So her tablet, her writing, supplied her with clarity. The notepad that she had brought out to make journal entries sat under the table, untouched, since she hadn't experienced any downtime.

With battery-operated fans and an ice-packed water cooler filled with Ozarka, Autumn felt like she had already reached one of her goals for the year - shedding pounds (just from baking in the sun.)

It was seconds away from 12:30. She had another hour and a half to go. The yard sale started promptly at eight o'clock, which are the numbers she wrote neatly on the signs. She had made $277 so far and that was more than enough since she hadn't been picky on price. Everything was going for a dollar and Autumn felt lighter by the moment as she watched items disappear from her life.

Activity suddenly slacked up and Autumn took advantage of the first real break she had experienced that day. She walked around the table she had set up and took a seat in front of the garage - which was the closest thing to shade. She panned the driveway to see how much had been sold. Her mother, inside the house, was only a cell phone call away, but things went so smoothly she hadn't had to dial for assistance.

Autumn was proud of the yard sale layout. She had taken putting her junk out seriously, hoping that it would be seen as someone else's treasure; she focused on organization. The driveway had been a mini version of Sampson's Department Store; posters hung from tables separating her things. By season, her clothes were sectioned off from the other departments: trinkets, shoes, jewelry and accessories, entertainment items, magazines and books.

Mentally, she was even more organized. Once a sensitive subject, she laughed at how she couldn't fit most of her clothes; so it was good to see people take them off her hangers. She was going to get in shape and get a new wardrobe that would compliment her new and improved attitude.

She had brought out her favorite CDs. Corrine Bailey Rae, Chrisette Michele, Jill Scott, Musiq Soulchild, Anthony Hamilton and Carrie Underwood kept her good company.

She had mentioned the sale to her two close friends who were now starting to seep back into her life; she was really happy about their return. Surprisingly, seconds after turning up the third track on Corinne Bailey Rae's album, Autumn saw the *Bat Mobile (*Autumn's nickname for Kennedy's Mustang.)

Autumn quickly stepped from behind the table to meet Kennedy.

"What! You actually cleared your schedule to come out here and *bake*!" Autumn asked while walking to meet her friend.

In her designer, black-wedge heels, Kennedy made her way up the driveway to meet Autumn. Autumn was shocked to see Kennedy had on something less business and more casual. 2009 was *definitely* a year for change. Autumn eyed Kennedy's fitted crop jeans then her snug white knit tank that read *Ambitious Bitch.*

"Hey, Mama!" Kennedy said moving her big designer bag out of the way so that she could hug Autumn.

"Oh, I thought I would keep you company. Of course, I brought some work, though. Can't leave home without that," said the current events queen who always had a way with keeping Autumn grounded; Autumn was all about fiction and Kennedy was all about fact.

Autumn laughed. She brought out an extra chair from the house.

Then moments later to add to the surprise, both women recognized the Navigator that slowly approached Autumn's mother's residence. By the jerky, unsure movements, quickly, they knew who was behind the wheel. Kyla, the other twin, had somehow made her way to Autumn's house.

As the two women moved to greet her, they could see that Kyla was too far away from the curb. Kyla finally opened the door. Wearing a lavender cotton silk baby doll dress, Kyla slowly and carefully stepped down from the SUV. Kennedy held out her hands for her twin's keys and she naturally handed them over. As Kennedy re-straightened and re-parked her sister's car, Autumn and Kyla hugged and squealed.

***

It had been some years since the women were together - on one accord. Autumn always felt like the *honorary triplet.* Being with her friends, like old times, took sentimental Autumn's mind off the rejection letter she had received from the reality show the day before.

Despite the closed door, she was optimistic and looked forward to a great new year. It wasn't long before the girls were all seated, watching the time melt away.

The women couldn't wait to catch up.

"I know Deon is suffering, but by the looks of everyone's hair, I can truly say we all are, as well," Kennedy said.

She knew Deon's condition had improved since the almost-fatal fall.

"That is just awful, especially since all of this happened on her birthday celebration," Kyla said with sympathy.

"That is just extreme. How do you just *fall* down the stairs," Kennedy frowned while shaking her head.

"Believe me it is possible," Autumn explained.

"I still think someone pushed her," Kennedy said. "It just didn't seem right."

Autumn felt disturbed, hearing the words.

"Oh, Kennedy, please don't think like that. I am sure it was just an accident," Kyla said.

"What if it wasn't? Then, we would have a really serious problem. Hope she remembers the details leading up to the fall," Kennedy added.

"Word is she was upstairs by herself for some reason," Autumn said.

"I heard that, as well," Kennedy said remembering the night she saw the horrific sight of Deon tumbling down. "But still…we don't know for sure."

"She was pretty tipsy that night," Autumn added.

Kyla shook her head.

"We certainly need to keep her in our prayers," Kyla suggested.

They all agreed then there was a long silence.

"On a lighter note, how is everybody doing?" Kennedy asked rubbing the palm of her hands together.

"You go first," Autumn said, curious about what the shirt was all about.

"The talk show is doing great, better than I expected! I finally got the independent production company going," Kennedy said. "It's been doing well. Thank you guys for watching the shows and continuing to spread the word. Network stations are actually looking interested."

"That is great, but must you cuss?" Kyla asked, looking at the word *bitch*. "I mean, don't you think that is a little bit much?

Kennedy looked at her twin for a good minute.

"No," Kennedy responded.

Autumn couldn't help but laugh.

"Oh, speaking of the logo, I actually saw the man who *inspired* the name when I was at Deon's party," Kennedy continued.

Autumn's heart sank at the thought of JT, a *mutual friend*. She tried to remember she met JT through Kennedy; turned out JT and Kennedy had something serious going on back then that Autumn didn't even know about until later.

"How is he doing?" Kyla asked.

Kennedy sat blank for a moment. Autumn braced herself.

"I am not sure. I wasn't even trying to talk to him. We have nothing to discuss, personally. I kept it professional as usual. I did hand him a business card though."

The girls laughed.

"But word is that JT has a baby that he is not claiming," Kennedy added.

Autumn shook her head in disappointment.

"Speaking of babies, how are you and Hilton coming along with your baby-making pursuits?" Kennedy asked.

Kyla smiled and shook her head.

"We both are doing well. We still are trying to conceive, but when it is the right time it will happen. Hilton is fine; he is busy as usual. I will be expecting you two to visit our church service soon; also, bible study is held every Wednesday at 6:30."

"Will do!" Kennedy said while putting the reminder in her phone.

"Of course," Autumn added, excited. She had been visiting churches for quite some time and still hadn't found the right fit; maybe this would be it.

"How are you, Kyla - you the person?" Autumn asked.

Kyla blushed, but quickly recovered. "I am actually great! I have almost finished completing some alternative teaching certification courses. By the grace of God, someone is looking out for me at a high school on the other side of town. There is an opening in the English department that I may be able to interview for by June."

Autumn clapped. Kennedy gave her a high five.

"Finally," Autumn said. Suddenly Kennedy frowned a bit.

"You sure *you* want to do that?" Kennedy asked.

"I think this is where He wants me to be. I sort of stumbled upon the situation rather than me looking for it," Kyla justified.

"Have you checked out the school?" Kennedy asked.

"Once or twice," Kyla said.

"Did you see the janitors?" Kennedy asked.

"Janitors?" Kyla wondered if she had heard correctly.

"Wherever you are thinking about working, you better study them - see if they seem okay. If they look happy, you're good. If they look like a miserable mess, just trying to make it through the day, you better pass. Pass until you see happy janitors," Kennedy expressed.

Kyla's eyes raised.

"I will make sure that I find the custodians before making final decisions," Kyla said.

Kennedy held her hands up.

"Enough said," Kennedy replied with a smile.

Suddenly the twins looked at Autumn, prompting an update from her. After changing the CD, Autumn took her cue.

"Well, I'm moving out soon. I am thinking about taking the managerial position that they offered me in the juniors department."

"Look at you, Miss Independent," Kennedy teased, bringing over ice cold waters.

Kyla clapped her approval.

"And for fun, once I move, I want to start a small book club that will be held in my apartment," Autumn said.

"Aside from that, I told myself that I needed to get in shape," Autumn said, before taking a long sip.

Kennedy jumped. "Say no more. I was looking for a workout buddy, anyway. I joined L.A Fitness as soon as I moved back. They have a special running for those who refer others. So you two need to get signed up."

Kyla frowned.

"Hey, we'll be at church on Sunday. You will be in the gym on Monday!" Kennedy pushed. "Soon we will be attending Autumn's book club. Ladies, this is our year! It's all about the mind, body and soul!" Kennedy chanted and lifted up her water.

Autumn smiled; Kennedy always knew how to make an event out of everything.

"Cheers to that. Mind, Body and Soul," Autumn agreed.

Reluctantly, Kyla raised up her water bottle. "Alright, alright. Mind, body and souuuuul!"

"Corny ass," Kennedy said laughing. Kyla finally joined in with the laughter.

Faithful fate

Sweet memories circle me
Childish dreams and fantasies
Elate me
That day

Thoughts of you run by
Trespassing pleasant times and sunshine
When you were mine
That day

You are not here
To hold me, console me
Can't nobody replace you, erase you
Any day

Save me a place
With you,
Some day

It was a bright Sunday morning. The three women sat in Mount Gerizim Baptist Church in Sugar Land. This was the church Kyla and Reverend Hilton got married in during the summer of 2005. In Autumn's mind, Kyla's wedding was still very vivid for a number of reasons. For Autumn, ever since Kyla's wedding, two questions still remained. When her time came, *who* would walk her down and *who* would be standing there at the end waiting for her?

While remembering the saintly bride the day of her wedding, Autumn thought Kyla and her sister Kennedy did not know how lucky they were to have a father in their lives. Thoughts of how Mr. James had walked Kyla down the aisle stuck in Autumn's head because she knew she would never have that opportunity. Autumn didn't cry tears when Austin White died. It was a silent weep that grew as time went on.

Reluctantly, Autumn did what she didn't want to do - she thought about Hendrix. At the time of Kyla's wedding, Autumn and Hendrix were so close, so close Autumn could envision spending the rest of her life with him. He had attended the wedding with her and was the perfect date.

As much as they felt for each other, their relationship was always hard to categorize, so neither one of them tried. They were friends, but more than. Neither wanted to say it, fearing they could mess up what they had - something special. Ever since the early days of their freshman year, spending whatever time they could together, seemed like a given. Every day with him was a celebration. After the storms of fall '05, the celebration ended. To this day, she missed his radiant eyes, his modest voice and his gentle touch. She missed her best friend.

Devastated, she knew after Hurricane Rita, she would have to move on and accept that maybe he was just there for a season, not an eternity. The concept of discovering her soul mate was always central to her, but now, she needed to soul search. Autumn turned her attention to the preacher who stood smiling at the congregation.

"On a scale of one to ten, how strong is your faith in *Him*?" Reverend Hilton asked the church. He was not the tallest man, but he stood taller than many. "You know it's funny. It may be easy for some of you to answer that if I rephrase the question - replace Him, with your mother, your father or your husband or even wife. Replace him with your financial adviser, your favorite athlete, your doctor or even…your preacher." Hilton started to walk from one side of the stage to the other.

The church responded well to the traditional, mature looking man who smiled evenly.

"It says in Numbers 23:19, 'God is not man, so he does not lie. He is not human, so he does not change his mind. Has he ever spoken and failed to act? Has he ever promised and not carried it through?'" Hilton recited as he started to walk the stage, looking at the church that showed they agreed.

"In 2 Corinthians, 5:7, it says, 'we live by what we believe, not what we can see.' So what do you believe? We live in a world where *seeing is believing. The eyes* never lie. What you see is what you get! So in a world that relies on sight, what do you see?"

"Preach preacher!" said one of the members. Hilton continued.

"I'm here to tell you, sometimes looks *can* be deceiving; and many times you are one step away from being a victim of your sight."

"Amen," shouted the church.

"Eyes aren't everything, but faith, faith is. How strong is your faith when you are left in the dark, when you are directionless? When things go wrong, what do you do, where do you go, who do you believe? Do you secretly ask God why? Do you question his ability to guide you into the light, into the right direction - or do you gladly accept that you know a good doctor, a good expert, a good adviser, a good teacher or a good preacher? Who do you have 100% faith in?"

"We know that in Hebrews 11:6 it says, 'without faith no one can please God. Anyone who comes to God must believe that he is real and that he rewards those who truly want to find him.' So that means that we have to truly want to find him, honestly want to seek him and have pure faith in him!"

***

After church, Kyla invited the two ladies over for dinner at her home. After the delicious Italian meal, with full stomachs, the women moved to the living room - the girly, cozy, sophisticated room with the invisible sign of no boys allowed. Somehow, Autumn found herself with Kyla's ivory-colored wedding album in her hand. She stopped at the first picture of the bubbling bride and the mellow groom.

"This was such a storybook wedding," Autumn said starting to flip to the next page.

Kyla took a long slip of her lemonade tea. She wanted to quote her husband earlier with, *looks can be deceiving*, the story of her life.

Kennedy, who served as the Maid of Honor, peered over at the album Autumn placed in her lap.

"My nerves were so bad. I remember hoping that Bootleg Craig got everything on tape," Kennedy said. "While the wedding was taking place, my eyes were on Craig the whole time."

"You should see yourself on tape. Looks like you are staring directly at me when I watch it."

The women laughed, imagining the sight.

"As nervous as I was, I am so glad I got my vows out," Kyla said. She is known to sometimes stutter when she is nervous.

"You couldn't tell," Autumn said.

Autumn had reached the reception pictures in the book; the pictures showcased the nice banquet hall that was a block from the church.

"Remember the deejay!?" Kennedy asked.

"Boy, do I," Autumn, not much of a dancer, said.

"I was Harlem Shuffled, Electric and Cha-Cha slided out." Autumn remembered how her and Hendrix danced to Zydeco and Stepped in the name of love!

Soon, after all of the moving, Autumn found a seat to collapse in. She had worked up an appetite. As the party kept going and the music kept pumping Autumn remembered she kept munching.

"Then the *bouquet toss!*" Kyla gasped while smiling at Autumn. "The floor was bum-rushed so quickly, the deejay couldn't even get it out. Oh, and I sure did like how you tried to position yourself in the back," Kyla said to her sister.

"Hey, what can I say?" Kennedy said making Kyla cringe. Kennedy began to look up at the ceiling.

"I let the other solo stars shine. I don't believe in that superstitious stuff anyway. But I was alone; who knew a bunch of flowers could mean so much," Kennedy said. "Bringing crowds together," Kennedy said laughing at a concept she took part in. "I need to research the origin of this silly tradition so I can know who to blame."

Autumn laughed. "My heart raced a mile a minute when you were about to toss it. I had all these random thoughts," she said.

"What's new," Kennedy asked playfully.

Autumn laughed. "It's funny if you think about it. I was just thinking about how there are so many single women who seemed to want to be married. More than likely that is going to happen for *any woman*, whether she wanted it to or not. So really, whoever catches it, there is still the possibility of five or even more women getting married *next*. So was it really accurate to look at it like hypothetically *she's*, as in whomever catches it, is next...to get married?" Autumn explained.

"Yeah, I know what you mean," Kennedy agreed.

"You sound like Kennedy now, taking the fun out of everything," Kyla said.

"You play around enough for everybody. Remember how many times you kept acting like you were going to toss it. You kept turning around so much," Kennedy said to her sister.

"I was looking at all the restless women who were awaiting the fate of the bouquet. It was priceless," Kyla said.

When Kyla did send the flowers into lift off, Autumn remembered the bouquet drawing an imaginary rainbow in the air. In that split second, squealing women of all ages and sizes jumped and pushed, pushed and jumped for the gold to land in their pot. But only one woman managed to hold it in her hand. The room went silent as they awaited who would emerge from the pile.

Like an Olympic torch, burning a flame, Autumn stood proudly for all to see; she held the bouquet like a champion! She knew she caught it - fair and square.

There were several pictures in Kyla's book to prove it.

Colossians 3:23-24

The next morning, Autumn had passed the mirror in the jewelry section of Sampson's Department Store in Sugar Land, and she refused to look at her reflection. She figured she didn't need a glass smothered by bright lights to tell her she looked a hot mess!

Working at the store that had kept her employed since her freshman year in college, like her clothes, she had started to outgrow them. And her hair, *that was another story.*

The juniors section was her normal area. That is where she started as a part-timer early on in college and Drumsey, the manager who was leaving in June, knew she could count on Autumn.

"Girl, you look like shit. What is going on?" Roxie asked when she first saw Autumn earlier that Saturday. The Asian girl didn't know Autumn from Eve, but she always talked to her as if she had known her from way back when. The two had been working together as floaters. Roxie was a senior in college.

Autumn didn't know what to say to that, so she stood speechless. The girl reminded her of Kennedy - someone who told it like it was, no matter how you took it.

"You going through something or is this just how you put yourself together?" Roxie asked point blank.

Autumn blinked at the question and nonchalantly, laughed. She knew she looked like a Raggedy Ann doll. She couldn't wait to go shopping and try out a new beautician.

All week, successfully flat ironing her hair seemed like an impossible task, considering the humidity had a field day as she sat outside for the yard sale, Saturday. Somehow, she managed to put her thick tresses in a puffy ponytail that violently flopped around on her back, which was still sore from working out for the first time with drill sergeant, Kennedy.

"Whatever it is, girl, I hope you get it together," Roxie said.

Roxie spotted a woman who was holding a pair of earrings up to her ear in the mirror.

"For real, does it really take that long?" Roxie asked Autumn as she peered over at a customer who had been there for awhile.

"Stop," Autumn said. "You need to leave people alone!"

"Look at her," Roxie pushed. "It's not like the earring is going to change," Roxie said to Autumn.

Suddenly the woman, while still studying the jewelry, walked over to where the women stood. She took one look at Autumn and turned her smile to Roxie.

"Look at this, does this look crooked to you?" the woman said handing it to Roxie.

Roxie took one look at it.

"Under a microscope, maybe," she said dryly.

"I beg your pardon, look!" said the customer.

The part that goes in your ear, right; the part you never see?" Roxie asked condescendingly.

Autumn could see that the customer looked insulted. She walked away to see if she could quickly find another pair in back-stock trays.

"Do you have another pair that isn't crooked?" the customer snapped.

"I'm sure that is the last pair," said Roxie.

"Did you even look?" she asked.

Autumn could still hear the two.

"I still don't want to pay for something that is crooked in the first place," said the customer.

"Then don't," Roxie suggested.

Autumn's eyes widened as she tried to quickly find another pair.

Roxie looked around and saw that the crowd had lessened. "Autumn, I am about to take my 15. Did you want me to bring you back anything from the snack shop?

Autumn shook her head and emerged from the other side of the counter. She found a similar set. "No, thank you," she said looking around for the woman.

"Where did she go?"

Roxie pointed to the woman who had stormed off looking for a manager.

"Alright, I'll be back in a few," Roxie said and she was off.

It had been a long draining day, but it was finally getting slower to where she could catch her breath. She still wasn't jumping up and down at the thought of being manager of the juniors section, but she knew it was time for her to grow up and she knew it was a job that she could do well.

Autumn thought about the last time they had worked together; it wasn't pretty. They were both pulled from the jewelry department to be floaters in juniors - a floater's biggest nightmare.

"I will not be doing this the rest of my life, thank you very much," Roxie informed. "I am going to have my own boutique."

Autumn started to straighten up the cluttered jewelry area she had just straightened a minute ago, which now looked like a war zone when she heard someone.

"Hello...hello," a voice called out faintly from the purses section, which was right next to jewelry.

Autumn looked up to see a scrawny middle-aged woman, about as big as her finger. The shopper was in what looked like her children's clothes and her wet hair dripped down her back while she wandered around in the purses area with no shoes on.

As the woman continued to call out faint *hellos*, Autumn could see that the usual purse department lady was nowhere in sight. Autumn put up the jewelry as she walked over to tend to the lost woman. Autumn frowned. The girl in purses had been disappearing all day.

"Ma'am did you need any help?" Autumn said finally approaching the spectacle.

As the woman, with slurred speech, told Autumn what she was looking for, she followed Autumn throughout the section to the specific brand. She still didn't seem satisfied as Autumn finally diplomatically excused herself to tend to the growing line of customers in the jewelry area.

The woman kept talking to herself as Autumn walked off. After she rang up the customers, she tried to finish straightening up as much as she could before her manager came to check in with her.

"You don't have any good sales today!" a tall big-boned woman with a bad case of sunburn, whined.

Autumn smiled as the woman continued.

"I am disappointed by your poor selection!" the woman protested.

Autumn smiled. *This lady was serious.*

"How much is this; is it marked down, anymore? We are in a dog-on recession!" with her southern drawl the woman said as she tossed the necklace in Autumn's face.

Autumn continued to smile as she read the price tag that stated the markdowns and she looked back at the shopper.

"Can you check for me, on the computer?"

As if reading the ticket wasn't good enough, Autumn checked on the computer, knowing that the price would stay the same, since she knew the mark downs.

"Sure," Autumn said with a smile.

As Autumn checked the necklace that was priced correctly, the woman handed her a handful of other pieces of jewelry she pulled out from somewhere.

"Can you check these as well?" the woman said irritably.

Autumn looked at the pile of tangled necklaces on the counter then up at the woman who had placed them there.

"Sure," Autumn said.

After Autumn checked all 10 of the gaudiest necklaces she had ever seen, the tomato colored woman decided to take none.

"I didn't like any of these prices. I'll just leave them here with you."

Autumn chuckled.

"Oh, thank you so much," Autumn said as the woman walked off. "You have a great day." Autumn started to untangle the chains and strings.

This was the usual customer, and Autumn was relieved she finally left. Smiling to herself, she laughed at how people were. If she wasn't mistaken, there was a price checker at every mirror; they were working just fine. They were all blinking the words "SCAN HERE FOR PRICE CHECK."

Then she heard it - the sound of kids. Not just any kids, but unattended kids. The sound of their feet running around on the tile floor made Autumn look up just in time to see one little girl with colorful bows in her hair, swinging the jewelry stand as if she was spinning the big money wheel on *The Price is Right.* Before Autumn could move, different sets of earrings went flying in every direction imaginable - Kenneth Cole, Nine West, Liz Claiborne and Tommy Hilfiger would all cringe at the sight.

Autumn rushed over as the girl's mother finally pulled the little rascal away.

"Sorry," the young woman smiled, a bit embarrassed.

"She could get hurt you know," said Autumn with concerned eyes.

The parent smiled as if she felt the same way.

"Excuse me," a strained, high-pitched voice called from behind Autumn as she started to pick up the items.

Autumn, with a handful of packages in her hand, turned to face a man dressed in women's clothing.

"Yes…" Autumn hesitated, not wanting to say sir or ma'am.

The *person* had on tight denim overalls and enough lip-gloss to add sheen to the dull floors.

"Do you have any more of these in the back?" asked the man, holding up fuchsia earrings.

"No, everything is out on the floor," Autumn said.

Literally, she thought.

The guy went on looking at other showcases.

"Can you show me a watch, ma'am?"

Still with a handful of earrings that formerly decorated the floor, Autumn followed a middle-aged man to the far watch counter where she was previously.

As Autumn set out the watch he asked for, she almost gagged at the sight of his hands. The man had a fungus growing on his nails; looked like he hadn't tended to it at all. She kept her composure as he tried on several watches before choosing the one he wanted to buy. His hands didn't look like they had been exposed to water in years. She wanted to ask him what *happened* as she fiddled with taking out the extra links but she wanted to forget the sight altogether.

After the man left, Autumn was relieved to see Eva, the associate who was supposed to be in handbags, come back from her lunch, which she extended 30 minutes. Roxie came back from her

15, but it seemed like eternity. Autumn walked to the escalators to get to the restrooms. She held on tightly to the rail as she was lifted up slowly. As she approached the restroom door, she knew she needed to sit down in the lounge area. There on one of the couches, a woman sat breastfeeding her baby, smack dead in the seating area.

As Autumn walked towards the downward escalator, she carefully looked down to make sure she stepped on it correctly. She knew she was clumsy. Looking down at the first floor, which seemed miles away, she could see Eva ringing up customers and the wet-haired woman wandering around *still* in purses *still* talking to herself. Autumn took a deep breath.

In that same breath she happened to glance across at the other side of stairs; her heart almost stopped. Autumn didn't want to blink as her eyes settled upon the boy who had her heart. His sandy locs were pulled back and his trendy glasses framed his face. He looked clean in his dingy, urban chic attire. Her heart almost melted when, much to her surprise, he returned her gaze.

No! was all she could think.

A few things had changed, but it was the same JT Hudson. The one who stopped her fluttering heart the very first time she spotted him across the patio on her lunch break while working at her Aunt's salon. Autumn became nervous because he looked as though he *recognized* her. She had promised herself to not *want* - not today, not ever. She for so long thought about the day they would see each other again, *but this was not the day.*

Autumn wanted to die of embarrassment when she remembered how dreadful she looked, but her pity party was interrupted when a bunch of hooligans came running up the wrong side of the escalator. The three pre-teens didn't touch her, but just moving out of their way was a challenge. She held onto the rail trying not to tumble down the remainder of the stairs.

She continued to hold on for dear life, knowing that falling could have been bad, and humiliating. The last person she wanted to see was JT. *Funny how time can change things.* Finally she reached the bottom step. As she stepped off, somehow a hem in her pant leg got caught in the escalator's moving grooves and she quickly was able to jerk it out, but the abrupt move caused her to trip over her own feet and crash to the ground.

It ain't over till it's over.

***

No! Autumn pouted.

Her squished up face touched the tile.

She was so careful! She opened her eyes to see it actually *had* happened. She swallowed hard as she just lay there. Suddenly she felt the warm familiar touch that made her skin crawl. Autumn looked behind her to see exactly what *she didn't need.*

JT, up close and personal now, had come to her rescue. *He always saw her fumble.* Something she regretted.

***

"You sure have a way of seeing me at my worst. What is up with that?" Autumn asked JT who sat across from her in the mall's food court. She was still on her lunch break.

"That may be how you see it," JT said and then took a sip of his fancy named drink. Autumn wasn't into all the different ways to say caffeine.

Lunch with JT probably wasn't the best idea, but Autumn prompted herself she would keep things short and sweet.

"Why weren't you at Homecoming? It was really nice," JT said referring to the 2008 event.

Autumn continued to finish off her Chick-Fila sandwich. Going back was nice. The thought of moving on seemed nicer. She often wondered if she was always revisiting her past, how far would she progress.

"Just wasn't up for it," she answered.

"So what have you been up to?" JT asked.

Autumn laughed at the thought of *trying to get over you.*

"Life," Autumn said, proud of herself for keeping it short and sweet.

JT looked at her, not recognizing her. He just kept sipping, trying to figure out who sat before him.

"I'm sorry," JT said.

"About?" Autumn asked.

"Just how things turned out. I hope we can still…be friends."

Autumn nodded and she was done with her lunch. "Was that what we were, JT? Friends."

Autumn was mad at herself for traveling back in time, but her heart thought there was more to them than that. She thought about the beginning, hoping to spot red flags that she would make sure to spot if she met someone new.

JT was ruining her appetite. The thought of what had happened between them disgusted her more than the sight of herself. She needed to shut the door for good. She kept letting him crawl in every time he wanted. This was not going to happen this time.

"Bye, JT," Autumn got her trash, and threw it away.

ILLUSIONS OF THE PURE

The Story of Autumn and JT

"The heart that loves is always young." - Proverb

Some things never change and some things can't help but, Autumn thought to herself as she sat in a familiar place. Since she didn't work for Deon anymore, it had been awhile since she had eaten at her favorite seafood restaurant in the Rice Village area. JT had been out of sight, therefore out of mind. Seeing him again, despite her efforts to avoid him made her go back down Memory Lane.

If she never laid eyes on JT then she wouldn't have fallen for him and he wouldn't have been the one who laughed when she fell. She would be living happily ever after with Hendrix.

The event that marked the beginning of JT and Autumn was the summer of 2003.

College-bound, seventeen *year-old Autumn casually measured the assorted couples that strolled by while savoring the last bites of her spicy seafood etouffee from Cornelius's Cajun Kitchen. Her intrigued eyes panned until her mind felt fulfilled. Some pairs navigated with an equivalent pace, while many sort of stumbled through with unmatched steps. It wasn't everyday that she could smell or even breathe clearly through both nostrils so Autumn was wholeheartedly taking advantage of all of her senses. Her usually annoying allergies were under control for the moment and for her, that meant it was a good day.*

Autumn continued to enjoy the beautiful and breezy outdoors. Her naturally curly auburn tresses blew effortlessly in the wind and tickled the sides of her face as they fell on her sensitive caramel skin. She had been outside only thirty minutes and she was already three shades tanner. Every blue moon, Houston would get a day like this - no frowning faces bearing the sun and no pedestrians making their way through a polluted maze of popped-open umbrellas. Every person walking, whether on their break or a shopping spree, looked like they were pleasantly floating on cloud nine. Anxious to read her fortune cookie, Autumn cracked the shell in half. "Avoid confrontation" was printed on the tiny strip. Autumn chuckled as she bit into one half of the sweet hard shell.

Her chuckle gradually stopped as she tried to convince herself she should take the written message as a warning. She gazed at her watch knowing she needed to be heading down the block to Deon's Hair Divas Salon sooner than later, or else she knew who would confront her.

As she gathered her stuff, the college-bound girl focused on something that occupied her mind and notebook pages. Autumn took one more desperate look across the street from the food court area where she stood, but she didn't see him. Her heart sank. She had practically spied on him all summer long when she came and sat for lunch. This was the first day she couldn't.

Her mind started racing. Where was he? Suddenly the thought of everything else seemed so minimal. The crystal clear skies and scrumptious food wasn't enough.

As good as the day was, a lump of disappointment settled in her stomach; she carried its load along the way and dumped her trash in the nearest bin. Here I go again. Another stranger she let leave a lasting impression. She was amazed at how she let herself get attached to people - people that didn't even know she existed. It was easier that way, she figured.

Though not present, his golden brown, even tone skin, Greek-god like features and his gritty, sandy dreads that hung down his back, lingered in her pre-meditated mind as though he was in her very sight.

The thought of him, made her melt faster than the ice on the city's sidewalk and made her imagination run faster than elementary kids at field day. She felt like a silly little girl when it came to him. Autumn inhaled the eclectic scent of the food court before leaving.

She didn't know this fella from Adam, and didn't necessarily feel she could handle knowing him. Knowing her goofy self, she would probably fumble in front of him or embarrass herself by some other freak accidental way and have him looking at her like she was stone crazy. Guys she liked never saw her because "the real her" froze up. It was a shame, she thought.

As she gave one more desperate glance, she left the courtyard. She laughed to herself at the thought of the guessing game she played. She settled with the thought that it was always safer to observe the game from the sidelines, especially if the other team plays dirty. From what she heard and observed over the years at the salon, men just seemed to all play by the same rules. Somehow they always won.

Moments later, after finally leaving the crowded block of patios, Autumn made her way to the salon as her naturally-tan skin glistened along her crème colored fitted tank top. As she passed several people, her lightweight long brown bohemian skirt blew against her thighs. She looked up at the sky's puffs and the moving pictures they formed. It was a habit she had never let go of, but she decided to for the moment as she picked up her natural pace determined to get to work on time, for a change.

But before she knew it, she was side-tracked, as usual. By passing Lety's Flower Shop, Autumn couldn't resist glancing over at the rainbow garden from Lety's Flowers. She quickly spotted the most unusual purple and orange flower she had ever seen. It looked like a bird with its spiky petals. She had to stop and take it in. It would only take a minute, she convinced herself; besides, the smell had to be delightful.

Then she saw what she was looking for – the most beautiful flower in the garden.

A Dime a Dozen

Before Autumn realized it, she was flipping her calendar to December 2003. Her first semester at Prairie View had zoomed by. Both she and her roommate, Tara, were preparing for final exams.

"I will see you later," Autumn told her.

"Where you headed?" Tara asked, still a little bitter by Autumn's non-conforming ways.

"Off to the library," she said bundling up.

"You and that library!" Tara said never looking up from her computer. "You act like it's your boyfriend."

Autumn fanned her hand at her roommate. It was something about the smell of books that made Autumn feel happy and the tall shelves that made her feel safe. *She kept that one to herself.* To be surrounded by so much knowledge, so many secrets waiting to be found, Autumn would spend all day there if she could.

***

Autumn rode the elevator to the third floor where it was usually quieter than quiet. She found it was the best place to study because something was always going on in their freshmen building and PVAMU was the campus that never slept.

She found a table and plopped her backpack on the marble table. She started pulling out her books and notes for her first exam – history. After working through a number of pages, Autumn was in total absorption mode when she was interrupted.

"How are you?" a guy implored.

"Fine," Autumn spoke before looking up to see the guy who stood behind the camera that infamous day.

"Oh, so you can talk," he laughed cheerfully.

Autumn's face was flushed with red as she remembered how embarrassing the moment was at Homecoming.

"Don't worry, I get camera shy too. That's why I am always behind it," he reassured.

Autumn felt she was imagining the moment.

"I'm JT, I saw you awhile ago. I was the one videotaping at homecoming," he said.

"Nice to meet you, I'm Autumn. I was the one who sort of lost it when you were videotaping."

She laughed uncontrollably.

"So you're a freshman here?"

"Wow, is it that obvious?" Autumn asked peeping around.

"No, I just remember Kennedy saying that."

"You mind if I sit down for a sec?"

"Sure, I mean, no I don't mind."

JT sat, making himself at home in her space.

He sat looking deeply in her eyes before flinching. She sat, watching him, wondering what he was going to do. Autumn swallowed as she imagined what he could be thinking. He seemed to look right through her.

"I didn't want to interrupt your studying or anything like that. I have been meaning to ask you something since the day I saw you."

Autumn's was certain JT could hear her heart pounding as she awaited his question. She knew that if he asked her out they would have to kick her out of the library for all the screaming she would do! Autumn looked down as she waited, trying to hide her nervousness.

***

"A Dozen Dimes! They want you to pose for a Dozen Dimes! That's a big deal," Autumn's roommate gasped, hoping the rather aloof roommate understood the honor. Autumn was picked to pose for the 2004 calendar! Tara frowned but her voice was high octane. She wondered if Autumn knew what to do with the opportunity, because she sure could think of many things.

"So how did it happen? How did you find out?" Tara asked, still frowning a bit as she parted her hair while sitting in her twin bed over by the window. She sat, attentively watching her roommate warm up Hot Pockets in the mini-microwave that sat on top of the mini fridge in the middle of the room.

"Please don't let anyone know because, I am still trying to decide what to do," Autumn pleaded.

Exposure

December 2003…

"I really appreciate you coming," JT said to Autumn as he picked up his camera in his personal studio, located in the back of the home he rented.

JT looked at her as she looked down at the painted white cement floor; she sat, trying to find something neutral to rest her eyes on. She didn't wear a lot of makeup, but the little amount she had on was sweating off.

"Do you have an example calendar I can look at, by any chance?" she finally asked.

JT paused for a moment. He nodded his head eventually. It took him some time to locate the past calendar.

Autumn didn't know what she expected to see. She just needed to look at something other than the floor and him. As she held his previous calendar, she flipped through it slowly; she felt a lump form in her throat that reminded her of why she wasn't thrilled about the idea of being photographed. All of the girls were women she had seen on campus: women in pageants for different organizations and fraternities and popular sorority girls. She remembered a lot of her freshman friends and building mates trying to impress these girls that graced the pages in order to score some points for when that time came around to make the real impression.

Autumn frowned and shook her head.

"That was last year's," JT said humbly. "So, keep that in mind."

"The quality is really impressive, and the people in it are as well!" Autumn laughed to try to ease her nervousness. "I can't help but feel out of my element."

"Please don't," he said.

"This is really nice; I mean these girls look like *real* models," she said.

He laughed. He found the lens he wanted to start with.

"None of them are real models. Many of them came to me and they wanted to take pictures – for this and for that."

Autumn wondered where she fit into all this.

"Difference is, I came to you," JT answered as if he had read her mind. He came to Autumn front and center and kneeled down. Autumn looked at him closely for the first time that evening. They held the gaze longer than she expected. Sheepishly, she turned away and he pulled his camera to his face. He adjusted the lens to get the right focus.

"Look at you," JT said under his breath with a smile that he didn't know escaped his lips.

"I just don't see exactly what you plan to do, you know," Autumn said.

JT nodded understandingly.

"This year, I wanted to take things to a different level. Everything is so political here. I ain't into all that."

JT started clicking, and kept clicking.

"These made-up girls, yeah of course, they are popular, but people want something different. People need something different. It keeps it real. Sounds cliché, but authentic is the route to go. You are a new face, a beautiful one at that. Not everyone can do the natural thing."

Autumn listened to his voice since she couldn't see his full face.

"Who is truly the person in front of the lens? When that camera flashes, do you have a story being told besides, *oh I am running for this, or oh I am trying to get on the next sorority line* or whatever. Artistry is more what I want," he said to his subject.

Moments later…

"Focus on me," said JT who moved around Autumn who continued to sit on a crate covered with a white sheet, even though her cheeks were numb. As she followed him behind the camera, Autumn tried to not let her thoughts go in directions outside of the ones being tossed from JT.

As nice as JT was being, Autumn still felt out of place in her own skin in front of him. To have someone staring, *twice*, at her, she hoped that what they saw now and later was good enough to capture. Everything she would naturally do seemed dull. She was hoping she miraculously channeled Tyra Banks or something, but she still felt like someone making a bad parody of what modeling was. She just hoped they weren't able to see how ridiculously uncomfortable she was.

"Relax," JT urged, still covered by the antique film camera.

Autumn continued to do what she couldn't.

Autumn smiled nervously and then a slight frown wrinkled her forehead.

He looked from behind the camera.

"I'm sorry," she apologized.

He flashed the camera.

"Please, don't be sorry."

Autumn really wanted to get up and gather her things.

"So tell me about you. What is it that you want to do?"

"Certainly not model."

The two laughed.

Autumn really focused on the question and for the first time wasn't focused on him.

"You know that is a good question," she said.

JT snapped away while his reflective canvas pondered.

"A question I don't have an answer to," Autumn said.

JT paused for minute to refocus.

"Really?" He seemed shocked. "What is it that you are passionate about?"

Autumn smiled.

"I think that is my problem." Autumn's smile faded as she shook her head. "It's hard to choose, you know."

JT remained quiet.

"I know so many people who knew at a young age what they needed to do in life. Their purpose was so clear. They were so focused. I envy that tunnel vision that they have," Autumn revealed.

Autumn sat looking through the lens at JT as random thoughts floated in her head.

"I used to ask God, why do I have so much going on in my head? Why couldn't I have this one thing to do well?"

She paused.

"Were you like that - knew you wanted to be this great photographer?"

JT laughed. "Greatness, I haven't acquired yet," JT continued snapping away.

"But in a sense I have been doing this since I was three. JT stopped for moment to remember his father who placed his first camera in his hands. "Then at 8, he gave me the camera I hold today."

"That's like Kennedy. She is so dedicated to the journalism thing. Whenever I see her, she has a mic in her hand, interviewing people - or typing up more questions and more interviews." Autumn smiled.

Autumn caught a glimmer in JT's eyes before he lifted the camera back up to his face.

"Yeah, she is *always* on her grind. That's my dog."

Autumn remembered what she was doing when she was three; *savoring every bite of her grandmother's soul food cooking.*

"My aunt is the same way. She knew she wanted to be in the beauty industry since she was a little girl," Autumn added.

"So what are the many things you are passionate about?" JT said. "We have time."

Autumn laughed.

"I love books."

Autumn couldn't believe she said it out loud.

"I probably sound like such a nerd."

"Hey, that's okay," JT reassured. "That's cool."

She took a moment. "My imagination is out of this world. That is why I started to write. It's funny, but I have kept a journal since I could write, not that my life is all that interesting. I have so many notebooks of unfinished stories."

JT clicked away.

"I did finish one, in third grade. It actually placed second in the school competition they put it in. I couldn't believe it," Autumn said.

Autumn laughed at the thought of the outrageous tales about *Tori, The Green-Face Girl.* The character had brain fever and was ostracized at her new school for being different.

After chuckling about the story she had written in elementary, JT found his serious side again.

"I love the arts. I adore poetry, I am obsessed with music and I am such a television junkie. So I take my stab at creating different pieces."

"You could do so many things with those interests, Autumn." JT contributed, matter-of-factly.

"That's not what my mom says," Autumn explains.

JT smiled sympathetically.

"How many people do you know actually made a career out of writing?" Autumn said mocking her mother.

"But there are few," JT said. "Even if it is what makes you happy, just continue."

"When I was little, I wanted to be a teacher. Then a nurse. I just wanted to help people."

JT managed to get some shots of her when she paused. Autumn had forgotten about the camera by this point.

"That is until Claudine stepped into the picture. She lived a few houses down and was ten years older than me. Talk about lasting impressions; when you witnessed her passion for her dream, you realized that there was more to life than the obvious. She had dreams of being an actress. She was always the star of the show at her school. I would go see her perform in plays at the High School of Performing and Visual Arts, better known as HSPVA. Then, I just wanted to be a part of that world. When she passed away at such a young age, I was terrified."

JT clicked away while he listened.

"You know, it really opened my eyes. I have never been able to close them."

Autumn smiled. "So that summer, what did I do? I tried to go after my dreams. I got into the Young Performers Program at The Ensemble Theater. *Me and my shy self.*" Autumn rolled her eyes. "I don't know what I was thinking. I soon found out, I was no Claudine."

"I just remember it like it was yesterday. As all the other girls played popular entertainers like Diana Ross, Tina Turner, and Whitney Houston, I portrayed Lorraine Hansberry."

"To be young, gifted and Black," JT recited.

"Yeah!" Autumn smiled.

JT kept snapping.

"I realized that even though it got me to speak, I knew I was not actress material. I no longer wanted to chase that dream. I had a new dream now. Lorraine Hansberry showed me the reality of another vision."

"So I left the idea of being an actress on the stage and went after the dream of storytelling."

JT went back to clicking; he captured the now, animated gestures that contradicted the former uptight ones.

"It's a side of me that wants to be a writer, but we know it is not that simple."

JT stopped.

"Why not?" he asked.

"It is so overwhelming to want to do this one day then the next day, do that. So many dreams and not enough time to choose."

"But why do you have to?" JT frowned trying to understand. "Why can't you just go for it all?"

Autumn laughed at the idea. It was a good one though.

"You are going to be just fine," JT reassured. "Just fine."

Later that night…

JT watched as Autumn's eyes slowly penetrated through the dripping, glossy paper, revealing her soft facial features.

JT smiled. He had gotten more than what he wanted. The array of emotion was more present than in any of the other girls he had photographed. He took it all in as the image grew more sharply while he stood in a closet in his studio. JT had never captured a subject so open - open with vulnerability. The strength in her almond-shaped hazel eyes lit up the dark room.

A.D.D and Pedigree

Two weeks after the photo shoot…

"Well, hey superstar," Tara said, as Autumn met her for lunch in Alumni Hall.

Autumn laughed. The calendar was out and floating around more than the Panther Newspaper's, *20 Questions* – a juicy gossip column.

As the two strolled through the downstairs portion, as usual, Tara looked around at some of Autumn's new spectators.

"Girl, everybody been talking about you and your pictures," Tara shook her head recalling the latest events.

"See, aren't you glad you went along with it? You were trippin' so hard; in the end, you got some attention and a man out of it."

"*A man*?" Autumn spit. "Girl please, JT ain't worried about me."

Tara pierced her lips together.

"He is not." Autumn said convinced. She knew the last thing she wanted to do was jump to conclusions.

"In fact, I haven't even seen the guy since the shoot."

"Whatever, Autumn. You in the door. I say go forward. It's not everyday a nigga just pick ya out of a crowd *of beauties*."

Autumn looked then listened to Tara.

"He had plenty to pick from. *Plenty*. So to say you were selected, must be nice." Tara laughed. "Have you seen the brother - talk about fine!"

Autumn hadn't really thought much of the photograph. She saw herself, but she wondered what so many other people were seeing. There were many people making a big deal about it, but she kept focusing on other things. JT was one of them. He had been on her mind since the moment she saw him on the patio during the summer. She never thought she would see him outside of that context. Autumn had promised herself, to not let herself get beside herself, but the thought of him made her want more.

As they reached the upstairs of the dining hall, there wasn't much of a line. Once they were on the actual second floor, it was crowded at every turn. Autumn wasn't too fond of congestion. She dealt with it on a daily basis with her allergies. Tara, on the other hand, seemed to live for the packs. She would walk around like she was putting on a show. The wanted attention made Autumn a bit uneasy, but she and her roommate had similar schedule breaks.

Tara strutted around and Autumn walked by her side. All the lines were long, making it not too easy to decide what to settle on.

"Girl, my stomach is growling," Tara said.

Autumn wasn't as hungry because she had been snacking all day.

The tables were filling up as they stood around.

"I will go find a table," Autumn said trying to sit down.

"Cool, I will get in the line then," Tara said.

Autumn walked randomly around the cafeteria.

Many people were aware of her. The same amount since her beginning freshmen days and then some.

"Hey, Miss December," a boy called out at her. "You make me want to jump to next year so you can keep me warm."

Autumn looked to see who made such a *lame* comment. He was nice looking. She had seen him around, but she didn't care to see much else of him.

She walked on. She could feel his eyes on her round rear. She walked to the other side of the cafeteria hoping to find a small table or at least two empty seats. There was a lot on her mind. She quickly realized she had possibly made a mistake. And for what? Autumn stood first scoping out the scale of the room before walking. Then all of a sudden, she felt two warm hands slowly cover her eyes. The body stood close behind her taking her completely out of her element.

"Guess who," the voice whispered, tickling her ear.

Autumn smiled unconsciously.

"Hey babe, you doing alright?"

"Yeah," Autumn answered without thinking.

JT turned to face her. He beamed from ear to ear.

"See you around," JT said.

Realistically, she knew that JT was not for her and she was not for him.

But maybe she was being too realistic, she figured.

"Okay," Autumn said trying to refocus her attention on finding an empty table so she could sit down somewhere; instead, she found several eyes on her that could burn a hole in her skull. It was going to be a long couple of years.

Later that evening…

Autumn wished he had seen more in her than just a model for his stupid calendar.

Coming to terms with the fact that JT was not feeling her was hard. He was nice to her, but not "into" her. She was just a subject for his camera.

She saw how guys, for instance looked at her aunt Deon. They had a certain glimmer in their eye that would give you all the reason in the world to know that this guy is really digging Deon. JT just didn't give Autumn that look. He rushed around her. It was just business. She knew she should be happy that she had gotten more out of it than she could have ever imagined. This was just a guy she had a crush on. Crushes weren't really worth anything.

***

Autumn started walking from her last class. It was a beautiful day. She was focused on making sure that she appreciated it.

"Just the person I wanted to see."

JT stood smiling at Autumn.

"Hey cutie, what is your Friday afternoon lookin' like?"

Autumn's eyes rolled to the top of her head. She knew she wasn't doing much; she had a math test she planned to study for since it was her most challenging subject.

"Cause I was doing a photoshoot," JT explained.

Autumn inhaled deeply. *Not this again,* she thought. She was certainly not interested, now.

"And afterward, I had something else in mind. I have been working like a mad man." He shook his head. "You know, I hated that we haven't been able to really spend any time together. Since the shoot, I had really been thinking about what a cool person you are. So afterward, I was thinking about us hookin' up so we can hang out a bit."

Like music to Autumn's ears, she beamed at the idea of the two of them getting to know each other better. Besides, he had been on her mind.

"So what kind of stuff do you like to do around here?" he asked.

PV didn't have much to choose from. Everything was about a good hour away. JT seemed to read her mind.

"How you feel about us going to catch a movie?" he asked the movie buff.

"That sounds good."

"Well then, I'll come and get you after the shoot."

***

After touching up the lip gloss that she rarely used, Autumn answered the room phone.

"Hello," Autumn said.

"Autumn, I'm on my way," JT said.

Autumn smiled. "Okay."

He could easily hear her smile.

The house he stayed at was right outside the campus. She figured she'd walk out earlier to try to avoid her nosey neighbors.

"Where you going?" Tara said before Autumn slipped out the door.

She was shocked Tara even cared. Lately, she had been in her own world in comparison to how it used to be. In a short period of time, their friendship changed; there were fragments thrown out at each other from time to time, but no longer full conversations.

"I'm sure it's not to the library," Tara said.

Tara tilted her head down keeping her eyes fixed on her roommate.

"Where are you going and with whom are you going?"

Autumn wondered when she had become a parent? Autumn paused.

"With just a *friend.*"

"Oh, so we ain't revealing names now?" Tara smirked. "I see how you being now. Got you some shine and now you too good."

Autumn rolled her eyes and shook her head while her hand stayed gripping the door knob.

"For one, it's not a big deal, so why are you making it into one?"

Tara eyed her up and down. She checked out her shiny pout all the way down to the way her skinny jeans showcased her coke bottle frame.

"Judging by your outfit and the scent of Curve, it looks and *smells* like a big deal to me."

Tara shook her head and looked away while pursing her lips together. She looked like she was grunting something under her breath.

Autumn laughed out of pure frustration. *The nerve*, was all she could think.

"Now you better be back by curfew. I don't want to have to come trying to find you.

Look who was talking, was what Autumn wanted to say as she thought about all those nights she unwillingly went looking for Tara. Tara owed her one, Autumn thought.

***

Autumn swiftly walked past the downstairs building mates who did nothing but look at her and then each other - this was the usual since the calendar.

Where she going? Some of the girls from the TV room asked when she passed by and walked out the door.

The sky was turning jetblue. Normally she would really study it. There was a nice breeze in the air that helped dry her all of a sudden damp skin.

***

Minutes later, Autumn continued to sit quietly as they rode down Highway 290 since she really didn't have anything to say out loud. She just looked at the road as JT passed trees. There was nothing but a couple of stores along the highway; other than that, it was pretty dead. One of her thoughts was *what was JT thinking.* JT sat and did not give off much emotion. He looked over at her suddenly.

"Now you gonna have to loosen up over there," he said playfully while reaching over to touch her arm.

She made her own self nervous; and she didn't understand what she felt around him.

He looked back at the road and his hand seemed to calm some of her uneasiness, but not all. He turned up the volume to his Jay-Z CD.

Autumn was far from a hip-hop fan, but she was getting more used to it being at PV.

For some reason, she felt that JT was probably never going to want to spend time with her again. There was something really forced about them.

She had forgotten the movie title that they were going to see, but she remembered it was something she had never planned on seeing, based on the trailers. She'd watch anything, though.

She looked over at him and quickly away.

"So how was the shoot?" she asked.

"Cool. For one of the pageants coming up. You know, I could see you doing a pageant."

"Oh no," Autumn was adamant and knew she was not putting herself out there. Nobody was seeing her cellulite - under all those lights.

"I wouldn't even know what to do for a talent," she said.

"Oh please, you would have so much to do. With writing and stuff - dramatic interpretation, poetry. That is up your alley." He laughed. "I know for the swimsuit competition, there would be no competition."

Autumn thought that was funny.

"Yeah right, I know how to wear the right things to disguise the wrong things."

JT shook his head.

"There is nothing wrong with that body."

She knew he had eyes, but hearing how his eyes saw her, was a bit much.

JT exited unto Highway 1960. There was so much traffic.

***

As the two walked out the movie together, JT mentioned something about going to film school and Autumn thought that was the coolest thing.

The ride home was unfortunately shorter. JT was polite. The music played. As they reached her dorm room, Autumn sat in the passenger seat for a moment before letting herself out. JT came around and walked her to the front door.

She was grateful that there wasn't much activity going on in the downstairs TV room.

"I had a good time," she said.

"I did too. We got to do this more often," he decided.

They stood and looked at each other for the longest before Autumn reached into her purse, and got out her gate card reluctantly. JT stood there until she was in and the door shut in front of him.

As she walked up to the third floor, Autumn couldn't believe it was over. She wanted more than what she was getting.

"You coming to the sleepover night right?" Tara questioned and some of her building mates waited for answers as they passed each other in the hall.

Autumn wasn't in the mood, for she was really tired. The capricious way her friends were acting lately drained her enough as it was, but she found herself there with the girls.

Everyone brought their sleeping bags to the third floor TV room. There were chips and drinks out. There was a lot of talk. Some other girls from other dorm buildings were there.

This chick who claimed to be a tarot card reader was sitting in the center of the room when Autumn entered in her bed clothes. Everyone was attentive.

"Autumn get yours read. She's the real deal," Tara challenged.

"No, that's alright. You get yours," Autumn cautioned.

Tara sat before the girl.

The tarot card girl dealt the cards then studied a couple.

"Tara, be careful. There is trouble coming your way if you don't," she said to Tara.

Tara laughed.

"What. Is that the best you can do?"

"I didn't do it; it's all in the cards."

"In the cards, my ass. What kind of trouble?" Tara burst.

The girl laughed.

There were plenty that got readings and a plethora of answers amazed the group because they had possibility and they could see the truth in the cards.

Tarot girl was about to leave.

"Alright ladies, y'all have a good night."

"You didn't want to see what's in your future?" Tarot girl asked Autumn once more.

"She already knows her love forecast!" Tara shouted from somewhere in the back of the room.

"Oh that's right, the goldilocs right?" someone else chimed in, referring to Autumn's crush.

"So what's the deal with you and oh, boy?"

Autumn blinked. Soon, it seemed that everyone was throwing questions and comments at her like they were throwing balls at a dunking booth.

"Nothing," Autumn began.

"You are such a bad liar," Tara laughed.

"I'm wondering what is there to lie about." Autumn defended. There is nothing going on. Do you want something to go on?"

Autumn hesitated. She knew the answer was simple.

"He doesn't like me like that." Autumn pleaded.

Tara rolled her eyes.

Autumn knew it was the truth. The truth was, she wished it were a lie.

***

For the girls, going to Alumni Hall was a ritual in the beginning of the year, but to get all the gang back in effect had become a task for a miracle worker by the end of their second semester. All their lives started to kick into full gear and they weren't able to catch up as much. Today was different; they all were able to go together.

Autumn was surprised and pretty happy to have that family-like time again. She saw the good in people, despite their far-from-favorable actions.

As they walked from the dorms, the girls carried on what seemed to be separate conversations, unlike when they first met.

Once in the cafeteria, they all split.

Autumn was out of the food line first so she and Tara found a table for the bunch, like old times. Little by little, the other building girls filled up the table and before they knew it, it was like previous times - loud.

There wasn't much to talk about, but there was conversation.

"So we know somebody's been getting some," one of the girls who lived down the hall from Autumn and Tara jeered.

All eyes were on Autumn suddenly. She gulped.

"Yeah, didn't take no time, Mona Lisa."

"Whatever," Autumn implied.

"So what is he like?" insisted one of the girls.

"Like I said, I don't know what y'all are talking about."

"Yeah right, coming home all late. You gotta know something."

"Word is JT has a girl, at UT," said one of the girls.

"I heard JT was seeing some girl at TSU," said another.

"Well that is funny; I heard he had a couple here," insisted another. "I saw one at the laundromat earlier today."

Suddenly, someone she was usually happy to see appeared. JT was walking into the cafeteria with a couple of his friends. Autumn pretended to not see and focused on finishing her meal. Most of them were the guys who were playing video games the night she came for the photoshoot.

Tara hit Autumn. "Look at him! There he go. Your boo!"

Heads started turning at the girl's table.

"Why don't we just ask him, to set the record straight," said Tara. "I am tired of hearing all these rumors.

Autumn shook her head in shame.

“What are y’all trying to do?” Autumn frantically asked.

Autumn wanted to die as the guy seemed to head in that direction, toward all the hoopla.

“Hey, lover boy,” one of the building girls coaxed and there were several echoes.

JT turned around and looked at one of Autumn’s building mates. He smiled to some extent. Autumn was so ashamed and beyond words. She swallowed hard. He never looked at her though.

What's wrong with a laughing smile?

It had been weeks since her building mates had put their immaturity on display. She couldn't believe they actually had the nerve to ask him to explain who he was talking to and in some warped way, they tried to make it as if they were looking out for her. She was going to have to put the whole idea of him out her mind. It would be for the best.

As soon as she was over the idea of him asking her out, he did.

***

Movie night at his house made her a bit edgy. His video playing guys had found another pad to crash. It was just them. He was quick to make her comfortable. It didn't really work. Autumn was so in her own head, trying to stay two steps ahead of him while the movie played. It played, serving as a neutral distraction, something she could once again rest her eyes on and look occupied with.

Love Jones was her favorite romantic movie. She knew it like the back of her hand, so she really didn't watch it. She, instead, battled with the emotions she felt building up inside as they sat side by side, together on the couch. She wondered what he could be feeling, or if he felt anything at all. Once it was at the closing scene, she searched for conversation as he sat there letting the movie play out to the credits.

"I wonder where are they now. Like, did they make it?" Autumn said at the end.

JT just sat, still letting the movie run.

"You never know if it ended happily or not." Autumn continued.

Suddenly, he budged from his zombie state. JT kept the lights on as he moved away from the couch they sat on and into walked the kitchen.

Autumn, for a change, witnessed how JT looked uneasy.

As he returned to the couch, his eyes roamed around aimlessly. Autumn looked at him yearning for a look in return, something that could clue her into him. She didn't understand what was missing exactly - but something was. *How did he feel exactly? At this moment,* she wondered.

She all of sudden laughed.

He looked concerned.

"You know what is funny. You don't know this, but Homecoming was not the first time I saw you."

JT was all ears.

Autumn explained how on her lunch breaks at Deon's salon, she spotted him across the way and never imagined that she would wind up at the same school as him.

JT couldn't believe that their paths could have crossed earlier.

"It's a small world," he said.

There was awkward silence.

"Well I'm glad we met," he said.

JT was driving her crazy without even trying. She could only imagine what his touch felt like as she sat right beside her.

She didn't want to just imagine. She had never thought being close in his presence would be like this. She felt like she was tugging a limp expectation. Just knowing him for surface value wasn't enough, but what would it take to know him deeper. How was it possible to miss what you never had?

Suddenly Autumn's cell phone rang. It was Tara, needing her to come and get her from the police station.

After rescuing Tara from the police station, JT drove them both back to the dorms. Turns out Tara's brakes ran out and she happened to run into the police station.

JT and Autumn were hanging out again the next weekend. Again at his house. They had come from a long day of just being out and about together. Once they plopped down on the couch, in front of the TV screen, there was nothing really pulling them anywhere, which Autumn thought was strange and unexpected.

No real direction, good or bad...no momentum to swing them anywhere. Their stagnant existence was driving her mad. She knew she had other things she could be doing with her time. She didn't want to be just another number thrown into the equation. She understood that he was not into her. He probably did have *girlfriends*.

Then all of a sudden, JT turned to face Autumn.

There were no words; a look of ambiguity in his eyes spoke volumes. It was a look that pushed her to lean into his space. He crept up closer to make her lips meet his.

***

Moments later, her skin against his was like nothing she could have ever imagined.

It happened so fast; and at times there was a pinch of déjà vu that teased her mind.

What they did, was nothing like the movies. It was nothing like the sweetest love song, but more like a lifeless beat with no soul.

Once she got back to her dorm, she locked the door behind her, stripped off her clothes and stared at her reflection in the full length mirror. In seconds, she cried; she sat on the cold ground. She didn't know why she was weeping. But it was the only thing she could do.

***

One day after English class, Hendrix stopped Autumn to see what was wrong with her. She tried to not involve him with her affairs, but she couldn't help herself. He lent his ear. One evening after dinner at Alumni Hall, in route to the dorms, Autumn needed a male's opinion. The two freshmen found a bench in the central courtyard of the freshmen community. For awhile Autumn sat, ashamed, but ready to let it out. He was the only person she could share her feelings with. She could trust him in a way that she never thought she could trust anyone.

"I made a fool of myself with someone who doesn't even care," she cried. She gave details of how JT acted the night they were together.

Hendrix looked hurt, but found some words to share with her. "There is that old saying, Fool me once, shame on you, fool me twice, shame on me. We all make mistakes. But we need to make sure we learn from them so we won't continue," he said.

"The games. Why do guys play them?"

"It happens, but there is someone out there for you, someone who will treat you right. You got to believe that."

Autumn felt that it was nice to know someone was optimistic about her situation.

"I didn't ask for JT. I didn't go around hunting him down to be in my life. I was happy just observing from the sidelines."

Autumn knew she didn't like herself when she was with JT. He had a way of making her feel entirely beside herself.

"The sad part is, I didn't for a second mind being a fool for him," she told Hendrix.

It was really hard for him, but he continued to be her support.

That was then and this is now.

Options (open)

"If you love something, let it go. If it comes back, it's yours. If it doesn't, it was never meant to be."
- Anonymous

April and May 2009 had been great months for Autumn, Kennedy and Kyla. The three ladies were focused, feeling good, looking good and getting ready for summer.

The church had two visuals at the front – two boards that represented two doors. They were labeled door number one and door number two.

The preacher looked at the congregation. "Which door would you choose?" Hilton asked.

Sensing the hesitation, Hilton added another question.

"What's behind them, you wonder?"

"Yeah!" said the church.

"That is thc thing. *You* don't know. So I ask again, *which* door will you choose? Door number one or door number two."

"Behind door number one, *could* be a monetary prize that gets you out of your credit card debt."

"Hallelujah!" someone from the crowd shouted. And several echoed the words.

Hilton continued.

"Maybe even one that puts your children through school, or even you."

"Yes, Lord!" said one of the choir members.

"Door number two *could* hide a brand new sports car that lets you ride clear across town. One that is guaranteed not to break down and have you pull over to the side of the road, hoping for a rescuer."

There were some claps.

"Behind door number one could be something you didn't need, but you could certainly find handy - like a flat screen television. Or a barbeque grill for your block parties."

The church laughed.

"We have no idea what each door holds until we make the decision to open it. You can't straddle the fence. Believe it or not, making a decision is a reward in itself. So *make up your mind!*"

Autumn chuckled.

"We must remember that making decisions aren't difficult if we know who to consult with. There are ways to know what God is telling you. He can make the elimination and selection process easier, *if you let him.*"

Autumn focused on the preacher.

"We all want to move forward in life, but sometimes there are things that have us standing still. In life, we may approach doors that have us dealing with different dilemmas. Remember though, before we can take steps forward, we must first make a choice of what direction we must go. That is the nature of the game."

The church agreed.

"So make up your mind! Don't just stand there. What is the point of keeping options open if you never choose? What is the point in wondering if you never seek to find out? Make up your mind!"

Hilton took a sip of water as the crowd shouted.

"When you trust in him completely, making up your mind is *easier.* When you lean not on your own understanding, making up your mind is *easier.* When you trust in God, he will reveal His will, and this makes it *easier.*"

"Yeah!" some of the church members shouted.

"In Psalms 32:8, the Lord says 'I will make you wise and show you where to go. I will guide you and watch over you.' So let him make things *easier.*"

The church responded.

"We owe it to God and to ourselves to study the word day and night because *confusion* should not be an option. We are reassured that 'If you go the wrong way – to the right or to the left – you will hear a voice behind you saying, *This is the right way. You should go this way.*' We find this in Isaiah 30:21."

Autumn wrote down the verse.

"So the next time you are approached with door number one and door number two, don't let confusion be an option. Let God make it *easier* for you. You can stand there without knowing what is behind either, but knowing that if you listen to the voice inside of you, you will know what door to choose. Let the spirit and your faith lead the way. *Make up your mind.* Step forward!"

Autumn finally knew who she chose.

SOMETIMES I FEEL LIKE A FATHERLESS CHILD

Autumn and Hendrix's Story

Father's Day seemed to always be non-existent for Autumn, but this year was the first year she made a conscious effort to celebrate the holiday. Tearing up the angry letter she had written to her biological dad, Austin White, she decided to write a new one.

A LETTER TO MY FATHER

You have been the Father my own father couldn't be. No man on Earth can be who you are to me. I am proud of who I am because of you, today. You have and continue to bless me with your angels I've met along the way. The present holds so much more than the past can because of you. Day to day, I will take with me the lessons of the past. I've made the mistake before, but I won't make it again, I will never forget you. You are the one I put my faith in.

She thought about all the times she looked for love in all the wrong places - wanting people to rescue her from her own heartache. She had a new approach to life. She knew who she needed to surrender to.

Suddenly her phone rang. As Autumn read the name of the caller, she held it together. It had been months since IKE and their reunion. She tried to not get herself too excited. Tried.

Song in my head

As Autumn drove her hybrid over to Hendrix's place, she hummed a tune that she couldn't get out of her head. She didn't know exactly what Hendrix had in mind, but she looked forward to seeing him.

As she walked to the door of the patio style home, Hendrix met her with an unassuming look. "When I did this, I knew you were the perfect person to call," he blurted.

Autumn blinked.

As they walked through the house, Hendrix thanked her for coming. Autumn was so anxious to see what he insisted that she see, she didn't know what to do. She took in the house slightly, but more or less wandered beside him, wondering where they were going.

Then suddenly, they approached a door; it was to one of the bedrooms in the one story house. Hendrix slowly opened the door to reveal something that made her heart beat faster. Hendrix watched Autumn slowly walk around taking in the room he had gladly transformed into a music studio.

"This is essential!" Autumn said. "I am in love with this!"

Hendrix's doubt was washed away and he felt so much better seeing that she was pleased.

***

Hendrix sat in front of a keyboard, computer and other machines that were somewhat foreign to Autumn. Hendrix normally didn't like people around while he played, but Autumn had always been an exception. Autumn got comfy on the sunken-in couch as she curled up and watched Hendrix in action. Hendrix modestly said he was experimenting, but Autumn knew it was more than a hobby; the man played with too much intensity and heart for it to be just to fool around. The last music session she had sat in on was in 2005, before Hurricane Katrina and from what he said, it was the last time he had one. It touched her soul to see him return to his passion.

Autumn closed her eyes as Hendrix layered - he stacked soft sounds on top of a raw Zappish synthesized beat. After a few minutes of mixing this with that, he turned to her with a big grin.

"Wanna hear what I got?" he asked, not wanting to show how excited and nervous he was. Autumn opened her eyes.

"Of course!" she said, sitting up straighter so she could digest it all.

For Hendrix, there was always a bit of apprehension when he played music for Autumn. She was always eager to lend an ear and offer some encouraging feedback, but he was still uneasy. He dragged the cursor back to the start and pushed play.

"It's a bit different for me," he said, as the music started, trying to prepare her.

A very taunting, textured and intense horn seeped through the speakers filling the room. Then other mysterious and manipulated sounds pulled her in automatically. Autumn's juices were flowing as she could feel the story already forming. It was a story that rang very familiar. It was a story starring love, and the villains were heartache and pain. She heard the vulnerability of the strings and the reasoning piano. And soon Autumn understood what lay behind the guitars' sly interjection. The beat kicked in and was steady, slick and tempting. Autumn moved, rocked to it, without even realizing it. It *was* different for Hendrix, normally a ballad maker.

When the music stopped, Autumn sat there, still engrossed in the musical voyage she had taken.

All she could do was nod.

"Is it okay?"

"It's more than *okay*."

Hendrix was in heaven; he wanted her stamp of approval.

"You are not just saying that?" he asked.

Autumn shook her head.

"Of course not. So what is this for?" she asked, willing to support his new project.

"Just playing around."

"Doesn't sound like playing to me. Sounds real serious. And it is such a new sound for you."

"I know, huh." Hendrix agreed.

"People do evolve," Autumn said.

"Ain't that the truth," he answered.

"You know it's funny, I wrote this poem, not too long ago."

"You still writing?" Hendrix asked.

"Got back to it," she said, remembering how she hadn't shared those details. "I was in a different state of mind. I called it *tangled web*."

Hendrix continued to be all ears.

"At the time, I felt so caught up; all the conflicting emotions trapped me. It really sounds like it would fit the tone."

Hendrix nodded.

"You got the words?" Hendrix was curious.

Autumn hesitated for a moment. "Yeah." She realized what she had gotten herself into. "I actually do."

"Want to try to see if we can put something together?"

Singing wasn't her thing, but she was in her element with Hendrix; this felt like the good ole days for them - when the duo was back in Hendrix's apartment. She remembered when he used to let her fool around with the computer keys while he was creating beats for his demo, when he had big dreams of being a big time music producer. Although Hendrix could compose, he wasn't the best writer. He relied heavily on Autumn's keen sense of storytelling and her imagination to fill in the beats. *She did every time.* She had a way of having the words that gave the song the meaning he felt was missing. She was the icing on his cake. Sometimes, he even felt like she was the cake.

During their "on-the-yard days," once Hendrix had the music and once Autumn had the words, Hendrix would invite their friends from the school's Baptist Student Movement over to sing. The singers would arrange the vocals and drop their heartfelt voices on his R&B tunes. That was the life they knew and the life they loved. Other times, it would just be Hendrix and Autumn in the studio. Those times, they both made music that only they heard.

It felt good to return to something that mattered to both of them. Autumn could carry a tune, but she would never claim to be able to sing. She cleared her throat and apologized for the fact that it was not going to sound like the singers they used to be impressed by back at PV.

Hendrix waited patiently to hear the story.

Autumn began. Hendrix listened intently as Autumn tried her best to transform her poem into a song. Right off the bat, the words struck a chord. He related. He wondered. He felt.

The two meshed magically; it was as if they were created simultaneously.

After Autumn concluded the lesson-learned themed song, both of them sat for a moment, looking at each other. With no words, no music to interfere with their thoughts, they just sat.

Moments later, Hendrix finally came out of the trance and gathered his thoughts.

He nodded his head.

"You still got crazy skills." He knew who inspired her words.

"You don't have to use that you know. I just thought it seemed to go."

"Oh, it really does," Hendrix said.

Hendrix was happy that they were back being creative together, but he couldn't help but realize who seemed to still be Autumn's muse. JT was the thorn in his side that just wouldn't quit. He wondered would he, personally ever replace the *other he* and have that role in her life? His mind always drifted to what the *other he* did or didn't do; he didn't know what to do.

He needed to know, but he feared what could be revealed, uncovered. He wanted to pick up where they left off, but he knew that the truth may hurt.

On the other hand, Autumn didn't want to lose this moment again. She looked at the song as closure. She looked forward to what lie before her and the man of her dreams.

Summertime

The summer was passing by so fast. Autumn and Hendrix were in the studio so much they had over a 100 songs written and composed. They were going to start getting some singers to make the words come to life.

The retail industry was still struggling because of the recession, but Autumn was actually in a good place. She was actually enjoying her job as juniors department manager, especially since she had music to turn to after her shift; not to mention she had stories for days from all the characters she had come across.

Aside from the bright side of summer, hurricane season was not yet over and Houston knew it wasn't over till it was over.

Autumn was happy to be around Hendrix. His girlfriend Martinique, who had just started practicing law, was another story. When they were working in the studio, the Thurgood Marshall Grad was not a happy camper.

Autumn tried to stay clear of any trouble and wanted more than anything to be respectful of the two. She also tried not to dip into Hendrix's love life. She was happy for him if he was. He didn't seem to be too elated about Martinique's presence, but Autumn figured it was none of her business. She knew who she was focusing on. Hendrix and JT were no longer contenders.

***

Martinique and Hendrix had an ugly break-up, but Autumn was there for him, like he he'd always been there for her.

The good, the bad, and the ugly

It was Autumn's birthday and Hendrix wanted to treat her to something that she would truly enjoy. Both found themselves in *Build-A-Bear* Workshop in First Colony Mall. Autumn had picked out a round-faced brown bear and was waiting eagerly in line to stuff it.

Even though Hendrix was in high spirits, there were concerns going on in his head that wouldn't let him settle down. His heart needed a release. Being friends with her was harder than he thought it would be.

Hendrix knew that they needed to have a little talk – he didn't want to spoil her birthday, but the time was now.

Autumn stood as the biggest kid in line. She looked up at Hendrix who had never been to the place before and couldn't help but smile. Finally it was her time to stuff the bear that had fur the same color as her caramel skin. The worker handed her a satin covered heart she would soon place in her bear's chest after two rituals were completed; she had Autumn do a "silly little dance" and recite something. Autumn cheerfully cooperated.

Soon she and Hendrix were finding clothes for the stuffed bear whose back was now stitched up and fastened. She picked out an outfit she could see Hendrix wearing. They were now moving to the birth certificate station - giving the bear a name. Autumn sat for a moment, having a hard time deciding on a name – finally she typed in the word *Beary White*. Hendrix chuckled and soon they both stood in the checkout line. After leaving the bear factory, the two headed to one of Autumn's favorite restaurants in that area. They sat on the patio of PF Chang's and enjoyed the Chinese cuisine.

Before they realized it, their day was coming to an end.

"This is really the best birthday I have ever had," Autumn said, while Hendrix was reluctantly driving her back home. She had enjoyed being with him.

He smiled while keeping his eyes on the road.

"I am so glad to hear that."

"I really have missed us hanging out, Hendrix."

They were approaching a railroad track, a landmark indicating that he was five minutes away from her house. Hendrix let out a long breath. He had not been able to get out his feelings and now it would soon be too late. As luck may have it, a train's whistle blew and suddenly the red lights started to blink.

The two sat in silence for a moment as a slow train started to pass in front of them.

Hendrix swallowed while he watched Autumn pull out Beary White to examine him. Hendrix finally worked up the nerve to ask a question he had wanted to know the answer to since 2005.

"Autumn, what about the night of Rita? The night I walked in on you two?" he finally let slip from his lips. He looked over at her, trying to prepare himself for the truth he avoided.

An uncertain Autumn held the bear tightly as she sat beside him, wanting to be careful with her words. It was hot in the car, but manageable. Once again, Autumn traveled back to a place that made her uncomfortable, but she was very much willing to put Hendrix's mind at ease in order to get things back to normal. If he wanted the truth then she wanted to give that. She started with the days leading up to the event Hendrix needed to know about.

Autumn's night with JT was a night that she would never forget, for JT was different in the dark; with nobody around and in the light, it was another story.

Her mind resentfully traveled back to that night when it was pitch black in her apartment on the campus of Prairie View A & M University. She had just checked on the five residents that had her staying on duty during Hurricane Rita. Her mother nearly had a heart attack when she told her she wasn't coming home to be with the family the day before. Her mother had plenty to worry about, considering weeks before, Hurricane Katrina had made more than an infamous name for its destruction. It had turned the whole south upside down, and allowed the whole world to see the world the way it really was. Three weeks had passed since the unnatural disaster and people tried to flip their lives back upright. Work and helping others adjust were taking up most of Autumn's time. She needed something to keep her mind off the fact that she was losing Hendrix in the process. Katrina had taken him and his Louisiana native family by storm and he had pulled away from her caring embrace.

During Katrina days, what Hendrix was going through really took a toll on Autumn. It was a very emotional and hectic time and she had never expected Hendrix to shut her out of his world during this time.

"He's never been like this, mom," Autumn remembered crying to her mother.

Precilla listened from across town.

"He won't let me in. I have called him and if he answers, I can really tell he is so down," Autumn cried.

Autumn was scared that door was closed forever.

"What if this is how it's going to be? What am I going to do?"

"Honey, it just goes to show storms can test the strength of any relationship. Let nature take its course." Autumn turned her attention to caring for those who let her. She and other PV students took shifts volunteering at different shelters, helping many Katrina survivors get back on their feet. Things finally started to get better. However, they would soon take a turn for the worst-for the entire Houston area that sheltered a number of Katrina victims. Autumn thought about what she remembered hearing earlier in the week on the news. "Houston, we have a problem – and one that may have us running for cover," said the local reporter on one station. "Texas is expected to be hit with a category 5 Hurricane that is stirring in the Gulf," the newscaster said.

Still early in the week after the announcement, serious precautions were taken. Mayor Bill White urged evacuations and made a clear picture of where to go for the local residents in Houston and smaller towns and cities outside of it.

"Here we go again," was all Autumn could say as she signed out many of the residents of the building as they started traveling home or wherever they thought they would be safest. Her mind was on Hendrix. She missed being close to him. She missed hearing his voice that gave her the security she longed for. He wouldn't let her be there for him. Autumn was still trying to help Hendrix cope with his distress of his family losing valuable things to the storm in their home in St. Lourdes, Louisiana. Now this time, things were hitting even closer to home. Hendrix was not there for her to lean on. Fear mixed in with desperation and a touch of hope. Devastation was what she felt in her heart as she thought about how whenever they tried to be together, something always seemed to pull them apart. She needed another miracle. She knew so many things could go wrong, but she prepared herself to be ready for anything.

By Wednesday, everyone in Houston was trying to leave. Autumn watched on television how the traffic was unbelievable. The gas pumps were a crazy mess! As three million people tried to get out of one of the largest cities in America, emotions ran high. Suddenly Autumn's phone rang and the tune, Erykah Badu's *Love of My Life* played. She perked up, knowing whose ring tone it was. Hendrix called to check on her from Dallas hours before the storm.

"Hendrix!!!" Autumn screamed. "How are you?"

"Fine. I am more worried about you. Where are you going?"

"I...I don't think I am going."

"What do you mean? You heard the news."

"I am staying at PV. I have some residents who aren't able to leave. My mom and the family are at home."

"You know hurricanes aren't a joke…"

"I know, but something in my heart is really telling me to stay put. I mean, it's really not safe anywhere."

"You know your residents can follow you to another area. I know your family wants you to be with them, just in case."

"I know, but…"

Hendrix knew it was a no-win situation. He would just let her be and hope and pray for the best. He had to admit this was a very emotional time for him. He wanted to be with Autumn. His family needed him with them. He tried to not be torn, but he was. He wanted to be strong, but he felt like things were out of his hands.

All he could do was shut down emotionally, just to cope. He regretted every second of his reaction; but this was the only way that he could deal.

"I love you!" Hendrix said, with all his heart on the phone.

"I love you too, Hendrix," Autumn cried.

There was silence. Hendrix tried to get himself together. He couldn't say another word because she would be able to hear the sound of his tears. The distance that had formed was driving him crazy. He wanted to close the gap, but it was beyond him.

He hoped that Autumn would continue to be supportive, and not take him not being able to talk to her prior to the phone call as a seasonal thing. But he was never too sure when it came to them and what they had.

"Hendrix, you okay? How is the family holding up?" she asked.

Hendrix was about to lose his mind. What was he going to do? He wanted to be with her if she had to stay there alone. Hendrix thought out the plan of traveling back to the yard so he could be with Autumn. He still had time.

"They are…holding up."

"Don't worry Hendrix, I will be okay. Take care of them. They need you."

"I need…you," Hendrix said.

The words broke her heart.

"The storm will pass and things will return to normal," she reassured.

They both knew this was not possible. Things would never be exactly the same. Hendrix's family had lost so many of their possessions. They loved Louisiana and they weren't able to be home.

Hendrix couldn't even handle the idea of losing Autumn. He didn't know what the storm would be for her. He just wanted to be there to protect her. All he could see was his sister Veronica weeping, his mother lying in the hotel bed emotionless and he could hear his father on the phone with FEMA. He had helped keep them get going, but Hendrix needed some help.

By Friday night, the clouds had started to turn a mix of purple and red before the sun disappeared completely. It would have been a beautiful sight if it weren't for the sound and sight of trees whipping their arms violently to remind you what was going to happen. The town was solemn. After Katrina, everyone was expecting the worst with Rita. The sound of howling winds roared through the house.

Autumn jumped then suddenly she realized it was only a knock at the door.

Probably one of the residents deciding that it was a good idea for them all to bunker down together.

She opened the door without looking out the peephole, only to find a co-worker with flashlights in his hand.

JT stood with a smile that brought some light to the dreary forecast.

"Just came from Walmart," JT shook his head. "It's literally a ghost town."

Autumn was a bit surprised by the visitor's relaxed nature. They weren't exactly on *friend* terms.

"I can imagine," she said, trying to not stammer as JT invited himself in.

Autumn closed the door behind him.

"I wanted to come by and check on you. We are the only two fools that didn't tell our residents to get the hell up out of here."

Autumn produced a laugh.

"So you okay?"

"I actually am. Just really not doing much."

"Yeah, don't think you have a choice, huh?"

"Guess not."

JT looked around her apartment.

"I was just checking on ya. Seeing if you needed anything. I got a lot of flashlights and a battery-operated radio."

"The lights seem like they are about to go out soon."

"I appreciate it. I actually got my own stash," she informed JT.

JT stood waiting for something.

"Okay. Well you know where I am if you need me."

Autumn nodded.

Autumn stood looking at JT.

"You gonna be okay over here?" he asked again.

Autumn, at this point, didn't know. She knew physically, she would be, but emotionally, she was a wreck and wouldn't mind company - being in the dark was not the best to be, literally.

Suddenly the lights went out.

The two stood in the dark until they could make out each other's silhouette.

"Well, you are welcome to stay over here if you want. I can imagine it may be pretty hard to navigate back to your place in the shadows."

JT laughed.

Soon the two, with handheld flashlights, set up the room to endure the storm. Autumn hated to admit it, but, she was pleased to have company.

After settling on her couch, somehow the conversation hit a subject Autumn never expected to hear.

"I still remember the first time I saw you," he said.

Autumn was fortunate he couldn't see her blush.

JT went on.

"It was just something about you and I couldn't keep my eyes off you."

Autumn was speechless as the moonlight soaked into the room.

"Once I got to know you, I was pleasantly surprised to know you actually had a good spirit. Some girls with pretty exteriors don't have much of an interior."

Autumn carefully listened, for she knew it was just the full moon talking through him. For this night might not come again. Autumn chose to be quiet during this. She didn't want to mess up anything with her words. When it was her time to speak, she was going to use her words wisely. She didn't want to reveal too much, putting herself out there for no reason. The lesson was learned from doing that in the past with JT.

"I really liked you a lot," he said.

Autumn couldn't help but laugh as she skeptically wondered how much.

"Could have fooled me," she accidentally let slip out.

"What do you mean?" JT asked with concern.

Autumn smiled trying to be meticulous with her words. Somehow, the two seemed like they were the only two people in the universe. Revisiting their ambiguous past made Autumn very tense. She needed to be very conscientious about what she allowed in her ears and heart. She had moved on a lot from the many questions she had about what she and JT had and now she may get some of those answers she longed for. She wondered right then and there were they actually worth having? Maybe this was the time and the place to have closure - the closure she had given up on. Maybe then she could shut out the idea of them, altogether.

"I didn't get that impression, JT. Didn't seem like you wanted me to either," she finally decided to say.

JT sat for a moment to think.

"It's really hard sometimes to act on what you feel. There were a lot of things holding us back - some things you didn't understand."

"Like what!" Autumn jumped, losing some of her new-found composure.

JT shook his head, wondering if he should say.

She needed to know now.

JT licked his lips slowly.

He searched for the words.

"I had to grow up a lot to realize how I felt about you. I didn't want to hurt you," JT said.

She knew he could sense how vulnerable she was at this point.

"You did though," Autumn informed.

"That was not my intention. It was a lot more to it than what you thought."

In the midst of the storm, the two community assistants still felt like they were the only two people in the world.

"I miss you," he said.

Autumn wanted to tell him how she was trying to move on and felt life was more than questions. She had found answers in other people, like Hendrix. Then the thought of Hendrix made her feel uncertain – the old Autumn took over.

"JT, I used to spend hours…I wasted so much time wondering about *us*."

JT listened.

"I really wanted to be with you, but…"Autumn swallowed her pride. "I would talk to other people to see what they thought I should do. Nothing worked. You didn't care for me the way I cared for you."

"You don't know how I felt about you, Autumn. You will never know how deeply I felt for you. Sometimes, people can't express themselves through words - like you can."

Autumn didn't want to buy his words now.

"I used to have strong feelings for you, and it seemed you punished me for that," Autumn explained.

"Things have changed. We can make it right now," he said.

Autumn couldn't believe her ears or her eyes that watched him move closer to her.

"Are your feelings gone?" he asked urgently. Autumn turned away from him.

"I have tried so hard to let go of the idea of you in my life. You didn't have a place for me in yours."

"I am sorry, Autumn, for not being able to show you how I felt. But I understand if you don't have feelings for me anymore."

"JT, I have feelings, for you. I just know that, with you, there is so much confusion. I don't think that confusion can produce anything great."

"I want to sort through the confusion, though," JT said.

Autumn thought about Hendrix, the person she wanted to be with. Was he hers though? That was the question. What would happen with them after the storm? She wanted things back to where they were, but they both knew nothing would be the same. Hendrix was allowing the distance to tear through what they had built for years. Their friendship was solid and crystal clear up to this point. She could not imagine life without Hendrix. But Hendrix seemed to be able to deal without her. She thought back on the days she had not heard from him. She thought back on them as a whole. They were best friends. They loved each other, but were they in love with one another?

JT was someone she fell for years ago. She shook her head at how she still was in the same place of confusion with him. She hated being in that place, yet she couldn't resist what happened next. He brushed her hair out of her face. Just the simple gesture seemed untimely. She sat stiffly. She didn't want to make the same mistake twice – fall for him.

"You may need to go," she said, remembering how he had led her on in the past.

Soon, they both walked carefully over to the door, but somehow, being the klutz that she was born to be, Autumn hit her shin bone on a table in front of the couch.

JT quickly turned to see what had happened.

Autumn fell back on the couch, holding her leg close to her chest. She grimaced in pain.

"You okay?" he asked.

"Yeah," Autumn lied.

He sat directly in front of her. He held his hand out.

"Here, stretch your leg out."

Autumn slowly stretched out her leg.

He started gently massaging her leg.

His touch overwhelmed her as the pain eased away.

"Does that feel better?" he asked.

"Yes."

JT rested his hands on her leg. Autumn didn't stop him from letting his hand rise to her thigh. In that moment, Autumn surrendered. This was the touch and emotion she anticipated years ago. When she least expected it, it was there. *But was it the right timing for her heart?*

He saw her squirm to be released then all of a sudden her eyes urged him to try again. He tried to regain the moment they had years ago, when she was open to him.

Suddenly, Autumn became putty in JT's hands as he pulled her closer. As he explored the outline of her fully-clothed body, her natural defenses began to shut down at every stroke. She realized she was not fully over him. She wrapped her legs behind his back. Her hormones got the best of her and soon her reasoning had taken a back seat to the temptation that sat at the steering wheel. As they hugged each other tightly, her emotions were all over the place as she thought about the way he made her feel from the very beginning.

Autumn allowed her mind to wander as she ran her hand through his locs.

Autumn wondered if he really cared the way he seemed to at the moment. As her lips met his, she hoped to feel something that would let her know the answer to her question, but she was disappointed that she didn't and couldn't feel him. JT assertively caressed her tense body. She didn't enjoy the thrill of the moment, a moment she felt she formerly deserved. She wanted more. As they continued to lock lips, his tongue began to explore her mouth forcefully. She wanted him to slow down but his pace excited her. His frustrated hands moved rapidly trying to catch up with his hormones.

Autumn's senses were heightened by his demanding hands and she tried to not react to them because she knew what that would lead to. Soon buttons were unbuttoning, zippers were unzipping and garments were being pulled off to expose both of their vulnerable sides. JT and Autumn were so caught up in the moment they didn't even hear the unlocked door open. Before things moved any further, JT and Autumn knew something was missing. JT reached for his pants pocket to pull out some protection. Finally, the two realized they were not alone; Hendrix St. John stood at the door.

***

The extensive and sluggish train finally passed, but the conversation seemed to just start. Hendrix hesitated before he started back up the SUV, for he knew he couldn't keep his eyes on the road; his eyes were fixed on Autumn who sat ashamed of the past, but ironically relieved to come clean about what happened that night before he stepped in. She knew that Hendrix had every right to hate her and think less of her commitment to what they had; but she hoped he knew not only what happened that night, but more of how she felt.

"It was not something that I planned to do, Hendrix. In fact, it felt all wrong being that close to him. The whole time, I thought about you. The whole time I was wishing that you were there with me. The whole time, I was feeling that the connection was not there," she said, thinking about the event itself.

This was hard for Hendrix, but he continued to listen.

"I'm not driven by what JT and I were doing that night. Yes, I wanted more, but *not sexually.* I wanted more of the spiritual link that *we* share, Hendrix. It is a funny thing; I was actually glad you walked in when you did. I am grateful that JT and I weren't able to go forward with our actions. They weren't responsible."

Hendrix swallowed. He remembered what he saw and how he saw her the moment he walked into her apartment the night of Hurricane Rita. He didn't understand how his heart could continue to produce love for someone who continued to break it.

"If I was so important to you, how could you do that to me – how could you end up in his arms that night? I was coming to see about you in the middle of a storm only to find someone I didn't recognize. I wanted to be there with you and just like that, you found someone else; someone you have always seemed to want *more* than me."

Autumn didn't want to give up.

"Hendrix, when I said that I loved you, I meant it with all my heart. I know that many times JT has gotten in the way of us. I can't stress enough, my frustration with myself for letting that be. Based on the past, I know that you have every right to not trust my words or actions."

He wished he could look at her differently, he wished it were that simple.

"That storm has passed; and my feelings for JT are dead."

"So where does this leave us, Autumn?" he asked.

"That is a good question, but for the first time in my life I will not push myself for the answer. I won't be selfish and say what I want because that is not fair to you. The truth is, I don't expect anything from you or anyone else right now. I do expect more from myself."

Hendrix frowned.

"Being in love with others is always a piece of cake. Being in love with me has always been a challenge. Since IKE, I have been really focused on committing more to God; and he has allowed me to embrace this testing journey. I know that I hurt you because I didn't love myself enough. I now know I can't treat you the way you deserve until that happens."

Autumn held back her tears.

"Therefore, I trust that you will make the best decision regarding us; the ball is in your court," she answered.

When I think of homecoming

I AM
Am I good enough to make it in this world?
Am I wise enough to let go of that little girl?
Am I talented enough to make my dreams reality?
Or am I weak enough to give into the fears of me?

Am I strong enough to handle all this pain?
Am I bright enough to shine through all this rain?
Am I bold enough to wash away all doubts and fears?
Am I willing to work hard throughout the years?

Am I open enough to let people in?
Am I wise enough to keep out those not genuine?
Am I free enough to trust my intuition?
Or am I going to ignore all that information?

Am I wise enough to outsmart manipulators?
Am I forgiving enough to forget the haters?
Am I brave enough to stand up against what holds me back?
Am I courageous enough to step outside and lead the pack?

I am! and I want you to see it!
I am! I'm gonna make you believe it!
I am! everything that I want to be!

I am! do you want me to prove it!
I am! you know I'm gonna do it!
I am! ALL that I can be!
There is no stopping me!

Driving like a bat out of hell in her black Mustang, Kennedy's speakers rattled. Like old times, the three amigas were all in the Bat Mobile – going to Homecoming 2009, Kennedy was playing her favorite old MJ cuts.

Autumn had taken the whole day off from Sampson's. Kyla, enjoying a teacher's schedule, was taking advantage of the Saturday. Kennedy had her camera and equipment in the back because she planned for Bootleg Craig to help her gather great footage at the game.

Kennedy was more than half way through the hour drive. They all were grateful Highway 290 was clear of traffic, considering it was the final hours of Homecoming Week.

Although the college supplied them all with great memories, Kennedy's gas tank was probably more relieved she no longer commuted.

"I am so surprised that you two came with us," Autumn said, looking from side to side, grinning.

To Autumn, it was a given that Homecoming documentary queen Kennedy would be in attendance, but somehow U of H Cougars Deon and HBU Huskies Kyla trailed along on the breezy Saturday to come down with the two proud PV Panthers. Deon had recovered from being in a coma, but she still wasn't herself – Autumn actually missed the old Deon. The women secretly couldn't wait until she felt comfortable talking about the fall at the club. Deon had said it was off subject for now. "*We are almost there*," Kennedy reassured the passengers.

As they got closer, Autumn remembered a conversation she had with a proud Panther like it were yesterday - the day she knew it was official that she would be going to PVAMU. She remembered the conversation she had with Mama B.

"So, you got a boyfriend, yet?" Mama B asked college-bound Autumn. Smiling with curiosity, this seemed to be Mama B's favorite question.

"Last time I checked, you didn't," is what her grandmother said in a matter-of-fact way.

Autumn smiled. It was funny how her grandma had a way of remembering *certain* details.

Autumn could still see Mama B sitting there knitting a purple and gold scarf, and how she looked down at what her crooked hands produced.

"Prairie View has a very rich history. Therefore it will have a rich future," her grandmother told her.

Autumn valued those words then and now.

"So many of these HBCU's that are still standing, the reason they stand is because of greatness. There is a story behind them all. Nothing is in vain," Mama B continued.

"PV is where I met your grandfather," Mama B said with a nod, while threading.

"Max. Yes I did. He was the most handsome man on the yard."

Autumn knew the pictures showed the same.

"You'll meet your husband in college," the woman said, with a girl-like grin and a starry look in her grayish brown eyes. "I just have a feeling."

As Autumn continued to ride, she laughed to herself at how her grandmother was right about many things, but she was way off with that one.

While seeing that they were passing the Kickapoo sign, she knew they had about ten more minutes before approaching Prairie View A&M University.

***

As Autumn sat with Kennedy, Kyla and Deon for Prairie View Homecoming 2009 game, she appreciated the atmosphere. The morning parade was pleasant because the weather was just right: a hint of sunlight and a cool breeze.

Autumn and Kennedy saw a lot of their former building mates passing through the crowds – many were with their sorority sisters. Old teachers were there among what seemed to be the '03 through '07 grads. It was a huge turnout!

As Bootleg Craig approached the women, Kennedy started to help him get the camera equipment out and situated. As Autumn looked around, she shook her head at how she had skipped some Homecomings after graduating. She wanted to avoid going back down Memory Lane because of the fear of starting to regret her past. But now, she was in a better, more grounded place and embraced it. It actually felt good to return to the yard to see the *now* and remember the *then.* A lot had changed, but her love had surely grown.

After moments of the crowd reacting to the game plays, Autumn stood out like a sore thumb as she sat looking straight ahead at nothing in particular on the field.

"You sure are in a daze," Kennedy, who sat on her right, said. She had given Bootleg Craig the camera and he sat further down from them.

Autumn laughed at the comment. She couldn't help but be in the clouds as she thought about how she anticipated hearing the band play. Since her first Homecoming half-time, she was in love. When she found out Hendrix was in the band, she gladly came to support the performances and cheered him on.

"When is she not?" Deon asked, who kept moving around, taking phone calls.

Autumn offered them some popcorn. Kennedy, with her free hand, ate a handful as they could hear Deon on the phone.

As the game came closer to half-time, in between rooting for the team and talking to the girls, Autumn couldn't help but wonder if she would be able to spot Hendrix on the field with all of the other former drum majors.

Then someone caught Autumn's wandering eye. JT, wearing a crisp and clean Alumni shirt, walked up the steps, solo. Autumn made a point to not let her eyes follow him as he coolly strolled along the bleachers to the other end of the seats. Of all the sights before her, she would not see him. She looked elsewhere, fighting the heavy emotions of resentment that came over her in just an instant.

JT stopped and saw a crowd that urged him to sit with them. He smiled coolly, and took it all in. It was the crew he used to roll with –a mix of frat and party boys. Both Autumn and Kennedy continued to look ahead as others naturally looked to witness what all the hoopla was about; the rowdy group hugged each other.

"Look at you," Deon said looking at the stain on her friends' shirt from the grease. She had just finished returning a missed call.

Autumn looked down to examine her shirt. She eventually shook her head.

"As corny as it sounds, they always did call me butter fingers," Autumn said.

“Yeah, that does sound corny,” Kennedy said laughing, glad Autumn didn’t seem the least bit bothered by her old crush.

As the girls helped Autumn finish off the buttered popcorn, the crowd cheered as the players ran off the field. Half-time was about to begin. Autumn perked up.

They made an announcement, and soon the band began to March from the street and unto the field; they always made a grand entrance. Autumn looked in her binoculars, ready to see Hendrix perform on the field.

Meeting him was a blessing. Regardless of how things turned out. She respected him and his decisions. Knowing him had changed her life. *If I had been more mature, maybe,* then she stopped herself. *I just got to let it be.*

As the drum cadence continued, she saw a line of the old and new come to the middle of the field. She frowned when she couldn’t see anyone who fit his build.

Suddenly, the band started to play a slow-paced rhythm. Autumn took a sip of her soda. In the middle of taking a big sip, she started choking. Kennedy hit Autumn’s back with one hand holding her personal video camera with the other. “You okay?!!!” Kennedy asked frantically, while still holding her camera in place on the field.

Autumn coughing heavily, tried to tell her to stop, but Kennedy was on a mission.

“I’m…okay,” the words finally came out of her mouth. “Please, please spare me!”

“Do you hear this?" Autumn said pointing like a mad woman at the field below. She continued to frown as the band continued to play a tune that struck a couple of cords in her heart.

Kennedy smiled. “Yes,” Kennedy said, not knowing what else to say.

Deon watched as Autumn blinked furiously, searching her brain trying to place the song, a sound so distinctive. Finally it came to Autumn, but it did not make any sense. “Hey, this is…” Autumn started but couldn’t finish. She couldn’t believe her eyes. The band rocked and walked to the melody and in seconds, the gold band suits formed the precise letters out on the field.

As the women, along with the packed crowd, watched the action on the field, Autumn's mouth dropped as her very own name started to develop in purple and gold. Afraid to move or blink, Autumn remained confused at the surreal sight before her, as if she couldn't read.

She started to realize that the women she sat by were each beaming as things unfolded. The crowd started to react in *ohhs* and *ahhs*. People that knew her started to look her way - JT was one of them.

"What?" Autumn said not being able to understand all that was going on. The song continued as the band formed a sentence and the Black Foxes, the dancers, formed one letter in particular.

This song is for U!

Suddenly, Kennedy was in her face with the camera. The camera was the last thing on Autumn's mind this time. After capturing an utterly shocked Autumn on camera, Kennedy kept focused on her friend while Bootleg Craig kept his camera focused on the field in order to capture the whole experience. Many in the stands started cheering and contorting their bodies to find her. People from the other team were using binoculars to see if they could catch a glimpse of the action.

Autumn closed her eyes for a second, for she could not believe them. But when she re-opened them, everything was still the same on the field. Suddenly she, looking ahead, could see a tall shadow hovering over her shoulders. She certainly could feel someone behind her as the band brought down their volume. Autumn yanked her body around to face a smiling man standing there with a bouquet of Crane flowers, her favorite, and one hand behind his back. Deon carefully took some of the items from her niece to avoid any accidents.

"Hendrix," Autumn said surprised as she slowly and carefully stood to meet his gaze. She covered her mouth. As the bass kept the tempo, Hendrix placed the bright bouquet of her favorite South African flowers in Autumns' trembling hands. The sunlight hit his eyes perfectly as he tenderly put the last one in her hair.

Hendrix took a deep breath. Autumn's eyes reassured him. JT watched in what seemed to be disbelief.

"I always wondered how long it took some of the greats to create their musical masterpieces," Hendrix started to stay focused on the prize. Only the crowd close to them could hear.

"I may not have the intense ear like Stevie Wonder."

"I may not have the wise words of Curtis Mayfield."

"I may not have Michael Jackson's magic."

"I may not have *Kanye* confidence."

"And I know I don't have the many voices of Prince."

Autumn laughed while she stood looking at Hendrix who stood calmly and sure."I'm no musical genius, that's for sure. I just *love* music. And I *love* you."

"Awwww*!!!,"* there was hardly a dry eye in the stands.

"My song is far from being masterpiece material, but I do know one thing. You, you *are* great. You are a masterpiece that not even Picasso, not even Mozart, not even Beethoven could come close to painting or composing."

Autumn's heart was beating uncontrollably, she couldn't stop her body from trembling. Butterflies flew around crazily in her stomach. She couldn't believe what was going on – her dream was coming true. The words that came from his lips were heaven-sent. She continued to look deeply into the eyes of a man she loved so unfathomably, she couldn't even begin to explain how ecstatic she was to hear them, to know that this was her *actual reality*, not some dream she had conjured up.

"And I tried, I tried to get that song as close as possible to you," he said.

Autumn's ears danced with delight. She was truly touched and overwhelmed by his effort and his love displayed through every note played. To her surprise, she was without words. "Autumn, you have been my inspiration ever since the first moment I saw you." The girls, while tears ran down their faces, smiled at the two.

"When I met you, I knew you were going to have a special place in my world," Hendrix said. "You have made my world larger. With your laugh…with the way you see things. I have learned so much from you. Through your eyes, I see clearly," he said. "I can't live without your smile. I can't live without your wisdom. I can't live without *you.* Hopefully, I have been half of what you have been to me. You have been my best friend. And I just wonder, hope and pray," Hendrix took a deep breath, hoping that Autumn could make a decision that would make his heart sing. "I pray that you wouldn't mind being my best friend for life."

Autumn blinked causing a fountain of tears - tears of happiness, to stream from her hazel eyes to her rosy cheeks. Hendrix took his other hand from behind his back to reveal a black box as he began to kneel, keeping his eyes planted on her. He had never been so sure; he just prayed that the chance he was taking was worth it. He wanted nothing more than for her to be sure as well.

Autumn covered her chest as Hendrix uncovered a diamond that sparkled in the sunlight.

Deon screamed!

Kennedy laughed.

Kyla cried.

"Autumn, will you marry me?" Hendrix said with conviction. The band, who magically hung onto every word and every syllable, made a strong finish.

Autumn, with a certainty that reassured everyone, *even herself*, nodded her head and said… "Yes!"

From afar, JT could see the two figures like magnets, pull together to connect. His heart dropped as the two shared a passionate kiss.

Kyla clapped not even bothering to wipe her messy face.

Kennedy kept the camera rolling.

Deon smiled sincerely.

When the two turned to face the people around them, the crowd roared jumping up and down at the touchdown.

"Congratulations, kiddo," Deon said, hugging her niece. "I guess I could do one more wedding," Deon said smiling. Kyla hugged both of them. "Oh my God!!!! I am so happy for you two." Kennedy gave a thumbs up while still on the job of capturing the moment on film. The bride and groom-to-be were touched to see all the people they were sharing this moment with, in the place where it all started.

"Pinch me," she said.

Deon did the honors.

"Okay," Autumn said. "Just making sure."
Autumn was traveling light!

Birds of Paradise

Autumn was in heaven!!! To finally feel the timing was right for the type of love she dreamed about had her floating on cloud nine. Hendrix was there right with her.

Preparation for the wedding came quickly. Autumn knew before things got too hectic, she needed time to reflect, but the time never really was there. Everything was in a whirlwind.

She had bought a wedding planning book and she had already mapped out so many of the facts, leaving less to the imagination. Autumn wanted a small wedding, with close friends and family. The engagement party would be at one of the artsy lounges in the city. The theme of the wedding was *paradise.* Autumn could envision the wedding invitation. She could also smell the flowers she wanted to hold as she walked down the aisle - South African Crane flowers, like the ones she had seen years ago at Lety's. Autumn looked forward to all the events. Autumn and Hendrix were having a parent's dinner later in the week. As far as her friends, Autumn already had planned to take the twins along with her to find the perfect wedding dress. She was elated that Deon had offered to do her hair. She still couldn't believe her aunt; being in a coma had really changed her. She knew that eventually she would snap out of it fully.

Kyla's husband had already agreed to do the wedding at his church. It was a no-brainer that Kennedy was the Maid of Honor. Kyla and Deon were the other bridesmaids. The only photographer she knew was JT, but she figured she would need to get to know another one. Kennedy said she would help book a place for the reception. Cornelius Cajun Kitchen was catering the wedding reception and both were excited about that. Hendrix had a big family, but each decided on 50 people – they knew that the number would probably increase for both.

A month after Homecoming and the wedding proposal, the couple had planned to enjoy a day at Herman Park for a picnic. As Hendrix pulled up, the postman was also pulling up beside the

White's mailbox. After Hendrix took the mail, he picked up the paper that sat in the yard.

As she met her fiancé at the door, Autumn could already see the future with him. She *could* believe she was going to be somebody's wife! After their hug, Autumn invited him in. *It felt so right.*

"Here you go," Hendrix said handing the stack of envelopes.

"Thanks."

Hendrix spoke to his future mother-in-law who was walking past the lovebirds and soon they gave each other a hug. They began to talk as Autumn decided to peak in the envelopes before leaving.

They were going to start their marriage counseling next week and Autumn couldn't wait.

Most were for her mother, she realized, as she sorted through the stack. She took out her few.

She opened her three magazine renewal forms and the Sampson's credit card bill. Then there was one envelope she didn't recognize with a Los Angeles address. She frowned as she opened what probably was junk mail. As she read the first lines of the letter, she realized it was far from junk. All of a sudden her knees got weak as she read on.

Her eyes were able to read, but she wasn't quite sure if she was reading correctly.

Hendrix and her mother were caught up in conversation and Autumn was caught up in the words printed on the page.

Autumn kept reading, skimming even, at a fast pace.

Dear Autumn White,

Hello. Allow me to introduce myself. My name is Roberta Lopez-Brown, producer of the upcoming urban soap opera titled "Neighbors." It is a mini-series centered around an apartment complex located on a HBCU college campus.

I became familiar with your work when you applied for the reality show. I was one of the judges for the competition you had applied for last year. Although you were not picked for the show, I was really impressed with your writing ability and thought that you had a voice, style and energy that could help bring the soap opera to life. I held on to your contact information.

I too was from a small town and always look out for those small town girls!

Autumn gasped. She knew about Roberta Lopez-Brown. Just the idea that Mrs. Brown knew about her was the shocking part. She had followed her career and had magazine cut-outs to prove it. Mrs. Brown worked as a sitcom writer on some of her favorite shows, *Living Single, Different World, Girlfriends, Half and Half* and now she had her own show that she wanted *Autumn* to be a writer for! Autumn remembered reading about the San Antonio native and the developmental deal she had.

Her mom and fiancé looked back at her. Autumn could not believe her eyes. She had given up on the professional writing idea when she received that rejection letter from the reality show. She had let it be what it was. She felt so honored to be recognized after all for something that she valued.

Autumn realized the other details though. *So what did this really mean?*

Her life had changed so drastically since the show she applied to sent her a rejection letter three months after the IKE inspired application. Autumn, though disappointed, hung up the idea of going after that dream again. Reading that she was not picked for the reality show gave her closure and she never imagined another opportunity coming out of that closed door.

"You okay?" Hendrix asked.

Autumn looked up from the letter.

"Uh…yeah." She needed to finish this letter. "Um, give me a moment."

Hendrix frowned.

"Sure," he said, keeping his concerned eyes on her as she left the room and went into her bedroom.

She continued to read the letter in private in order to take it all in. She sat on the treasure chest of notebooks and journals that sat at the foot of her bed.

The letter was one of the greatest things she had read. But the timing sucked, considering there was more to it than what met the eye. She needed to come to terms with the terms herself.

If she wanted to take the opportunity, one that sounded like a dream come true, it would affect her *other dream.* She had to move, soon. To Los Angeles. Where would it leave her new life? She felt elated and sick at the same time.

So much had changed since she had applied for her dream, a job as a writer. She was ready to relocate if the opportunity presented itself - then. Since it hadn't worked out, she had had to move on.

When she had sent the application, she didn't think she would be engaged to such a wonderful man. They had planned to marry the summer of 2010.

How was she going to break the news to her *fiancé*?

Should she even break the news? Was it worth it?

She figured she wouldn't; she couldn't.

She knew it wouldn't be fair to Hendrix to just say *Hey, I am relocating to pursue my dreams whole-heartedly - here is your ring back. Take back my yes.*

Hendrix was moving up in his company and she wouldn't want him to have to mess things up with his job. Then he had built his home here. His studio. She didn't want him to feel like he was losing his home again.

Living on two different coasts wouldn't work either. Autumn remembered how she never wanted to be separated from Hendrix again after getting her taste of it during all the hurricanes.

Timing couldn't have been worse. Months ago, there was nothing to lose. She wanted to pursue her dreams. She was single. *Single for many years, even.*

Autumn folded the letter and placed it back in the envelope.

Concerned eyes met Autumn's when she emerged from the bedroom. She tried to avoid them as she gathered her stuff and said *bye* to her mom. They headed outside; she wanted to push it out her mind and enjoy the picnic Hendrix had planned.

Hendrix opened the car door for Autumn. He smiled as she hopped into the car that smelled really good. As he walked to the other side, she peaked in the back and saw the picnic basket sitting beside a blanket.

"You sure you okay?" Hendrix asked as he buckled up.

"Yeah," Autumn said reassuring. "I am just excited to be spending my time with you."

The two leaned forward to share a kiss in the driveway.

Autumn didn't want to be greedy. She knew from past experience she couldn't have her cake and eat it too. She needed to focus on what she needed. *She was on a healthy diet.*

Hendrix smiled. He believed her words, but he knew something was on her mind that she wasn't sharing.

The saga continues…

10 Year Anniversary

Special Edition

Acknowledgments

I thank God for all that He has done in my life, especially through storms. To all of my angels watching over me from above, and to all of my living angels who make my life here on Earth more heavenly - this book is dedicated to you!

***

Since 2009, I have seen the power of *story*. Ten years later, to Houston's passionate reading, writing, film and theatre communities – thank you for embracing me and helping me see these projects through.

Mimi, my rock: words can't even express my gratitude and admiration. You are an awesome mom. To my grandmother, Marian, I miss you dearly, but I know you are with me. I honor you both. To the rest of my family, I love and thank you for your support, especially my grandparents: Ethel and AY. Thanks for buying my books in bulk. Your enthusiasm to share with others makes my heart leap!

Early-on mentors: Thank you to the 1999-2001 Hightower High's Media Academy instructors for equipping me with a foundation that has never left and one in which I rely on as an "Indie". To the many people along the way, especially Angie, Norma, Angelo (RIP), Chandra: thanks for lending your ear at crucial times of me taking an abstract idea into a concrete space.

Gratitude also to my few friends, many associates and fellow authors who discuss books at our book club, BYOBook Club for Busybodies! Thank you for being a #litforlife booknerd right along with me!

Geri Felder, where have you been all of my life?! It has been a pleasure and an honor working with you as my editor for this edition!

Many thanks to my co-workers from various campuses who have been supportive! To the ten percent of my students who want to be writers, I am rooting for you and can't wait to buy your book! Students who hated writing and reading and have shared how I actually helped them come to appreciate the written word, even enough to feel empowered to write better and for *fun* – wow, you are giving me my roses while I am still here. That means *everything* to a teacher.

To young people with *any* dream: don't ignore the entrepreneurship pursuits God has placed in you. Hold tightly.

To my church-families, I can't not express how much it meant to be nurtured, supported and taken seriously stepping into this creative business lane. I love you. There were many who, behind-the-scenes, sowed seeds: Sister Washington, Glapion, Smith, Mathis and Grimes – the list goes on. Thanks for recognizing something in me. Serving in the church has brought me great joy and purpose. To my childhood church, Metropolitan C.M.E, and Bishop Lockett (RIP), Pastor Truelove, and Bishop Best, thank you for elevating God's people with your ministry. To my current church, Pastor Joel Osteen's, Lakewood Church – I have grown leaps and bounds as a believer and look forward to evolving even more.

Prairie View A&M University: The experience was priceless. I started becoming who I am most proud of, in college. To all the kindred spirits I had the privilege to celebrate creativity and Black excellence with, thank you for the magical synergy! God.Was.In.That.Place!

National Association of Black Journalists, Delta Sigma Theta Sorority, Inc., National Association for the Advancement of Colored People: to these dynamic organizations that I have been proud members of, thanks for grooming me as a storyteller for my community.

Diane Tezeno, you are a gem. And Empower Magazine: thanks for honoring me and covering my projects over the years.

It is nothing like your very first book launch and being able to embrace your first readers – Karen and Phelix, thanks for being my right-hand for the event. Thanks again to my mom. To my baby sister: Alex, over the course of your life, thanks for taking all the pictures I made you take as a kid, a tween, and a young adult. (I hope your training days serve you well in your upcoming career!) But on a serious note, use your God-given talent and He will keep you in perfect peace. Proud of you. Drew, thanks for giving me my bonus sisters. Jacquice and Jacquee, you are both awesome and I appreciate you *always* lending a helping hand. To my big cousin Terrance – thank you. Latricia, Diana, Zerlene, Rayneisha, Toni, Ashli, Kristina, Bettina, Gisselle, Faith, Mama Deggins, Candace, Michelle, Lori, Courtney, Natalie, Andrea, Ashley, Ryan and Damon, my fairy Godmothers, AKA the awesome DHS Biz teachers: Aunt Cyndy, Aunt MaryAnn, and Aunt Mary D (RIP) and Mr. D…thank you all for officially launching my writing career with me!

To the many readers I have met along the way – you have kept this story going. I honor you! Blessings to Mahogany Souls Book Club! I appreciate your longtime support and super-good questions! Also thank you to my hairstylists over the years!

To the awesome "Tangled Web of True Love Tales" short film series crew: with your time, talent and equipment…David, Hope and Darren, thanks for helping to get the production off the ground. To the amazingly gifted actors – you give me life. I am your biggest fan! To all who played a role in the project, the countless gracious location owners, my cousin Seeta, even those who attended the screening or watched and liked online…You made one of my biggest dreams come true! To my travel buddy Angelina Spriggs, I appreciate you helping me spread this #twotlt message even when we are off having fun in Miami and NOLA.

To the Mary Kay Inspiring Stories team and Tiffany and the Plenty Pennies team, thank you for picking my work for your mission!

To Alisha Brumfield, my HHS classmate, little sister on the dance team, and…the talented artist whose artwork graces this anniversary cover – collaborating with you to create portraits of these 7 ladies is one of my fondest and fun memories by far. You are SICK at what you do and I am ever-so grateful that you captured my characters with your gift and I look forward to future collabs.

To the libraries, the bookstores…like a fortress, keep standing. We need you!

To all mags, newspapers, podcasts, shows, stores, businesses, venues, conferences, platforms, and people who have featured my book – I am grateful!

Francis. You are the *purrfect* writer's pet. (Had to) You are my mascot!

To those who are new to me, I am thrilled that we have met in this way and I truly appreciate your interest. To all, holding this book right now, I would love to hear from you about your reading experience. In this 10-year anniversary special edition, you will also find Author's Q&A and book club discussion questions.

Hopefully this book will-m-power you to get untangled and embrace the love that sets you free!
- Micole Williams

Author's Thoughts and Theories

(These FAQs are from book club discussions and interviews with the author.)

What is your point-of-view as the writer?
I mainly have a journalistic viewpoint and like to examine topical issues from various vantage points and truths.

Through fictional characters, I wanted to explore seven love stories that have a universal message but also allow me to stay true to my Houston roots.

Would you consider this a collection of short stories or a novel?
This is a novel that introduces seven women who are searching for true love. You experience, through an ominous lens, a slice of their life in poetry, prose, vignettes and significant snippets. Each woman is connected in some way to the other. They are each intertwined in this web that taints the love they desire. I want the characters to represent different challenges women face in romance and life. Through social satire, or allegory even, I knew I was speaking for women, and also pushing them to speak for themselves.

What is the significance of, as you call it, *herstories*?
I write because I know we live in a world where a "woman's voice" is too many times hushed. I was finding my own voice ten years ago, and I continue refining it.

Why did you use the "seven deadly sins" as a way to present the women?
Given that I was inspired by folktales and morality tales, it makes more sense to see it from that context as opposed to romantic fiction. I was a fan of *The Canterbury Tales* by Geoffrey Chaucer. My first year teaching, I taught

seniors and I had to reread this piece and understand the text in a different way in order to teach it. I loved how when I had to dig deeper, these contradictory figures personified issues of the time. I wanted to do that as well but instead, through modern-day fatally-flawed examples of the seven deadly sins.

Although many people were interested in hearing the premise, I remember that just as many were leery about the subject-matter and asked: "Why would you have the women identify with the "seven deadly sins"? It was viewed as a very scary topic for a few. People were asking, "Are they all going to die at the end of the book?"

***Are* they all going to die at the end of the book?**
I won't spoil that either way. But what I will say is that I love figurative concepts. And I wanted to make a statement about the condition of relationships in a modern sense, in the digital age especially; although, I go into greater detail with that in the "Toxic Ties Trilogy" series.

How are the characters able to illustrate modern issues?
Autumn and Sheila deal with identifying their self-worth in order to assert themselves on a personal and professional journey. I love suspense and psychological thrillers, so I am able to play with these elements with the Nadia and Deon rivalry. Both ladies have triggers that become apparent when dealing with Houston's most eligible bachelor. Juxtaposing twin sisters, Kennedy and Kyla allow me to tackle issues within community and in society regarding race, religion and gender roles. Self-care also plays a huge part in our overall well-being and through Dr. Lynne, I am able to present this notion that

there should be a fight for mental health to not be a taboo subject.

What do you think about the state of *story* now as opposed to when you started?

Overall, now we are seeing more widely-different and dark ideas being brought to light and many are based on books. Studios and networks are taking more risks, like Indie and Artsy films did. So now viewers are displaying more of an appetite for novelty stories that are outside of the box. Because of that exposure, in mainstream media, we are hearing more interesting conversations and needed dialogues about our society and the sin epidemic in many communities. From an Indie perspective, there are so many more options and ways to get your story out there…even more are on the way. It is a pretty exciting time.

How long have you been writing? When did you decide this route was for you?

I was an avid reader as a kid. It was my favorite pastime. Like many of my peers, I read and loved *The Babysitters Club* and *Sweet Valley High* novels. At one time, a friend of mine and I were reading a book a day. Reading pushed me into writing. I have been telling stories since I can remember, but didn't realize it was a job until later in elementary school. So I had a lot of unfinished books and magazines I created around the house just for kicks. But when I won a shiny blue and gold ribbon in an elementary school writing competition, I got serious about the path ahead.

Writing is so broad - was it hard to decide what area or genre to focus on early on and throughout?

I agree. I wasn't sure in what capacity I'd be writing. I just knew it was a huge part of how I lived and wanted to live. In high school, I realized that storytelling also came in the form of news and news packages. Being on the yearbook and newspaper staff and in the broadcast academy in high school, allowed me to evolve my definition and I learned more about how to reach people. I still yearned for the artistic side and the desire to make films in high school blossomed. I still have a couple of trailers to short films I wrote and directed in college although the actual short films remain unfinished. As far as writing novels, reading Toni Morrison opened my eyes. I was an English minor and read some of her writing in an Afro Lit course in college. She indirectly gave me the courage to incorporate mystical aspects to what my characters go through. I used to write as a kid in a way that allowed my imagination to run free, but as an adult, I found myself second-guessing that freedom. I feel that, in reading Morrison, you, as a writer, understand that you are granted permission to tell the story you have in your heart. There are some metaphorical aspects to our reality and *this* story mirrors that.

How do you relate to the book you wrote?
Like many millennials, I too, was trying to find my own way after college. I graduated with a Mass Communications degree in 2005 and I, though previously invested and obsessed with journalism since high school, had some family emergencies and because of them, I made some decisions that changed the trajectory of my life. For the first time, I had doubted myself and my dreams and for many years. So I can relate to my characters in that sense.

What was significant about the time it was published?
In 2009, I had been teaching two years and after a super stressful start, I resigned at the end of the year with no

plans to return. The first thing on my bucket list was "write the book." So the stakes were high. The previous summer, I had just bought a house as a single woman on a teacher's salary and I had no back-up plan when I quit, just faith. I wrote it in the midst of trying to survive my own quarter-life crisis. Luckily, I was periodically writing this novel in college and after graduation, so it was a matter of completing it all while trying to figure out what I was going to do with my life. This book had me taking a giant leap and is a testament of faith still to this day.

What was your book publishing process like?
With this book, I originally self-published through a company that handled some aspects of production. As I gained more knowledge, I changed some aspects of how I published along the way. Being an indie author is not for the faint at heart. Thankfully, I got a lot of heart. There were many great aspects to going this route and just as many nightmares - I could write a book about that.

What was one of those publishing nightmares you could share?
During the time of wanting to publish, since I was no longer teaching, I ran the risk of losing my house. So let's just say, I had some pretty serious things on my mind. My mom helped me out tremendously during that time. I worked odd jobs, some were fun, then I eventually - in the nick of time - found full-time work - again, as a teacher, but I had to adjust to a major pay cut for two years until I got closer to my original salary. So unfortunately, when I did publish, I wasn't living off book sales. But I did accomplish getting the story out. That was big for me at that time. A lot of forces come against you when you are trying to accomplish a goal. But I had a dream that kept me alive. I know the power of God-given dreams…*and strong women.* In my books,

these women come from all walks of life. They are fighting, just like I was and have been ever since, for something near and dear to their heart.

In 2010, you independently adapted this book into a film and later web series while working behind the scenes as the director, and producer. With the lack of funds, how did you mange that? What challenges did you encounter doing a project on your own, again?
Turning this story into a film on a shoestring budget was a challenge and later a miracle. Prior to, I had worked with many productions that did not see the light of day. So as a realist I *really* knew the limitations of a small-budget project but focused on what resources and skillsets were readily available. I had a lot of awesome talent who auditioned, and they knew others who were perfect for the roles that were not yet filled. These actors were the pulse of the project. They gave it life. Ironically, I had planned to only start small with one short story and see how it went, but I met so many people who wanted to work with me in the future if I saw a part for them. So I got to work and instead of one short, adapted all seven stories to scripts. Casting was completed and the production commenced. We were super-invested. By the grace of God, the production successfully wrapped and screened at *THE Landmark River Oaks Theatre* in Houston for a One-Night-Only screening for a packed crowd during the month of February, a month of love and Black History. That was a labor of love on so many people's parts and I was grateful that I was able to keep my word. My small project only got my appetite ready for when I can really do the story justice.

Ten years later, what do you want readers to know and what are the plans for the future?
The sky is the limit.

I always saw this as a transmedia – from book-to-film, from film-to-TV transitioning and evolving. I always say, there is a void to be *filmed.* I wanted to see representation of a truth I knew existed. Publishing the book was more cost-effective at the time, and allowed me to understand myself as a storyteller, make a statement and continue making it. So I am excited about the next ten years and how it will keep growing, not just by my Indie efforts.

What advice do you have for inspiring writers?
Whether you go Indie or traditional routes, be ready to go insane.

Whether it is brainstorming, writing, revising, editing, publishing, promoting, selling, you will keep doing the same thing over and over and over again, expecting a different result. There is always room for improvement. We should all be students in this writing world and honing our craft is a never-ending process. So to future writers, I say, you have to love it and if you do, your hard work will all be worth it.

About the Author

Micole Williams is an eclectic force: a teacher by profession, writer by heart, and creative director by nature. She finds inspiration all around and storytells for a living. The native Houston, Texan started both her writing and teaching career over ten years ago and is the author of the satirical romantic series, TANGLED WEB OF TRUE LOVE TALES and creator, director and producer of the indie short film series under the same title. TOXIC TIES TRILOGY is her second book series. She uses writing to bring social and relational issues to the forefront in a fun, yet thought-provoking way. Williams has more creative directed workshops, coaching series and an upcoming book that is a personal account with more tips and strategies scheduled for the near future.

Micole Williams is available for select readings and lectures. To inquire about possible appearance, coaching and classes please contact info@micolewilliams.com.

Tangled Web of True Love Tales

Reader's Guide

1. Which character do you think serves as the symbol for the following sin: lust, greed, pride, anger, gluttony, sloth and envy?

2. Where is evidence of true love in the novel?

3. There are several messages in this book – one is *trauma triggers trauma*. How is this idea prevalent?

4. How are the characters expected to break generational curses? Face their own demons? Are they successful?

5. There seems to be an underlying idea that these are the "stories we tell ourselves" – how are the characters bringing this theory to light?

6. One theme for this novel is *ready or not; here life comes.* How is this displayed in the narrative?

7. Do you think Nadia is guilty of murdering her husband? What do you think happened the night of his death?

8. If you were in Kyla's situation, how would you handle the call from a possible mistress?

9. Do you admire the success of the alpha females in the book? Why or why not?

10. There are some lessons learned by the women and one happens to be *love is the gift to be cherished, not a game to be played.* How are the women and men playing games?

11. Seeking truth has hurt – who do you think has suffered the most from the truth?

12. What made you select this book?

13. What sin do you struggle with the most and why?

14. Were any of the women or men victims in your eyes?

15. Describe your reading experience.

16. Who do you think is the best example of the protagonist? Villain?

17. Who is your favorite/least favorite character and why?

18. How is the city of Houston playing a role in the story?

19. In regards to Q, were you #TeamDeon or #TeamNadia? Why?

20. How would you describe the writing style of the author? Did you notice any devices used to illustrate a tangled web of true love tales?

21. Who would you cast for the main characters in a movie version?

22. What did you think about the language and vernacular?

23. How reliable is the narrator? Whose point of view do you think is driving the story?

24. How does society view predicaments presented in the book?

25. Where you satisfied with the book's ending?

26. Do you think Hendrix deserves Autumn? What would you do in her dilemma?

27. What rating / review would you give this book and why?

28. In ten years, where do you see the seven women?

Visit

www.micolewilliams.com

for other books by Micole Williams:

Toxic Ties Trilogy: Queen D Syndrome (Volume 1)

and

Tangled Web of Poetic Confessions

Visit

www.eclecticallyyou.com

for other media projects, courses and events by Micole Williams!

www.ingramcontent.com/pod-product-compliance
Lightning Source LLC
Chambersburg PA
CBHW070638310726
48982CB00001B/323

* 9 7 8 1 7 3 3 3 0 2 3 1 9 *